SKIN

Small-town private investigator and part-time assassin Bonnie Parker isn't expecting any trouble at the boardwalk amusement arcade in South Jersey—until she meets Kyle Ridley, a renegade drug courier on the run, who desperately requires Bonnie's special skills to keep herself alive.

Going up against a ruthless drug syndicate isn't anyone's idea of fun and games, especially when the enemy is the Dragusha clan, whose graying patriarch–*Ujku*, the Wolf– has a penchant for shipping his victims out of Port Newark in a freighter's cargo hold, locked in a steel container where no one can hear their screams.

What started as another day at the beach turns into Bonnie's longest and most harrowing night as she tangles with professional killers, sadistic thugs, and a deeply crazy man out of her past. It's the ultimate test of luck and skill, with the odds against her stacked impossibly high, and Bonnie wouldn't play at all if she didn't have her own skin in the game.

USA Today and *New York Times* bestselling author Michael Prescott has sold more than 4 million books worldwide. *Skin in the Game* is his 27th novel.

SKIN

IN THE

GAME

Also by Michael Prescott

Manstopper
Kane
Shadow Dance
Shiver
Shudder
Shatter
Deadly Pursuit
Blind Pursuit
Mortal Pursuit
Comes the Dark
Stealing Faces
The Shadow Hunter
Last Breath
Next Victim
In Dark Places
Dangerous Games
Mortal Faults
Final Sins
Riptide
Grave of Angels
Cold Around the Heart
Blood in the Water
Bad to the Bone

SKIN
IN THE
GAME

MICHAEL PRESCOTT

In memory of my father

The wolf loves the fog.
    —Albanian proverb

PROLOGUE

SHORTLY BEFORE SUNRISE on a windy Thursday in December, Shaban Dragusha visited the Wolf in his den.

Ujku—the Wolf. That was what they called him. An old man now, who walked with a cane and sucked at his yellow teeth.

Still dangerous, though. A man who could kill with a word. A gray wolf, sure, yes—but with sharp fangs.

Shaban headed east on Lydig Avenue, his head down, hands in his coat pockets. The neighborhood around him, Pelham Parkway in the Bronx, was empty except for some men unloading crates from a truck outside a meat market. Burly, bearded men who watched him with insolent eyes as he went past.

They thought they were tough, because they stood tall and had broad shoulders and heavy beards. To them Shaban was only a wiry, nervous youth, clean-shaven and well groomed, easy prey. They were wrong.

The restaurant came into view. It was a narrow hole wedged between a flower shop and an electronics store. A sign said it did not open its doors to the public until 7 AM.

Shaban ignored the sign. He was not the public. He rapped twice on the door and waited in the winter wind.

The door creaked open. A white-haired woman in an apron stood facing him with a suspicious look. "Hello?"

"I have appointment," Shaban said in his rough English. He was sure the woman spoke Albanian, but using the language of his new country was a point of pride with him.

1

"You're his grandson?"

His head bobbed once. "Sure, yes."

Her expression softened into a wary smile. "Come."

The restaurant boasted four tables and a menu scrawled on a chalkboard. The place sold *bureks* stuffed with meat, cheese, and spinach. The mingled odors of grease and coffee took him back to Elbasan in central Albania, where he had spent most of his twenty-two years.

"In back." The old woman pointed toward a beaded curtain over a doorway.

Shaban went down the short hallway, past the kitchen, where a young boy was busy kneading and stretching phyllo dough. The boy kept his head down as Shaban went by. He had been trained to mind his own business when visitors showed up in the morning.

At the end of the hall there was a private parlor reserved for special guests. A single table with an inlaid tile surface occupied the room. At the table sat a very old man, sipping a cup of the frothy espresso called macchiato. Shaban hadn't seen it on the menu. Maybe they made it for him exclusively.

The man was small and frail, a bony figure in a loose-fitting suit and tie. His skull, with its high forehead and sunken eyes, seemed too large for his narrow shoulders. The scrawny stalk of his neck disappeared into a buttoned collar two sizes too big. By his side rested an antique cane with a silver handle, a relic of the nineteenth century.

Shaban stooped before the man and kissed him on both bearded cheeks—first his right, then his left. "Grandfather," he said quietly, being careful to meet his eyes as a sign of respect.

He pulled up a chair and seated himself opposite Arian Dragusha, the Wolf.

The old man sat unmoving, ramrod straight, silently

appraising him. "You get on well in your new country," he said at last.

Another head bob. "Sure, yes."

"This is good. Me, I am lost when first I come here. I leave my friends, my family—leave everything. For me, in the beginning, it is like being in exile."

"Did you not want to come?"

"I had no choice. There were people at home who had sworn a *gjakmarrja* against me. I was only a boy. I could run—or die."

"A *gjakmarrja*?" It was a death sentence.

"There was a girl." He waved an age-spotted hand. "It does not matter now."

"Who were these people?"

"They do not live anymore. I saw to that, when I had made enough money to pay for it to be done."

Shaban nodded. He was not surprised. He had once seen a sepia-tone photograph of his grandfather as a young man, and he remembered the lean face and sharp eyes, the unsmiling mouth. The hands jammed deep into the pockets of a thrift-store jacket. The subtle emanation of menace in his stiff, angular stance. It had never been wise to cross Arian Dragusha.

A memory of that pinched face still haunted the deep-set eyes and crêpe-paper flesh of the face before him. His hair was gray now and thin like iron filings, and his hands shook, and he breathed heavily through his mouth, each inhalation an effort. When he sipped the macchiato, he exposed a row of crooked teeth, and when he licked the foam, his tongue was as pale and glossy as a slug. But he was still the man he had been.

Arian leaned forward, hunching his shoulders, his voice lowered to impart wisdom. "In this world money solves all problems. Money makes all things right. A man without money is nothing. Don't let the priest at Saint Albius lie to you. God and Mammon ... If you must choose,

choose Mammon. Always."

His eyes were unnaturally bright. Shaban had seen that same fevered brightness in the eyes of feral dogs. Did those eyes ever blink? Their hungry, lambent gaze was unsettling.

He shifted in his seat, uncomfortable. "Yes, Grandfather."

"Enough chatter." Arian clapped his hands. "Make your report."

"The problem with the truck is taken care of."

"You have the merchandise?"

"The merchandise was already moved. But we are getting paid. The man who bought it, he did not know nothing. He pisses his trousers when he finds out."

"He should die anyway." Arian raised and lowered the cup, smacking his lips. "Let him be buried in his pee-stained pants."

"Is no need. He gives me the information. From what he tells me, I can track down the ones who stole from us."

"So this other man, the buyer—he is to go untouched?"

"Was not his fault."

"Fault! It is not about fault. It is about fear and respect. We kill him."

Shaban shook his head firmly. "No. I made a deal."

It took courage to stand up to the old man. But he would not back down.

"A deal with this man who robs us?" Arian growled.

"He did not rob us. He bought the merchandise from a third party. He did not know where it comes from. When he learns this, he is scared, sure, yes. He reaches out and makes amends. Full res—res—" His tongue struggled with the difficult word. "Restitution. In cash."

He laid the money on the table.

Arian studied the stack of bills. It seemed to fascinate him. "He reached out to you?"

"Through a, uh, intermediary, yes."

"What intermediary?"

Shrug. "A person of no importance."

"I still say he dies."

Shaban had a sense the old man was testing him. "I give him my word. Is on my honor."

"This is not Shqipëria. Things are different here."

"*I* am not different."

The old man raised his eyes from the money and took a long look across the table. Slowly he shook his head. "You are your mother's son."

"And my father's."

"Yes, *nip*." Grandson, it meant. "Your father's, too. You swore an oath to this man?"

"I did."

Arian's hand fluttered. A slender hand, all bones and liver spots and long, polished nails. The skin almost translucent, the pale blue veins showing through. "An oath given to one outside the *fil* means nothing. It is not a matter of honor."

"It is, to me."

"Stubborn boy. Principles, yes?"

"Only *besa*."

"You are old fashioned. You do not keep up with modern times."

"I come from an old country, *baba*." The word meant father, and sometimes grandfather—a term of affection.

Perhaps it was his use of this word that decided the matter. Arian shrugged magnanimously. "He lives. It is nothing to me."

Shaban nodded and stood, trying not to show his relief.

"But," Arian added, "the ones who sold him our product—they do not live."

"Already I am on their trail."

"You will kill them yourself?"

"Of course."

"I am told you do not like such work."

"This is so. But I will do it. Is my duty."

"Always with you, duty and honor. Is it duty that brought you to this country, when your mother wanted you to stay with her?"

Shaban thought about this. "No," he answered honestly. "Was ambition. There was nothing for me in Elbasan. Here—there is something."

"A great deal, perhaps." The old man stirred his coffee with one finger. "I was ambitious when I was young."

Again Shaban recalled the old photo, the scowling mouth and piercing eyes. "You had to be," he said quietly, "to build all this."

"Yes, all this." Arian sounded thoughtful when he said it, and unaccountably sad. "Someday, perhaps, you will sit where I sit now."

This was so unexpected that Shaban had no words for a response. He tried to make light of the remark. "Drinking macchiato in the back room of a shop?"

"Yes. And the young pups will report to you. Perhaps."

He waved again, this time in dismissal. His eyes were on the money again.

As Shaban left the parlor, he saw the Wolf reach slowly across the table with one long-fingered trembling hand.

1

THE FACE IN the rearview mirror was ghastly. It was a face in a nightmare.

Blood flecked the eyelashes, ringing her blue eyes in red rims. There was a spreading bruise on her jaw where one punch had landed, and a cluster of deep scratches down her neck, where clawing fingers had tracked ragged grooves in her skin. Glass splinters from the shattered carafe clung to her cheek. Her lips were bloodied and swollen—another punch—and two of her front teeth were chipped.

The rest of her wasn't in any better condition. Without looking, she could feel the deep bruise on her forearm where the first kick had connected, and the blister on her midriff where Ringo's cigarette had inflicted a burn. Her knuckles were skinned, her wrists badly chafed. And—oh, hell—she'd broken a nail.

"Yeah, I'm a mess," Bonnie Parker muttered. "But you oughta see the other guys."

It wasn't a joke.

She sped south as the sun emerged from the river, putting distance between herself and the terminal before the authorities showed up. Someone was sure to stumble across the bodies before long.

She wasn't worried about being connected to the scene. She'd wiped down both pool cues to remove any prints, and she'd retrieved Ringo's pistol, along with her purse and hat. The Walther she'd left behind. She couldn't take the time to look for it. The gun was unregistered, and it couldn't be traced to her.

7

There were no security cameras on the ship, but there might be some on the pier. In a closet she'd found a sailor's hooded jacket. It was too big for her, which was good; when the hood was up and her hands were in the pockets, she was completely unidentifiable. With the hat and purse concealed under the generous folds of oilskin, she wasn't even recognizably female. As she'd walked down the gangway, then past the towering cranes loading the last containers, she might have been any random dockworker. Whatever images were caught on camera would provide the authorities no help at all.

Nobody had noticed her as she walked away. So far, the violence aboard the *Mazeppa* had made no impression on the outside world. The gunshots had been fired below decks or on the bridge, the reports muffled, drowned out by the racket on the pier.

She'd found the Jeep where she'd left it. At this early hour on a Saturday, she'd encountered hardly any traffic during the half-hour drive down the turnpike and parkway. Now the only thing left to do was dispose of certain items.

She took a turnoff to Red Cliff, a medium-size town on the ocean. Red Cliff was like that old movie: a river ran through it. She parked on the south bank and made her way down a thickly overgrown incline to the water's edge.

By now the sun was up, the October day turning bright and pink, the weather still unseasonably mild. Shaded by trees, she sat on the bank and tossed Ringo's Sig Sauer, watching it sink in a mist of silt. Then she reached into her purse and withdrew the first of several thick bricks of cash. Hundred-dollar bills, neatly bundled in rubber bands. She'd noticed them when she'd taken out her car keys. A lot of money—fifty grand, maybe.

She peeled off the bills in twos and threes and tossed them into the river. She spent a long time doing it, like a child casting flower petals on the water. The bills floated downstream, toward the sea, slowly darkening as they became waterlogged. They might sink when they were soaked through, or they might vanish into the Atlantic. Or maybe they would wash up on the shore of the barrier peninsula that extended along this stretch of coast.

It didn't matter. She didn't want that kind of money. She never had.

When the last bills had been dispersed, she climbed the hillside and got back into the Jeep and headed home, taking the ocean road. She was too tired to return to the parkway. She was more tired, she thought, than she'd ever been.

She lit a cigarette and pulled in a deep drag, ignoring the complaint of bruised ribs.

A long fucking night. And yet by the clock it had been ten hours, no more. Ten hours that had begun in Wonderland—and ended in hell.

THEY REALLY DID call it Wonderland. It was a six-block stretch of kiddie rides and games of chance on a wide section of boardwalk in Point Clement, New Jersey. Mobbed in summer, shut down in winter, and in October— well, it depended on the night and the weather.

Tonight was a Friday and the weather was decent enough. The sun was down and the wind was up, the wet, salty breath of the ocean. The locals were out in force, riding the Tilt-A-Whirl and pumping quarters into arcade games and cramming piles of cotton candy down their throats.

Bonnie detested cotton candy. It was like eating cobwebs. She wasn't too crazy about amusement areas in general, or about this one in particular. But she wasn't here for fun. She was on the job.

Ahead of her, making his way through the crowd, was a married man by the name of Bill Mitter, who was suspected of cheating on his wife. It was Bonnie's job to turn suspicion into proof.

Yeah, it was a milk run, the only kind of assignment she'd taken on recently. Penny-ante stuff, straying husbands and background checks. Boring and not especially remunerative. No cases involving the special services she'd been known to offer as a sideline. Not anymore.

Bonnie felt sorry for Mrs. Mitter, first name Gloria. She was a dumpy middle-aged lady with bleached hair and an obvious facelift. She'd done what she could to hold her hubby's interest, but instead he'd decided to go tomcatting around, probably with some bimbo half his age. It just wasn't right. Though Bonnie herself had never been married, she was a stern respecter of monogamy in intimate relationships. She'd done a lot of things that weren't exactly on the up and up, but she could honestly say she'd never cheated on a guy. Then again, given her solitary nature, she hadn't had many chances.

In their meeting in Bonnie's office two days ago, Mrs. Mitter had said Bill was working late way too often and acting funny about it. Of course, she'd added with a kind of wistful optimism, there might be nothing to it.

Bonnie knew there was something to it. There was always something to it. She'd named her PI agency Last Resort for a reason. Anyone who came to her had exhausted all other options.

She told Mrs. Mitter to call her the next time Bill said he would be working late. That call had come in this afternoon. She had staked out Bill's office and followed him here when he'd left.

Now it was just a question of catching the bastard with his pants down. So to speak.

Her quarry was still progressing down the midway. His

rumpled raincoat was easy to track. The getup made him look like that detective on old-time TV. Columbo, right? Like the yogurt.

She followed him past a miniature golf course, a bandstand where two women were playing keyboards and singing "YMCA," and assorted game booths. He was moving fast, checking his wristwatch way too often. Like the white rabbit, Bonnie thought.

"He's late," she murmured. "He's late for a very important date."

Given the venue, it seemed appropriate.

Despite its name, there was nothing very wonderful about Wonderland, especially in the off-season. This late in the year, it was just about ready to go dark for the winter. Some of the rides were already closed. All the booths were still open, but that was hardly a selling point. She knew about carnies and their tricks, and she knew their games were a license to steal.

There was the basketball game—simple, right? Except the hoop was smaller than regulation size and was subtly bent into an oval. Kareem himself couldn't make those shots.

The dart game. Puncture a balloon, win a prize. But the balloons were underinflated, and the darts had dulled points.

Throw a ball into the tub. Anyone could do it! Not really. The setup was rigged so the ball would always bounce out.

At least that was how it was in other places. Maybe in Wonderland the games were legit. Maybe here the targets weren't gaffed and the prizes weren't fifth-rate crap that would fall apart as soon as you got them home. But that wasn't the way to bet.

Some folks, knowing the games were rigged, played anyway, just for fun. But the more trusting souls didn't know. She'd seen a news story about a guy in some other state who'd lost a couple grand—his life savings, sadly enough—on the ball-in-the-tub scam. How much did you have to lose before you realized you couldn't win?

She'd asked herself the same question earlier this year. And her answer ...

Hold that thought. Her quarry had stopped.

Twenty feet ahead, Bill Mitter was studying a map of the amusement area in a kiosk. There was a chance he'd made her. He might be testing her right now. She didn't think so, though. Any guy whose fashion sense ran to Columbo raincoats couldn't possibly be sharp enough to spot a tail.

Anyway, she was as close to invisible as she could be. Before starting out for the evening, she'd changed into blue jeans and a navy windbreaker. Her sneakers were dark blue also. It was a little-known fact that navy blue blended into the night more completely than any other color, even black.

She held back, adjusting her hat—a soft denim news-boy cap, also dark blue—while pretending to read the menu in the window of a snack shack. The place offered Mad Hatter burgers, Cheshire Cat shakes, and side orders of Tweedledee (fries) and Tweedledum (onion rings). The Jabberwock dogs sounded pretty good.

Then her gaze slid from the menu to the whirl of reflections in the glass. Amid the kaleidoscope of moving forms, there was one point of stability. A female figure, immobile, directly across the midway.

Watching her.

It was a truism in her business that the most boring job could get interesting in a hurry. She was reminded of that truism now.

Because while she had been tailing Bill Mitter, someone else had been tailing her.

2

BONNIE KEPT HER eyes on the reflection as she reviewed the steps that had brought her here. For an hour or so she'd sat in her battered puke-green Jeep Wrangler across the street from Bill Mitter's office building. Had the mystery woman been watching her then? Bonnie hadn't noticed her, but the street had been crowded. Someone could have parked farther down the block.

When Mitter had driven out of the parking lot behind his building, Bonnie had followed. He'd taken Highway 71 to Route 35, over the bridge into Point Clement. Rush hour. Heavy traffic. A vehicle tailing her? It was possible.

She remembered a white Hyundai Accent that had idled behind her at a red light on 71, a girl at the wheel. Young. Dark hair. Big eyeglasses, the squarish kind favored by smart people, or at least by people who wanted to look smart. Bonnie hadn't thought anything of it. She'd made the observation only out of habitual alertness. The Hyundai had continued behind her after the stoplight. When the highway had opened up into four lanes, the car had dropped out of sight.

Hiding behind other traffic? Following at a safer distance? Maybe. If it was the same girl. And she thought it was.

Bonnie took a closer look at the reflection without being too obvious about it. The girl wore a padded bomber jacket striped in red, white, and blue, one of those polyester things with foam lining. It was bulky enough to conceal a firearm. No handbag, though. That was where Bonnie kept her gun, a Smith & Wesson M&P 9 Shield, in a special compartment.

A few yards away, Bill Mitter was in motion again, having located his destination on the map. Bonnie went after him. She didn't glance back to see if the girl was following her. She already knew the answer, and she didn't want to tip her hand.

The three of them would have made for quite an amusing little parade, if anyone around them had noticed. Mitter in front, Bonnie behind, and the girl in the patriotic parka taking up the rear. What was that old song? *Me and my shadow, strolling down the avenue ...*

Mitter had just about reached the end of the amusement area. All that was left was the food court pavilion, and naturally that was where he went. Bonnie entered in time to see him climbing the stairs to the second floor, where a sign advertised Mulligan's Bar & Grill.

She'd eaten there once. Nice enough place, a step up—literally—from the steam-table ambience of the burgers-and-pizza operations on the ground floor. He must be meeting his date there. He'd be occupied for some time.

That was good. She wanted to take care of this other little problem right away.

She left the pavilion, her gaze ticking from side to side as she looked for the girl.

There. Twenty feet to her left, just standing around, making no effort at concealment or diversion.

Either her technique was poor, or she wasn't worried about being spotted. Which could be because she was about to make her move.

Yeah, she could be a shooter. That heavy jacket might be the tipoff. The night was chilly, but not really that cold. On the other hand, some gals just had thin blood.

Bonnie headed north, retracing her steps, walking fast. When she looked back after intentionally dropping her purse, she saw the girl closing quickly. A rapid, purposeful stride.

A hitter's stride? Maybe. There was a moment in any hit

when you gave yourself the go signal. Then you went on autopilot, completing the job with robotic efficiency. Bonnie knew all about it. She'd been there, done that.

Now maybe this girl was coming for her.

To her left, a side plaza crowded with carnival rides came into view. She went through the gate. This area was better lit. She didn't think the girl would do anything under the lights, in front of witnesses.

At a vending machine she purchased a roll of tickets. Paper tickets, the old-fashioned kind. She handed a ticket to a wizened carny running the carousel and boarded just before it started to spin. She swung onto a painted zebra, rode it for a couple of turns, then dismounted and hopped off the moving platform, violating the rules. She alit on the opposite side and lost herself in the cluster of parents watching their tykes.

When she looked back, she saw the girl glancing around in confusion, a hunter who had lost the scent.

Time for a quick change. Bonnie reversed her windbreaker so the shiny lining was on the outside, stuffed the cap into her pocket, and pushed her hair under her collar. Instantly she was a new person—different clothes, different hair.

Sidling up to a mom and dad, she took out her cell phone and pretended to be snapping pix of rotating rug rats. Actually she'd switched to the front camera view so the image in the viewfinder was her own face. She wasn't really that vain. She wanted to scope out the people behind her.

In a minute the girl made her appearance. Her gaze panned past Bonnie without stopping. Having completed her circuit of the carousel, she moved on.

Bonnie followed. She was the hunter now, a role much better suited to her taste.

Near the line for the Ferris wheel she came up fast and shoved her purse in the girl's side. Her hand was inside, gripping the Smith, and she knew the girl could feel the hard circle of the muzzle through the fabric.

"Looking for me?" Bonnie said.

To her credit, her quarry hardly flinched. "I'm not here for the popcorn."

Up close the girl was even younger than Bonnie had thought. Barely out of high school. But this was no child. There was something hard about her, a toughness and a high-strung wiry energy.

"Keep your hands in sight and come with me. Don't say anything and don't scream."

"I never scream," the girl said calmly.

Bonnie nudged her into the line and waited in silence till they reached the gate, where she handed over two tickets.

Her captive seemed more amused than afraid. "The Ferris wheel?"

"That's right, kiddo. I'm taking you for a ride."

3

SHABAN DRAGUSHA GUIDED his Porsche across the George Washington Bridge, feeling troubled. His day had not gone well.

First there had been the problem with his courier, a problem still unresolved. Then, less than twenty minutes ago, a message had appeared on his phone. Five cryptic words.

Third man found. St. Astius.

He understood the message well enough. Perhaps he should even be pleased about it. The third man had eluded him for nearly a year. Now the whole matter could be laid to rest.

He didn't like it, though. The prospect of killing never cheered him.

He crossed the river into the Bronx, fingering the crucifix around his neck and wondering how many Hail Marys and Our Fathers he would be made to recite by Father Gjergj. Very many, he was sure. But it was a small price to pay to save his soul.

His mother had always been deeply frightened for Shaban's soul. He had been an infant, only six weeks old, when his father, Sokol Dragusha, had died under circumstances of extreme violence in a bus depot in Rome, New York. After that, his mother Saranda had taken him back to Albania, to her own family, where she had raised him to be a good Christian, honest and unashamed of poverty, a boy who wanted nothing to do with gangsters. She had prayed over him. And when, at the age of twenty-one, he'd told her that he was going to

17

America to join his paternal grandfather in New Jersey, she had screamed, a keening wild-animal cry, and lunged at him with a knife.

Naturally she could not have hurt him. He'd swatted the knife away, then held her as she wept and begged for strength in Jesus' name.

He had never wanted to bring her pain. But in the end he was Sokol Dragusha's son. Blood would tell.

Even so, he did his best to be a Christian. He was not a cruel man. He did no more than what he must.

ST. ASTIUS WAS an Albanian Orthodox church on Rhine-lander Avenue. It was, in fact, Father Gjergj's church. But the priest would not be there tonight. He always made himself scarce at times like this.

Shaban parked around back and entered through a rear door, which had been left unlocked for him. Lou and Joey were already here; he'd noted Lou's late-model Chevy in the lot.

Todd Patterson was here too. Shaban could hear the man's hopeless pleading voice from the janitorial supply room next to the sacristy.

He opened the door and found Patterson spread-eagled on the concrete floor, wrists and ankles crudely tied with knotted rags. The overhead light was on, pouring down its fluorescent glare on his sallow face and dishwater gray eyes.

He had been stripped naked. That had not been necessary. Had Shaban been present earlier, he would have forbidden it. But Lou and Joey must have their fun.

"He's been crying like a baby since we picked him up," Lou said in their native language. His given name was Luan, and he had emigrated from Kavajë at the age of sixteen.

"Fuckin' pussy," Joey added in English. He was Jozef by

birth, but he'd been born in America and had no accent.

"Please ..." Patterson craned his neck, trying to meet the newcomer's eyes. "I didn't know, I didn't know ..."

"We don't give a fuck what you knew," Joey spat.

Shaban touched Joey's arm. "Let me talk to him."

The whole situation made him deeply uncomfortable. He did not like the man's nakedness or his obvious fear. He did not like the stink of sweat in the air, or the smirk on Joey's face, or Lou's dead eyes. Above all, he did not like what he would be required to do.

Kneeling beside Patterson, Shaban asked, "You understand why you are here?"

Patterson nodded. His tongue flicked at his lips, lizard quick. "Yeah."

"That shipment you hijacked was one of ours."

"I didn't *know*."

"I believe you. Your two friends didn't know either. But they have paid. Now you must, too."

"I'll pay. Anything you want. Any amount."

"Is not about money. Is about honor. We cannot let our merchandise be stolen. We must send a message."

"I'll never do it again. I swear." He was a man who thought he could talk his way out of trouble. A man with a quick wit, perhaps, and a grifter's dubious charm. But it would not help him now.

"This is not the point." Shaban sighed. "You ran away, sure, yes? We could not find you. Your friends, they were easy to find, but not you."

"Yeah. I ran."

"But you came back?"

"I thought it had been enough time."

Shaban shook his head. That was their mistake, always. They came back, seeking familiar territory.

"If you had stayed away, you might have been okay." He spread his hands in a gesture of futility. "You see how it is, right?"

19

"I didn't know it was you guys' stuff," Patterson said hopelessly. "I never woulda touched it if I knew."

The conversation was pointless. Shaban reached into his jacket and drew his FEG 9mm. The gun was a Hungarian import. He'd seen it in the movie *American Gangster* when he was a boy, and he'd always wanted one. It had been his first purchase when he came to this country.

He looked around for an apron or a coat, something he could use to prevent the blood spatter from soiling him. His suit was new, a jet-black Giorgio Armani, and he preferred not to ruin it.

"Don't," the man whispered, his eyes on the gun.

"I do it quick," Shaban promised. "No pain. Never do I cause pain. Is not my nature."

"I don't care about pain. I can take pain."

Shaban plucked yesterday's *Daily News* out of a waste-basket. Not ideal, but it would serve to keep most of the blowback off his clothes.

"Will be no pain," he said again. "I am not a cruel man."

"I got a kid." Patterson was crying. Wet streaks ribboned his face. "Little girl. I wanna see her grow up."

Shaban smoothed out the newspaper. "That is a lie."

"No lie. Really."

"We researched your background, your family. There is no child."

"She doesn't have my name. She was born, you know, illegitimate. But she's mine. It's true. It's true."

"So it is true. So what?"

"Do anything you want, but don't kill me. Bust me up, teach me a fucking lesson, but don't ... don't ..."

Shaban paused in the act of draping the newspaper over his arm. "Teach a lesson," he said softly.

Patterson seized on that. "Yeah, that's what I'm saying. Hurt me bad as you want. Then I tell everyone—don't mess with the Albanians. You know?"

It was a possibility, Shaban reflected. A beating that

was sufficiently severe would send the same message as a killing, and it had the advantage of allowing the victim to spread the word.

True, his grandfather had said the man who had taken the truck must die. But two were dead already, and if the third ended up a cripple in the hospital, it ought to be enough.

"Perhaps so," he said slowly. "Sure, yes."

"It's not a good idea, Shaban," Lou said firmly in Albanian. "*Ujku* wants blood."

"There will be blood," Shaban answered in the same language.

"You know what I mean. He wants this one in the ground like the others."

"Besides," Joey added in English, "the guy's an asshole."

Shaban knew Todd Patterson was an asshole, but even an asshole had an immortal soul. And a man could be condemned to perdition for killing an asshole, could he not? Sure, yes, he could count the rosary and make absolution, but was he entirely certain God would let him off the hook so easily? Perhaps God would not prove as forgiving as Father Gjergj.

Damnation was nothing to fool around with. And Todd Patterson had offered him another way.

"I think I follow his suggestion," Shaban answered, still speaking Albanian. "It seems right to me."

"It won't seem right to *Ujku*," Lou warned.

"I take responsibility. If my grandfather is angry, let him talk to me."

He holstered the 9mm and picked up a broom. The long wooden handle would make an adequate instrument of torture.

"Okay, Mr. Patterson. I go with your idea."

Patterson's eyes brimmed with tears. "Thank you. Thank you ..."

"Do not say this. Is nothing to thank me for." Shaban

pursed his lips. "Will be much pain. Very much."

"I know."

"You are sure? You can have a quick death, no pain—or this way. This way is harder."

"I don't want to die."

Shaban nodded gravely. "As you wish."

He himself would have chosen death. To die held no terror for him. All living things must die. But to be tortured and crippled and left a broken ruin—this was a worse fate, he thought.

Lou and Joey stood back. Shaban knelt again and gagged Todd Patterson with another rag, wadding it tight to choke off his cries. There was no telling if any parishioners were in the church.

Standing, he went to work with the broom handle, cracking kneecaps, splintering fingers and ankles, snapping bone. The man's face was awful to see. His eyes bugged out in a silent scream. After a while he lapsed into merciful unconsciousness.

Still the grim business went on. It must be thorough. Shaban did the job impassively, with a focused effort of will. He was careful not to kill Patterson inadvertently. It would not do to snap a rib and puncture a lung, or crush the trachea and cut off breath.

Finally he was done. The naked man on the floor was a sprawl of twisted limbs slowly turning black and blue. Blood oozed from the deeper bruises, but there had been no spatter. Shaban's suit was unharmed.

He wiped the broom handle with the newspaper and laid it aside.

"Take him somewhere and dump him in the street. Make it close to a hospital."

"*Ujku* will be angry," Lou said with stubborn repetition.

"I am his grandson. He will do nothing to me." He hoped this was true.

Leaving the room, he proceeded to the front of the

church. The pews were empty. Stained-glass saints gazed down from above, and Christ on his cross hovered over the altar.

Shaban knelt by the altar rail. Head bowed, he prayed to St. Bessus, patron of soldiers. He prayed that he had done the right thing.

And he prayed also that when he found the courier, he would be forgiven for what he must do.

Because for her, there could be no mercy, no half measures.

For her, there could be only death.

4

BONNIE FOLLOWED THE girl into a swaying gondola shaped like a teacup, open to the sky. The girl went first. They sat side by side on a padded bench. The carny swung down a bar to lock them in their seats, then banged the door shut. After a moment the wheel began to rise.

"Why are we doing this?" her new friend asked.

"Privacy."

"*Quelle* dramatic."

"Yeah, I'm a real diva. Now let's talk. And in case you had any doubts, this purse is locked and loaded."

The girl seemed unimpressed. "You're Bonnie Parker? The PI?"

"No, I'm Bonnie Parker, the brain surgeon. Who the hell are you?"

"Kyle Ridley."

"Kyle, huh? Did your daddy want a boy?"

"Did yours want an outlaw?"

Kyle was quick. Young as she was, she knew about the original Bonnie Parker, the one who'd run with Clyde Barrow in the Depression, robbing banks and killing lawmen.

"Matter of fact," Bonnie said, "he did."

"From what I hear, he wasn't disappointed."

"Meaning?"

"You have a reputation."

"As an outlaw?"

"Of sorts. Mind if I smoke?"

Bonnie could have used a cig herself. Right now she was jonesing for one of the Parliament Whites in her purse, but she couldn't afford to get distracted. "Sure, light up."

The gondola swung in the breeze. It was cooler up here, high above the midway.

"Actually," Kyle said, "it's a vape pen. You know, an e-cigarette. There's no toxic output. But some people find them objectionable anyway."

"Some people find everything objectionable. Those people can go fuck themselves."

Bonnie studied the girl. She was small and slim, a tiny thing half-buried inside the smothering coat. Her face was impassive, hard to read. The eyes behind the big lenses in their thick rectangular frames were hooded, secretive.

The lights of the amusement area sparkled below their feet. Moonlight stippled the ocean and whitewashed the slender strip of beach.

"You smoke?" Kyle asked as she primed the e-cig with a quick puff.

"Yeah. Real cigarettes, not those bogus ones."

"When'd you start?"

"When I was fifteen."

"Me too. Vaping, that is."

"Hey, it feels like we're really bonding here. Now can you tell me why you've been pasted to my ass like a tramp stamp?"

"I want to hire you."

"You couldn't just come to my office?"

"I was watching your place earlier today, and it seemed to me the police are just a little too interested in you. I saw a squad car in your parking lot three times in three hours. It looked like they were writing tag numbers."

"Yeah, they've been riding me pretty hard lately. It tends to discourage a certain kind of client."

"My kind, apparently."

"I left the office a couple hours ago. Why didn't you talk to me once I was on the move?"

"I didn't want to get in your way. I could see you were on a stakeout. Then you followed the red Dodge Charger to the parking lot here, and on foot you tailed the guy in the raincoat to the food court." She expelled a jet of steam. "Your technique isn't very good."

"No?"

"That business of pretending to read the menu in the window lacked verisimilitude. And later, when you dropped your purse so you could check me out—it was too obvious."

"Anything else?"

The girl considered it. "The hat is a mistake. Besides being a fashion faux pas, it makes you too identifiable."

Bonnie didn't much care for the faux pas crack, but she let it pass. "My target didn't identify me."

"You were lucky."

"Meanwhile, I figured out you were tailing me and I maneuvered you into this little tête-à-tête. What does that say about *your* technique?"

"I wasn't trying to be inconspicuous. I just wanted to give you some space to do your job. As a courtesy, you understand."

"Nice of you. Did you let me get the drop on you as a courtesy too?"

"We had to make contact eventually. I tried to approach you after you left the food court. But you stayed ahead of me."

"Until I was behind you—and you got jumped."

Kyle chuckled.

"Something funny?" Bonnie asked.

"I shouldn't laugh. It's just the whole tough-gal vibe, you know? You sound like you're channeling Humphrey Bogart."

"And you want me to change the channel?"

SKIN IN THE GAME

"It's not a criticism. Really. You have a unique personal style. It's so unabashedly retro."

Bonnie took a moment to remind herself why she couldn't just shoot Kyle Ridley. "Let's try to stay on point. What do you need me for?"

The red LED on the tip of the vape pen lit up as Kyle took another drag. "I've gotten tangled up in a tricky situation. I think you can help me get clear of it."

"What situation?"

"It involves lawbreaking. I assume I can speak freely?"

"Just talk."

"For the past few months I've been working in the, um, transportation business. Carrying a certain item into the United States from Turkey, by way of London."

"Heroin?"

Kyle nodded.

"You're a drug mule?"

"Can't say I care for that term. I prefer to be called a drug courier. I've done six trips, plus a dry run. This was going to be my last time. At ten fifteen AM I walked off the plane at Newark with two kilos on me."

"And then?"

"I lost it."

"Yeah, I'm always losing stuff, too. I lost a hairbrush, still can't find the damn thing."

"You know what I mean. I got jacked."

"In the airport?"

She nodded. "Long-term parking."

"That sounds like more than just bad luck."

"I don't know what it was. It could have been a random mugging. Or it could have been someone from another organization who got wind of what I was carrying. Whatever the real story is, the son of a bitch took my carry-on, and I lost the haul. All of it."

"What about your employers? They know about this?"

"No. I was supposed to take the product directly to my

contact. That's our usual routine. Instead I went home, threw together some clothes and all the cash I had, and got out. Took my car but left my phone behind, in case he could track it."

"You don't trust him to take your word for it that you were mugged?"

"He won't care about that. I lost the shipment. That's all he'll need to know. Excuses won't cut it."

"What will he do to you?"

"Kill me. What else?" Her voice was flat, a dry mono-tone.

"You sound pretty sure of it," Bonnie said.

"I know the type of people I'm dealing with."

"Might have been better not to go into business with them."

"Yes, well, you know what they say about twenty-twenty hindsight."

Hindsight wasn't the issue. Simple common sense should have shown Kyle Ridley all the ways her business arrangement could go wrong, with results ranging from a prison cell to an unmarked grave. But it was a little late for that lecture.

"By now, of course, he'll be looking for me," Kyle added.

"Him and the rest of the crew."

"No, I don't think so. He'll want to handle it on his own. He won't want his superiors to know there's a problem."

"And you think he can find you."

"He can find me." Still no emotion. "He's not dumb, and he's incredibly tenacious. As long as I'm in the tri-state area, I'm at risk."

"Then go someplace else."

"I will, eventually. But all I have on me is a hundred dollars. I can't get very far on that. And even if I could leave, I don't intend to spend the rest of my life looking over my shoulder."

"They spread their net that wide?"

"They're national. International. The Dragusha family. Heard of them?"

"Albanian mob." Bonnie frowned. "So what is it you need me to do, exactly?"

"I thought that was obvious." She drew vapor into her mouth, let it rest there for a moment, then blew it out in a swirling cloud. "I need you to kill him."

Bonnie took in the remark without particular surprise. "Because you heard I do that kind of thing, huh?"

"I know all about your unadvertised skills. I know your rep as a hitman—or hit woman; I'm not sure of the preferred terminology. And I know what you charge. Three thousand up front, and thirty down the line."

"You seem to know all about everything."

Kyle nodded, taking it as a compliment, which it wasn't.

Bonnie looked down. The Ferris wheel had stopped, with their gondola at its apex. From this height it was impossible to make out individual figures in the crowd below. There were only drifts of movement, ripples of shadow, like crisscrossing currents in a stream.

"Just out of curiosity," she asked, "how am I supposed to get paid? You told me you've only got a hundred bucks to your name."

"A hundred on me. But there's fifty thousand dollars in a safe deposit box. In cash."

"How'd you get fifty grand?"

"I made six trips, counting today's. I was paid for the first five. I made ten thousand per trip. You do the math."

"Ten g's per trip? That sounds high."

"It's what I'm worth," Kyle said with a kind of childish pride.

"In that case, you shouldn't have wasted time at your apartment. You should have gone straight to the safe deposit box and cleaned it out. By now you'd be halfway to Florida."

"I can't go to the bank. My handler in the organization

helped me set up the account. One of the clerks is always watching me when I open the box. If I tried to clean it out, my handler would have been notified before I even had a chance to leave. But once he's been eliminated, it'll be clear sailing."

"Don't kid yourself, slugger. Nothing about this is clear sailing."

"You have no reason to refuse. The money is good, and after all, it's what you do. You *are* an assassin, right?"

"Hey, ixnay on the sassinsay. There's people around."

"Are you or aren't you?"

"I was. Not your ordinary kind, though. I only went after the bad guys. I had, you know, standards."

Kyle's eyes narrowed. "Why are you using the past tense?"

"Because whatever I might or might not have done in the past, I'm not doing it anymore."

"What are you talking about?"

"That part of my life is over. Finito. Kaput."

"You're saying you quit?"

Bonnie nodded. "Cashed out. Retired."

"I don't understand."

"I'll make it simple for you. Bang-bang go bye-bye."

Kyle was staring at her with the first real emotion she'd shown, an expression of horror that was almost comical. "You can't be serious."

"Afraid I am, kiddo. You'll need to find yourself another hitter, because Bonnie Parker is officially out of the game."

5

"THAT ISN'T POSSIBLE," Kyle said slowly, stuck in denial mode.

Bonnie smiled. A less than admirable part of her was actually enjoying the kid's anguish. "You hear any scuttlebutt about jobs I've pulled lately? Say, in the past six or eight months?"

"Well, no. But I assumed ..."

"Assumed what? No one needed anybody put out of the way anymore? There'd been a general outbreak of fellowship and good cheer? Nope. I've been turning down work, that's all."

"You're telling me you've—you've reformed?"

"Guess so. I'm learning to color inside the lines."

Kyle shook her head. "I don't believe you. People don't change."

"Some people do. And I've got a powerful incentive."

"What incentive?"

"For one thing, there's all the attention I'm getting from local law enforcement. You noticed it yourself. There are people in positions of authority who know about my former sideline. They can't touch me, not for the stuff they're already aware of—"

"Why not?"

"It's complicated. Let's just say I had a good lawyer and some bargaining chips to play. But that won't help me if I mess up in the future."

"So you're scared?"

"Of a life sentence? You bet. But I'm also seriously committed to making a fresh start."

"That can't be all there is to it. You're leaving something out."

Bonnie was leaving a lot of things out. She was leaving out her long talks with Frank Kershaw, the man who'd taken her in off the street when she was a teenager and who, in recent months, had been quietly insistent that her chosen way of life had no future. He was the one who'd told her to color inside the lines, a metaphor he'd repeated so often that she was now using it herself.

So there was Frank. And there was the whole situation with Streinikov's crew last winter, and the Long Fong Boyz and Frank Lazzaro before that. She might not be the sharpest quill on the porcupine, but even she could see that she'd used up her quota of good luck for this lifetime, and probably for several other lifetimes to boot. There was such a thing as quitting when you were ahead.

Which was not to say her fingers didn't itch every now and then as she contemplated her collection of black-market firearms. Nor to say she didn't miss the sizable addition to her income that her moonlighting activities had provided. But she was officially on the wagon, assassination-wise. Had there been an equivalent of AA for people like her—Assassins Anonymous, maybe—she could have honestly proclaimed, "I've been homicide-free for two hundred forty-one days."

And a smug little twerp like Kyle Ridley wasn't going to get her to backslide, no matter what kind of fix she was in.

"It's not gonna happen, slugger," she said with finality.

"It has to. I was counting on you to come through."

"Then you're up a creek, aren't you?" She couldn't keep the complacency out of her voice, mainly because she hadn't tried.

"Come on. It's one night's work. It won't even be that hard."

"Sure, taking out a mobbed-up drug importer is a walk in the park."

32

"Ordinarily, no. But I've got it all worked out."

"I'll just bet you do." Bonnie sighed. "Take my advice, free of charge. Hop in your Hyundai and make tracks for a warmer climate. Spend all your cash on fuel and drive as far as you can."

"And end up homeless, living in my car?"

"It's better than not living at all."

Kyle gaped at her. "This is *bullshit.*"

"Use your indoor voice. We're at a family place."

The girl was showing signs of real fear. That was good. Fear was what she ought to be feeling. Lots of it.

"Look," Kyle said, straining for a reasonable tone, "I can understand your wanting to reform. I get it. But this is different. This isn't some random hit. This is saving my life."

"You so sure it's worth saving?"

"What's that supposed to mean?"

"I'm not a big fan of heroin traffickers."

"Oh, come on. Not that just-say-no crap. People have a right to put whatever they want into their own bodies."

"Most of the H around here is scored by high school kids. Middle school kids, too. Twelve-year-olds."

"Children grow up fast these days," Kyle said indifferently. "Anyway, if some shop-class rejects want to try for a Darwin Award by shooting crap into their bloodstream, why should you care?"

"Oh, yeah. Way to win me over."

"You don't have to like me. You only have to work for me."

"Looks like I'm not gonna do either. You'll have to get yourself another hitter."

"I don't know any others."

"Then do the job yourself."

"It can't work that way."

"Then you're in trouble."

"You fucking bitch. You're willing to let them murder me?"

Bonnie lifted her shoulders. "Not my problem. I got no skin in the game."

The gondola was descending. At ground level the carny lifted the bar and set them free. Bonnie stepped out without a word and made her way back to the main drag. Kyle followed, her voice more urgent than before.

"You can't just walk away. I can't handle Shaban on my own."

Bonnie stopped, looking back. "Funny. I thought you could handle anything."

"Don't be a moron. For Christ's sake, how much do I have to dumb it down for you? He'll kill me for something I didn't even do."

Man, even when she was begging for her life, little Kyle couldn't find a way to be likable.

"Sounds that way," Bonnie said. She walked on.

Kyle caught up to her, clutching at her windbreaker like a kid clinging to her mommy. "But it's not fair."

"Life seldom is."

"*Please.*"

She looked down at the small figure wrapped inside her large coat. A girl who was afraid, really afraid, and not hiding it anymore.

"There's one other problem," Bonnie said slowly. "Even if we do take out your friend ..."

"Shaban."

"Right. Even if we remove Shaban from the equation, it won't help. The others will figure out what happened, and then the whole crew will be after you. If you think running off with a shipment is enough to put you on a hit list, just think about how popular you'll be once they've tagged you with the murder of one of their own."

"But that's the thing. They don't know about me."

"They may not know about the missing shipment, at least for now, but—"

"No, they don't know about me *at all*. Only Shaban

knows. He's essentially a cutout. He selected me for the job, and only he makes contact with me. The others don't even know my name."

"So you assume."

"That's how it works with the Dragushas. Their operation is hierarchical, bureaucratic. There's a leadership council that coordinates the activities of all the different families. Each family has its own executive committee—they call it the *bajrak*—sort of the inner circle. The *krye*, who's the boss, the godfather, runs the clan—"

"That would be Arian Dragusha," Bonnie put in.

"Right. The *kryetars*, the underbosses, report to him. And it's all bound together by family connections and by *besa*, a code of honor like omertà. You see? Everything is compartmentalized. Shaban knows who I am. No one else does."

"And with him out of the picture, you're home free."

"I thought I'd already made that clear."

Bonnie let a moment pass while the crowd swirled around them. "Okay, look. I'm not committing to anything, but since you said you've got it all worked out, I'll give you a chance to brief me on the details of your master plan."

Kyle showed no reaction. She had to be at least a little bit relieved, but she was damn hard to read. No wonder she'd breezed through Customs without so much as a second look.

"I suppose that's the best I can hope for," the girl said flatly.

"It's way more than you should've hoped for. Right this second, though, I gotta finish up my other job. How about we meet up at the Sand Bar in an hour?"

"The Sand Bar?"

"Right down there. Nice view of the water. We'll talk, we'll hoist a few. By the end of the evening we'll be friggin' sorority sisters."

"I don't approve of sororities. They're an expression of an outdated classist and sexist system."

"It was a joke, kiddo."

"Of course it was. I know that. I'm only saying—"

"I don't care. Get lost. I'm on the clock, and you're cramping my style, Kyle."

"Rhyme? Really?"

"What can I say? There's poetry in my soul."

6

ON HER WAY back to the food court, Bonnie shrugged off the windbreaker, reversed it again so it was no longer inside out, and pulled it back on. The newsboy cap went back on her head. She did all this unconsciously. Her mind was elsewhere, musing on Kyle Ridley.

The girl's story didn't pass the smell test. She got mugged on her last run? Like the cop who gets killed on the day before his retirement. A movie cliché.

And she knew exactly how much Bonnie Parker, PI, charged for a hit. That meant she'd done more than just listen to rumors. She'd done research, planning. She'd expected to need a hitter.

Something funny was going on. Even so, she was going to take the case. She'd already decided that much. She just didn't want to make it too easy. She wanted to make the girl sweat.

A patter of gunfire drew her gaze to a shooting gallery, a moving line of ducks, and a James Dean wannabe in a black leather jacket doing his best with a rifle. Not a real rifle, naturally; the days when carnival visitors shot .22 rimfire ammo had ended around the time when the real James Dean checked out in a car crash. This thing was a modified air gun that produced a flash of light when the trigger was pulled, enlivened by electronic sound effects of gunshots and ricochets.

In theory the targets would react to the flashes, but hardly any of the ducks had gone down. Either the guy was a crappy shot, or the game was rigged. Probably the latter. She didn't know how the scam was run, but she always assumed the worst. It was one way to avoid being disappointed.

The booth operator, a graying burly guy with an over-hanging gut, watched his latest mark impassively. She thought he had the look of a con artist. There was something about his too-casual slouch, his expressionless face.

She spent another few moments observing the carny—she wasn't sure why—then entered the pavilion. She climbed the stairs to Mulligan's, slipping inside while the hostess was busy seating someone else. A long bar with a mirror behind it stretched along one side of the restaurant. She scanned the room's reflection until she spotted Bill Mitter in a corner booth.

He wasn't dining with a secret lady friend. His companion was a man.

Well, that was a kick in the cornflakes. It looked like he really was working late, and this was some kind of business meeting.

Or maybe there was another answer.

She ventured closer, moving among the tables as if searching for someone she knew. As she got within a couple of yards of the booth, she did the purse-dropping routine again.

Kyle might not approve of her technique, but the gimmick worked well enough to give her a glimpse of the underside of the table, where Bill Mitter's hand rested lightly on the other guy's leg.

Not a business meeting. Apparently Gloria's hubby was keeping more than one secret from his wife.

A waitress breezed into view, carrying a tray loaded with glasses. Bonnie timed her own progress to intercept the girl as she came even with the booth. Casually she brushed a foot against the waitress's ankle, tipping her off balance.

Three glasses slid off the tray, and one of them splashed

Bill Mitter's friend in the lap, dousing him with what looked like a strawberry daiquiri.

Commotion. Flustered apologies from the waitress. Napkins were produced to dab at the stain. In the confusion Bonnie disappeared inside the ladies' room.

She gave Bill's friend a minute to decide to clean himself off in the gents' room next door. She used the time productively by taking a pee.

When she emerged from the restroom, Bill Mitter was alone at the table. She slid into the booth alongside him, partly to intrude on his space, but mainly because she didn't want to plant her tush on the daiquiri-slick cushions of the opposite bench.

"Hey, Bill. Enjoying your evening?"

He was scared, and he didn't try to hide it. This rendezvous was a secret. No one was supposed to know he was here.

"Who the hell are you?" he blurted. It was intended as a bulldog bark but came out as more of a Chihuahua yip.

"Bonnie Parker. I'm a private detective in Brighton Cove. You may have heard of me."

"Everybody's heard of you." The tone of his voice made it clear that not all publicity was good publicity.

"Yeah, I'm real popular. So here's a funny thing. Your wife hired me. She thinks there's another woman."

"There isn't. I'm here with a friend, that's all."

"Skip it, Bill. I caught the hand-to-knee action. I know he's more than a friend."

"Whatever you think you saw—"

"I don't just think it. I took a picture. See this pen?" She plucked what appeared to be an ordinary ballpoint from her purse. "It's a spy camera. Digital images, twelve megapixels, instant upload to the cloud. Snazzy little gizmo, huh? I got it at Sharper Image."

"What is this? You angling for a payoff or something?"

"It's not a shakedown. I just don't want you wasting my

time with stupid lies. Your boyfriend won't be indisposed forever. We need to get this done."

"Get what done?"

"There are two ways we can play it. I can tell your wife—or you can."

"What?"

"It would be better coming from you. This isn't the kind of news Gloria wants to hear from a hired hand."

"You want me to tell her about Phil?"

"That his name? So it's Bill and Phil? Cute. He seems like a nice guy. Didn't blow his stack at the waitress. And hey, don't stiff her on the tip, by the way; I'm the one who tripped her up."

"I *can't* tell Gloria ..."

"You can. Or I will. She has a right to know. And let's face it, Bill, you'll be better off if you can live your life honestly, won't you?"

He lowered his eyes almost shyly. "It's not just Gloria. I have a reputation in my town."

"So do I. Mine's not so good at the moment. Yours is probably better. Which gives you more to lose. But it also gives you more goodwill to fall back on. People can be surprisingly understanding about stuff like this."

"I don't know."

"I'll give you twenty-four hours. After that I'll check in with the missus. If you haven't had the talk ..."

"You'll show her the pictures?"

She tossed the pen onto the table. "There aren't any pictures. It's just a pen."

"So you can't prove anything."

"Nope. But you'll tell her anyway. Because it's the right thing to do. It'll clear the air and make things better for everybody. All right, here comes Phil. Cheers."

She left the table, ignoring Phil's suspicious stare. She was pretty sure Bill Mitter would step up to the plate. If he didn't, she would wait for his next liaison, and that time she wouldn't be so nice.

On her way out she circled back to the bar to avoid the waitress she'd encountered earlier. Halfway down the row of stools she spotted a familiar face. It was the fish market guy, the one who'd loaned her a camera a few years ago when she'd needed some video evidence.

"Yo, Sparky."

He looked up slowly. "Oh. Hi there."

She plopped herself down on the stool next to his. She didn't mind making Kyle wait a little longer.

Her companion stared down at his drink, a fizzy concoction that looked just a shade girly.

"You don't seem happy to see me," she said.

"Should I be?"

"People usually are."

"Really?"

She considered. "Well … no. Lately I've kinda been a local pariah."

"So I understand. There are, uh, certain rumors about you."

"You know what they say about rumors."

"So they're not true?"

"What is truth?" she asked philosophically. It was as good an evasion as any.

The bartender asked for her order. She was no teetotaler, but tonight she needed to stay sharp. She ordered a Sprite. When it was delivered, she jerked a thumb at Sparky. "Put it on his tab."

Sparky acquiesced with a weary nod. "What are you doing here on a Friday night?"

"Just hanging. You?"

"Uh, yeah. Me too. Hanging."

"Nah, I don't think so. You're trying to get your drunk on, and something tells me that's not your usual MO."

His gaze dropped to the cocktail again. "Leave me alone."

"Why so down in the dumps, chump?"

"If you must know, my wife and I are having some problems."

"What kind of problems?"

"She left me. I mean—we broke up. It was mutual."

"Good recovery. Why'd she vamoose?"

"It's personal."

"Obviously it's personal. You can't talk about personal stuff with an old friend?"

"Old friend? You don't even know my name."

"Sure I do. You're Sparky. So why'd the missus take off? She find someone better?"

"No."

"She turn gay?"

"*No.*"

"So what's her deal?"

"She said I wasn't going anywhere and I'd never make anything of myself."

She sipped her drink. "Hard to argue with that."

"You really suck at conversations like this."

"Okay, okay. You ever think about proving her wrong?"

"What do you mean?"

"Still working at the fish place?"

"Yeah. I'm an assistant manager. It's a good job."

"It's a go-nowhere job, like your ex says."

"She's not my ex. We're just sort of having a trial separation."

"Whatever. Look, what's the best you can look forward to in the fish game? Getting a promotion to full manager?"

"Mr. Brown is the manager. He owns the place."

"I remember." He was the guy who'd hired her to find out if Sparky was filching fish. Which he was. Bonnie had covered for him, because she'd felt sorry for the poor little schmo. "So unless he kicks off and you inherit the store—"

"I'm not going to inherit the store."

"Then you've got nowhere to go, Sparky. The wife is

right about that. What's her name, anyway?"

"Belinda."

She wrinkled her nose. "I don't like it. I'll call her Mrs. Sparky."

"You're really starting to annoy me. And what's wrong with the name Belinda?"

"Reminds me of that chick from the Go-Go's."

"So?"

"I hate the Go-Go's." She took another sip. She'd forgotten how much she disliked Sprite. It tasted like carbonated piss. "How about the ghost thing?"

"What?"

"Didn't you have some nutball idea about ghost hunting? I seem to recall that's why you bought the infrared camera I borrowed."

"I still do that. It's not nutty. I've captured some interesting anomalies—"

"Yeah, yeah. Save it for the Discovery Channel. Make any money off it?"

"It's not about the money."

"So ... no."

"It's a metaphysical exploration—"

"I don't care how metaphorical it is."

"Metaphysical."

Bonnie was pretty sure that was what she'd just said. "Mrs. Sparky wants to think her hubby is gonna provide for her. Chasing Casper with a camcorder just ain't getting it done."

He sighed. "That's one of things she said."

"Oh yeah?"

"She said I was spending too much of my time on that stuff. She said I needed to grow up."

"Yeah, it might be time to put away the Superman pj's and get some big-boy clothes."

"I don't wear—never mind."

"You don't wear Superman pj's?"

"No."

"Captain America?"

"I sleep in the nude, if you must know."

"Whoa. TMI."

He glared at her. "I can't imagine why nobody likes you. It's a real mystery."

She chuckled. "Hey, I like that. You're punching back. Felt good, didn't it?"

"A little."

"Punch harder, and it'll feel better."

"Is that what this is—some kind of therapy? Are you riding me so I'll assert myself?"

"I'm riding you 'cause it's fun and you make it easy. Any therapeutic benefits are purely accidental."

"Oh."

"But if it's working for you, I'm glad."

He looked away. "You might not be an entirely despicable person."

"No, I am. You just don't know me well enough, Sparky."

"Could you stop calling me that?"

"To be honest, I don't remember what you call yourself. It's been a few years."

"I'm Walt. Walt Churchland."

"Oh, right." She thought about it. "I like Sparky better."

"You're a real pain in the ass."

"That's the consensus."

He had to smile at that. "Have you always been this much of a hard case?"

"Ever since I can remember."

"Even as a kid?"

"I didn't have a normal upbringing. I did a lot of moving around."

"With your folks?"

"At first, yeah." Until they got killed, she could have said. "Then on my own. When I was seventeen, I lit out on a Kawasaki rice-burner to see the country and find myself."

"And did you?"

"See the country?"

"Find yourself?"

She shrugged. "Does anybody?"

She didn't know why she was talking about this. She wasn't the type to open up. For some reason her extended road trip had just popped into her mind.

"You bum around like that for very long?" Walt Churchland asked.

"Couple years."

"What got you to settle down?"

"Nothing in particular. It just got old."

This was a lie. But she wasn't under oath or anything, and there was no reason for Sparky to know about Palm Garden and what had happened there.

Palm Garden ... Funny. Something about that memory raised a shiver along her back.

She was just jumpy, she guessed. Tired of reminiscing, she switched the subject back to him. "How long have you and the wife been married?"

"Seven years."

"Kids?"

"No."

"She ever walk out on you before?"

"Never." His voice broke on the word.

"It's eating you up, isn't it?"

"I guess so. The worst thing—it's not the loneliness or even the uncertainty about my future. The worst thing ..."

"Spill it, Sparky."

"The worst thing is not feeling like a man."

"You're not the first guy whose wife has skipped out on him. It doesn't make you any less manly."

Not that he'd been all that manly to begin with, she almost added, but somehow she suspected that this observation might be unhelpful.

"I know, but ..." He shook his head. "I've lost my confidence, I guess. I need ... I don't know what I need."

"I do. A little of the old bouncy-bouncy."

"What?"

"You know what. Do I gotta spell it out for you?"

"You could be right." He gave her a sly look. "I don't suppose ..."

"Me? Uh, no."

"I was just putting it out there."

"Yeah, well, you can put it back in. I'm not gonna rock your casbah."

"Okay, okay."

She swallowed more Sprite, winced at the liquid-candy taste, and pushed the glass away. She thought about Walt Churchland and his problem.

"You know—and this is not an offer—but I just might be able to help you out."

He glanced at her. "What's that mean?"

"Can you meet me back here tomorrow around this time?"

"Why?"

"Don't ask so many questions. Can you or not?"

"Sure, I guess."

"Good deal." She got up. "Right now I gotta see a man about a horse. Well, technically, I gotta see a girl about some horse."

She thought that was pretty clever, though it helped if you knew that *horse* was street lingo for heroin.

Naturally, Sparky didn't get it. "What are you talking about?"

"Never mind. I need to get going, is all. Nice chatting with you."

"Yeah," he said sourly, "it's been magical."

She laughed. "Sparky, this could be the beginning of a beautiful friendship."

As she left the restaurant she realized the damn girl was right. She really was channeling Bogart.

7

SHABAN PARKED THE Porsche on a side street two blocks from Jay Sanderling's house. With his collar turned up, he walked along the sidewalk to number 421 on Egerton Avenue in Woodbridge. The lights were on, and there was movement in the windows. He circled the house, peering in, and saw a small boy playing with model cars in the living room and his mother preparing dinner in the kitchen. A nice domestic scene.

The father, however, was not in sight. Shaban moved to the garage, separate from the house and sitting well back at the end of a gravel driveway. He beamed a pocket flashlight through a side window and saw only one vehicle, a Chevrolet Suburban, in the two-car garage. The Suburban was the wife's car. Mr. Sanderling had not yet come home.

That was no problem. He could wait.

He positioned himself behind a screen of hedges in a drift of brittle leaves. The night was turning chilly, but he was indifferent to the cold.

The problem that faced him was unprecedented in his experience. Never before had a courier run off with the product. And this one, Kyle Ridley, was the last person he would have suspected of duplicity. An intelligent girl, reliable—so very reliable that he had not even insisted on picking her up at the airport. He had been content to let her come to him.

And now, on her sixth assignment, she had—what was the expression?—skipped out. At first he couldn't believe it. But when she had not arrived by noon and had failed to answer repeated phone calls, he had begun to worry. That was when he'd taken a trip to her residence. Her car had not been in its numbered space, and her apartment, which he'd accessed after jimmying the lock, had been empty. Many of the clothes had been removed from the closet. Some had been left strewn on the floor. She had packed in a hurry. She had left her phone behind, and the SIM card had been removed and smashed.

It was all very disappointing. He had credited her with more sense. Now he would have to track her down and recover the goods, and of course he would have to kill her. Later he would make his confession to Father Gjergj and say five Our Fathers and five Hail Marys to cleanse his soul.

The purr of an engine drew his gaze to the street. Headlights approached. Shaban eased closer to the garage wall, out of sight. The car, a Ford Taurus, turned into the driveway, and the garage door slanted open with a shuddering creak. As the Taurus eased inside, Shaban followed. When the engine fell silent, he moved up slowly toward the driver's door from the rear.

A man with a briefcase emerged. He turned toward the driveway and stopped, facing Shaban. A gasp hissed out of him.

"Hello, Mr. Sanderling," Shaban said.

"Jesus. You scared the shit out of me."

"Sorry for that. Was not my intention. It should not have been needed to meet you in this way. You should have taken my calls."

"I—I was busy all day. Didn't have time."

"When I call, you make time."

Sanderling set down his briefcase and pushed his glasses higher on the bridge of his nose. "Look, the thing is—I don't want to do it anymore."

"No?"

"It's too risky. I can't take the chance. The money is good, but if I lose my job ... You understand."

"I do not understand. We had an agreement. A man honors his obligations."

"I can't take the risk."

Shaban glanced at the clutter of tools hanging from hooks on the wall. There was no broom, but he did see a snow shovel. Casually he lifted it by the handle. The wide blade was aluminum, reinforced with a galvanized steel edge. He tapped it against his open palm.

"There are many kinds of risk." Tap. "When I could not get through to you, I took the trouble to find out some things." Tap. "Personal things."

Sanderling's eyes flicked to the shovel's blade, beating out its steady rhythm. "What things?"

"Your wife is Joanna. She is employed at Raritan Bay Medical Center as a registered nurse." Tap tap. "Is good to be a nurse. She helps people. She must have a heart that is kind. Your child is Joshua." Tap. "Joshua is nine years old and attends public school three blocks from here. Is allergic to peanuts. Is on the drug Ritalin for hype— hyper—" He gave up on the impossible word. "The drug Ritalin." Tap tap.

"How the hell ...?"

"You are not the only source available to me. I have friends in many places. I am capable of many things." Tap. "You understand me, sure, yes?"

Sanderling's voice was thick. "Yes."

"Good." He replaced the shovel on its hook. "I do not wish to be cruel. Is not my nature. But I'm a pragmatist. Your assistance is needed. So I obtain it. And you will be paid, like before."

"All right."

"I'm sorry, but you make a mistake to think you can go into business with us and, later on, walk away. Is not that kind of arrangement. Once you prove useful, you are called again. Is not a call you can ignore." He shrugged. "These are the rules. You should have known them."

"All right," he said again, and for a second time he pushed his glasses higher on his nose.

"So you will do it?"

"Yes."

"Can you set it up from here?"

"No, I need to be at the command center. It's not as if the system is on the web or something. It's our own network. It can be accessed only from our dedicated terminals."

"Then you go back to the office."

"You mean now?"

"Sure, yes."

"I can't go back now. My wife is making dinner."

"Dinner will be late."

"I'm off duty. It won't look right. It'll raise too many questions."

"You go back anyway. Make excuse. Get to one of your dedi—dedi ..." He tried again. "Dedicated terminals. And set it up."

"It can't wait until morning?"

"No. I already texted you the details. You will forward any hits to my phone, like last time. You will set it up to work automatically. You will not even have to make the calls yourself."

"I know," Sanderling said, sounding unhappy.

"No one will find out, and you will make money. You buy your wife and child something nice. New TV, maybe."

The man nodded.

"No hard feelings, Mr. Sanderling?"

"No, no. Of course not."

"Don't be scared. You do the smart thing, sure, yes. Believe this."

Shaban left the garage, satisfied. It was unnecessary to watch Sanderling pull away in his Taurus. There was no doubt the man would do as he was told.

He walked back to his Porsche, satisfied. He was sure

he would find Kyle Ridley now. The girl had been crazy to think she could ever get away. She'd been carrying two kilos of pure heroin, with a street value of at least $220,000 once it was cut. Her very life was not worth so much.

He would find her, and he would get the shipment back, and then he would kill her quickly and simply—a single bullet placed between her eyes.

No pain. He would be sure of that. He was not a cruel man.

BONNIE FOUND KYLE sitting alone in a booth in the Sand Bar, nursing a bright green cocktail and picking at a dish of pretzels. The pretzels reminded Bonnie that her only dinner had been a couple of candy bars she'd scarfed down while staking out Bill Mitter's office.

"Job done?" Kyle asked without interest.

"I think so." She shrugged off her windbreaker. Underneath she wore a form-fitting short-sleeved shirt that bore the warning *You Can't Handle This*.

Bonnie had been in the Sand Bar a few times, usually on a job. It was your typical Jersey Shore pickup spot, crowded and dimly lit and ridiculously loud. Tonight a local band that called itself Gas Station Sushi was caterwauling in a corner, the lead vocalist croaking inarticulate lyrics over a trainwreck of clashing guitar chords. On the plus side, the wall of noise meant nobody could eavesdrop on a conversation. On the minus side, it was barely possible to have a conversation in the first place.

A waiter approached. Bonnie couldn't stomach any more Sprite, so she relaxed her discipline a tad and ordered a Dark & Stormy, making a silent promise to limit herself to one.

"I used to be a Jack 'n' Coke gal," she explained to Kyle, "but I gave up Coca-Cola 'cause that shit strips the finish off cars. After that, I tried a whole slew of decoctions before I settled on this one. Basically I just like the name. *It was a dark and stormy night*—isn't there some classic novel that starts that way? One of those Russian ones, like *Madame Bovary*?"

Kyle lifted a bored eyebrow. "I can't even count the number of ways you're wrong. Do you drink a lot?"

"Only every night. And sometimes during the day."

"You could have an alcohol problem."

"You could have a lot of problems if you keep giving me lip."

"I'm just making an observation."

"Yeah. Me, too, Crocodile."

The eyes behind the square lenses were flat, uninterested. "I'm Crocodile now?"

"Rhymes with Kyle."

"Does it have to rhyme?"

"Not necessarily. But I always go the extra mile, Crocodile."

Bonnie's cocktail made its way to her from the bar, where patrons were standing three and four deep, yelling small talk to each other and watching hockey and baseball on a row of flatscreen TVs. She took a swig.

"Now lay some exposition on me," she said. "I want to know how you scored the starring role in *I Was a Teenage Drug Mule*."

"I haven't been at it long. Until recently, I was attending NYU. I ran into some money problems and had to drop out. Only temporarily. I'm still going to get my degree."

"Right, right."

"Tuition costs are so obscene. In enlightened countries, higher education is free. It's only in retrogressive capitalistic cultures that students are burdened with a mountain of debt. We're so backward in this country."

"Yeah, whatever. Get to the good part."

"I met a man at a party. He said I could make some serious money going back and forth to Istanbul."

"And this man was Shaban?"

Kyle nodded. "Shaban Dragusha. Heard of him?"

"I've heard of the Dragusha clan. Albanian mafia."

"That's right."

Bonnie frowned. "Nasty bunch. The Albanians are batshit crazy even by the standards of the other mobs. They still got that peasant vendetta thing going on."

"I wouldn't expect you to know it, but that's an example of repressing a socially marginal group by reinforcing cultural stereotypes."

"You're right. I don't know it. In fact, I don't know what the fuck you're talking about. But, hey, I never went to college."

Kyle was appalled. "Not even community college?"

"Got my education on the street. No mountain of debt for me. So you don't think the Albanians have that rep?"

"I don't look at people in terms of race or ethnicity."

"Yay for you. What's Shaban's place in the organization?"

"He's Arian Dragusha's grandson."

Bonnie shook her head in disapproval. "Nepotism. Very unprofessional. Aren't you warm in that thing?" She meant the polyester jacket, which was still smothering the girl.

"I'm all right. I get chilly pretty easily. Cold-blooded, I suppose."

"No surprise there, Crocodile. So you met Shaban and hit it off?"

"You could say that." The lilt in her voice was suggestive.

"Oh, yeah? You did the old in-out, in-out?"

"I'm not going to discuss my sex life with you."

"You are, if you want us to keep talking."

"We hooked up a couple of times. It was nothing serious. Just fooling around. I felt it might be expected under the circumstances. A quid pro quo."

"A roll in the sack in exchange for a job?"

"Why not? People do it for even more trivial reasons—as payment for a meal or a movie. The whole sexual act is essentially an economic transaction."

"It can be a little more than that."

"Not often. The idea that sex has some deep romantic significance is an archaic holdover from medieval times—"

"No history lectures. Was it just economics, or did you have the hots for this guy?"

"I suppose I felt something for him. Most men of my age are still boys. Coddled by helicopter parents, hung up on personal insecurities and uncertainties about their societal role. You can't really blame them. There's so much societal evolution in play right now about gender definitions and interpersonal boundaries."

"Yeah, yeah. I'm guessing a Dragusha guy hasn't got those hang-ups."

"No, he doesn't. He knows exactly who he is and what he wants. He makes no apologies and he doesn't ask permission. He just takes."

"You like that?"

"It was refreshing. Not like the others I've had."

"There've been a few?"

"I think I've shared enough of my sexual history with you."

Yeah, she'd shared, all right. But Bonnie had a feeling a lot of what she'd shared was bullshit. She was pretty sure Kyle was lying about her personal relationship with Shaban, but she couldn't say just what the real story was. The girl was too damn hard to read.

For now she let it go. "Okay, so you and him are cuddle-buddies, and then he sets you up as a drug runner. And pays you ten grand a trip. Which still sounds way too high."

Kyle shrugged. "Different couriers earn different rates. I'm not a swallower."

"Yeah, me neither. Wait, what are we talking about?"

"Someone who swallows pellets of heroin. Usually they're stuffed into condoms first. Some people can swallow over a hundred pellets. Fat people have the advantage; they can swallow more."

"But you didn't go that route."

She shook her head. "Swallowing is for losers. It's too easy for the condoms to rupture inside you. Then the shit floods your system and kills you. Even the bosses don't respect swallowers. They pay them less. There's a hierarchy in every human enterprise. We seem to have a hardwired need for social status."

"No anthropology lectures, either. Get back to the heroin."

"If you're not going to swallow it, you have to conceal it some other way. Package it in powdered milk, put it in shampoo bottles, hairspray cans, whatever. Or you dip your clothes in liquid heroin; it comes out in the wash. I had my own method. My carry-on's pullout handles were outfitted with lead-lined tubes. The packages went inside. No one ever noticed the extra weight."

"You told me you made six trips."

"Plus a dry run to learn the system."

"Seven visits to Turkey ought to have raised a few red flags."

"I had a cover story. I was an archaeology student studying ancient ruins at Yenikapi. It's a real place, a district of Istanbul that used to be a harbor, and there was a real dig going on there up until last year. The finds are still being catalogued. My specialty was tenth-century shipwrecks."

"Shaban worked all that out for you?"

"I worked it out myself. I even read up enough on the subject so I could talk about Byzantine galleys if I had to. It was child's play."

Bonnie had to agree. Kyle Ridley was a child, all right, and she was playing a dangerous game.

"And I wore this coat," Kyle added. "Red, white, and blue. Tacky, no? Not something I would ordinarily wear, except perhaps ironically. But it was part of my camouflage. I'm just your ordinary American girl."

"Now you're an ordinary American girl with a price on her head."

"That's not my fault. Anyway, if you do your bit, I'll have nothing to worry about."

"It seems to me you're not nearly worried enough."

"I'm an optimist."

Or a nutcase, Bonnie thought. She found the distinction between optimism and insanity pretty hard to pin down anyway.

An older overweight guy swung past the table, jiving to the beat. He gave a hopeful look in their direction. Bonnie deflated his hopes with an uninviting stare, and he sashayed on.

"Your whole plan," she told Kyle, "is based on the assumption that Shaban hasn't said anything to the others about you. If you're wrong and he ends up dead, you'll be in way worse trouble than you are now."

"I'm not wrong. He can't let the higher-ups know he was betrayed by his own operative. He would lose face."

"Maybe he doesn't care about that."

"He does. He's the product of a shame-based culture. I know how his mind works. I'm majoring in Psychology," she added, puffing up a little inside her coat.

"Somehow that fails to reassure me."

"You mean because I haven't earned my degree?"

"I mean because most shrinks are nuttier than a shithouse rat."

"That's another uninformed generalization."

"Yeah, I'm real good at those."

She took off her glasses and polished them with her napkin. "Well, you'll just have to take my word for it. Shaban is running solo for now. Eventually, of course, he'll have to admit that the shipment was diverted. Then the entire organization will find out about me. That's why we have to eliminate him before he decides to talk."

"And how am I supposed to get up close and personal

with this guy?"

"You won't have to. He'll come to you."

"I'm not so sure I like the sound of that."

"Oh, it's easy enough. I'll call him and arrange a sit-down. When he shows up, you'll take him out."

"Just like that, huh? And where are you planning to lay this trap?"

She shrugged, slipping the glasses back on. "A motel. Doesn't matter which one. Someplace around here, I suppose."

"Motel room," Bonnie murmured.

"Something the matter with that?"

"I haven't had the greatest luck in motel rooms. But don't worry about it."

"I never worry about silly superstitions."

"What if he enters shooting?"

"Why would he?"

"That's how I'd do it."

"He won't. He needs the heroin. He'll want to make certain I hand it over."

"He may anticipate a setup."

"Shaban doesn't see me as a threat. His overdeveloped sense of masculine pride wouldn't permit him to look at me that way. And he would never suspect me of hiring a pro." Kyle spread her hands. "Look, it's not a problem. I open the door, he comes in, and you pop up from your hiding place and take him out."

"Easy-peasy," Bonnie said dubiously, taking another swallow of rum. "And tomorrow we go to the bank and open up your safe deposit box?"

"Exactly. Thirty-three thousand dollars for you. The rest for me so I have some capital behind me when I start a new life. So are you on the team or not?"

Bonnie thought about it, staring into the black depths of her Dark & Stormy. "If I'm in, we do it my way. I'm not on the team. I'm coaching the team."

"All right."

"I pick the motel. And you don't open the door. I do."

"I thought you were afraid he'd come in shooting."

"I am. That's why I'll take the risk. I told you, we do it my way. *Capisce*?"

"I suppose so."

"Okay then. We'll have to stop at my house for a hit kit."

"Hit kit?"

"Small-caliber pistol and sound suppressor. Silencer, to the layman."

"Layperson," Kyle corrected.

"Shut up." Bonnie finished her drink and stood.

Kyle remained sitting a moment longer. "May I ask what got you to agree?"

"The knowledge that if I said no, you'd end up dead."

"And that would bother you?"

"Not as much as you might think. But maybe a little. You said you got a hundred bucks on you?"

"More or less."

"Then pay for our drinks, Crocodile."

THE GIRL WAS in motion.

Shaban received the first text at 8:45 PM, forwarded automatically from Jay Sanderling's account. Kyle Ridley's vehicle had been spotted in the northbound lane of Highway 35, leaving Point Clement in Millstone County.

The south-central part of the state. An hour away from Hoboken if he obeyed the speed limit. He wouldn't. His Porsche Cayman was built to move.

He settled behind the wheel, his cell phone in his breast pocket. There would be more texts. Thanks to Mr. Sanderling, he had electronic eyes on every highway, parkway, turnpike, tollbooth, and major intersection in the state.

Sanderling worked for the Turnpike Authority in Woodbridge, in an analysis hub of the E-ZPass system. Scanners installed in tollbooths recorded the signals of transponders attached to vehicles, debiting their accounts for each toll. As a secondary system, automatic license plate readers—ALPRs—took digital photos of the vehicles as they passed through the tollbooths.

All this information was available in real time. The system threw up an alert whenever a vehicle with an expired E-ZPass account went through a toll booth.

That was all well and good, but it was only the beginning. As Shaban had learned, few people truly understood the extent of technological monitoring in this country. E-ZPass was part of the story, but the ALPRs played a much larger role. While E-ZPass was deployed only at tollbooths and a handful of other locations, the license plate readers were everywhere. They dotted highways, bridges, tunnels, and surface streets in the form of traffic enforcement cameras that snapped thousands of images per hour, converting each photo to an electronic text document and comparing it to databases of missing persons, suspected terrorists, wanted criminals, immigration violators, sex offenders, and more. Even high-risk drivers could be flagged. That was probably the list Sanderling had used when adding Kyle Ridley's plate number to the system. And yes, she had an E-ZPass transponder on her four-door Hyundai Accent, a fact Sanderling had confirmed via text after looking up her name and address in the accounts database.

By tomorrow, the police would be tracking her also. It was standard procedure to download the latest version of the ALPR database to a patrol car's computer before heading out. How many police cars cruised the roadways of New Jersey? What chance was there to escape their notice?

Kyle Ridley could be driving down a city street in Newark or Camden or Trenton—or anywhere—and eventually one of the ubiquitous cameras would snap her plate and run it through the system. And Sanderling's computers would know about it. The alerts pinging Shaban's phone included the exact geographical coordinates of each sighting, allowing him to track the girl while she was on the move.

As he pulled out of his condo building's underground garage, the phone rang. He checked the screen. Ahmeti again. Third time today. Shaban let the call go to voicemail. He knew what it was about. Ahmeti was his immediate superior, and he wanted to know where the shipment was.

Shaban was not yet ready to share that problem with anyone in the organization. The situation was one he was fully capable of handling on his own. And he was Arian

Dragusha's grandson; Ahmeti would, as the saying went, cut him some slack.

He had been part of his grandfather's organization for a little more than a year now. It was not quite what he had expected. At times he reflected on the wisdom of his mother in trying to keep him away from this life.

Of course, he had known there would be bloodshed. What he had not counted on was the arbitrariness of it, the pointlessness, the sheer insanity.

That night at Hajdari's, for instance. He and a few other men had gone there for a drink. Tariq Dushku had consumed too much raki. He was loud and rude and when he started singing *Himni i Flamurit* in an off-key yowl, a baldheaded stranger at the bar made a comment.

"Freakin' guy thinks he's Pavarotti."

That was all. Just those words. A joke. Even Shaban, whose command of English had not been so good back then, knew it was a joke.

But Tariq Dushku, stupid with drink and, well, just stupid in general, didn't take it that way. He wheeled on the stranger. "Fuck you call me? Fuck you call me?"

The bald man forced a smile, trying to look friendly and apologetic. The tactic backfired.

"You laughing at me, you hairless fuck?"

Dushku's gun was out, and he was firing, and the bald man wasn't smiling anymore, because he had no face.

There was chaos then. The bartender reaching for the shotgun mounted behind the bar, and Cela and Berisha jumping him before he could use it on Dushku, and both of them beating the hell out of him, first with their fists and then with liquor bottles from the shelves, and Dushku still shooting up the place, spraying rounds as the other patrons hit the floor, bullets punching out the windows and setting off car alarms along the street, and in the midst of it, sitting shell-shocked, his drink still in his hand, was Shaban Dragusha. He was too amazed even to dive for cover. It was sheer good luck—or the protection of the blessed saints—that he wasn't shot.

They had all cleared out before the law arrived, and somehow his grandfather had arranged matters so that the police investigation came up empty. The Wolf hadn't even been angry. He had seemed to take it for granted that his men would get out of control once in a while. High spirits—that was how he seemed to think of it.

That wasn't the only such incident. Shaban had been present at other episodes of spontaneous violence, and had heard of many more. There was the time Adnan Bogdani conveyed his disappointment with a shopkeeper who was late with his monthly *gjoba* by nailing the man's hands to his cash register. There was the time Gjon Mehmeti and his crew thought a kid on the turnpike had flipped them off and answered the insult with a volley of small arms fire that left the kid's vehicle a smoking wreck. There was the time Fitim Zaharia, whom everybody called Timmy, came home from a trip to find his canary dead in its cage, a victim of starvation. He swore he'd told Leka Prifti to feed the bird, and Leka swore with equal ferocity that the conversation had never taken place. The dispute was settled only when Leka threw Fitim out of a second-story window, breaking both his ankles. It was said that Leka yelled down at his moaning victim, "Timmy, you like birds so much, I thought you could fly."

Over time, Shaban had learned why the Dragusha clan had a reputation for craziness, even among other criminal gangs. This was not entirely an undesirable state of affairs. It meant that Arian's people were largely untouched by the intimidation tactics practiced by their rivals. No one wanted to mess with them. Even the police—the few who hadn't been blackmailed or bribed—were unwilling to push them hard. It was understood that the Dragushas drew no line at killing a cop, or a cop's family. They drew no lines, period.

All this troubled Shaban. It was not the life he had hoped for, a life he had naïvely imagined to be grounded in *besa*, honor. A violent, hot-blooded life, sure, yes, but one structured by rules and discipline. The life of a mercenary or a crusader, not of a feral animal tearing out the throats of its competitors in squabbles over scraps.

He was not alone in this. Other men—mainly young men like himself, men of the new generation—felt likewise. Occasionally the issue was raised obliquely in conversation. More often it was expressed by other means. Much could be communicated with a nod of the head or secret smile.

On that morning in the back room of the bakery, Arian had intimated that one day his grandson might sit on the throne of power. Such an idea had never occurred to Shaban before. Since that day, it had occurred to him many times.

No longer did it seem outlandish. He was in the direct line of descent, and his murdered father was a martyr and a hero to the clan. The Wolf had sired no other sons. New leadership was needed, and a new vision. Order in place of chaos; honor in place of madness. With the right man in command, it could be done.

All that lay in the future. It was by no means certain. The next few hours might make the difference. There was far more at stake than one shipment of heroin. To be taken in by his own courier, outplayed by a mere girl—it would be unforgivable. Even Arian Dragusha's grandson might not recover from such a humiliation.

He steered the Porsche onto Route 9, aiming for the turnpike. Kyle Ridley had a head start, but he would catch up.

Soon.

10

IT WAS ILLEGAL in New Jersey to talk on a cell phone while driving unless you used a hands-free setup. Bonnie didn't have a hands-free setup, but she used her phone anyway as she sped north to Brighton Cove with Kyle's Hyundai on her tail.

The phone was a Samsung Galaxy named Sammy—or technically, Sammy II, the first Sammy having given his life in the line of duty. She brought up her list of contacts and dialed the number of Charlotte Webb.

That was what she called herself, anyway. Her actual name was Charlotte Finkelstein, and she was about ten years older than she admitted. Bonnie had once sneaked a peek at her driver's license. No particular reason. She just liked to know who she was dealing with.

"Hey, Char," she said, mildly surprised the call hadn't gone to voicemail. "How's it hangin'?"

"Girlfriend, it's a Friday night and I'm home with no one but Orville Redenbacher for company." The crunch of a kernel accented the remark.

"Business slow?"

"I think I'm just getting too choosy. I had a date tonight, but I ran for the exit when I got a look at the guy."

"Come on, Char. Uggos need love too."

"Oh, it wasn't that. Troglodytes I can handle. It was the snake."

"Snake?"

"Freakin' boa constrictor or python or something, I don't know. He had it wrapped around his neck, and he was feeding it something out of his pocket. I think it might've been a mouse. Who carries mice in their pocket?"

"Where was this? At his house?"

"Nah, I meet 'em at a public place now. Safer that way. This was at Alcatraz." A bar in Brighton Cove. Not one of the area's more refined nightspots. "So the whole evening was a bust," Charlotte concluded with another crunch.

"Well, how about tomorrow night? You booked?"

"Tragically, no. Why? You got something?"

"Friend of mine could use a lift. His wife walked out, and he's getting all mopey about it."

"What's his name?"

"Spark—uh, Walt. You want to meet him at Mulligan's in Point Clement? Say, around seven thirty or so?"

"Sounds good. So what's this guy's damage?"

"I told you, his wife—"

"Nah, I mean what's screwy about him?"

"How do you know there's something screwy?"

"Honey, there's always something."

"Well ... he's kinda into ghosts."

"That's not so bad. Wait, he doesn't, like, hang out at graveyards casting bones or anything?"

"Not that I know of. I think it's more like he goes to somebody's house with a special camera and tries to get the Headless Horseman on video. It's only a sideline."

"He ought to take up a different hobby."

"Maybe I can talk him unto collecting action figures."

"Oooh, I dunno. Did I tell you about this one john who had all these G.I. Joes in his house? Hundreds of them."

"Is that so weird?"

"It is when they're wearing ballet outfits. Freakin' tutus."

"It takes all kinds, Char."

"Some kinds I could do without."

"So you're okay with it? You'll be there?"

"With bells on. Why do they say that? Nobody has bells on."

"It's just one of those mysteries. Okay, the guy you'll be looking for is sort of a sad sack dweeb." Bonnie sketched out Sparky's physical characteristics as if he were a suspect in a bank heist. "Let him think it's a pickup. He'll figure I stood him up and then he got lucky."

"The girlfriend experience? Won't he get suspicious when I call in his credit card?"

"Don't. It's my treat."

"Seriously?"

"My good deed for the year."

She ended the call and put Sammy back into her purse, next to the Smith nine in its special compartment. Soon the gun would be replaced by a .22 with a screw-on silencer, one of many illegal firearms she'd stowed in a hidey-hole in her house. She hadn't looked at that stuff since last February. Vaguely she'd been meaning to get rid of most of it, but somehow she'd never gotten around to doing so. Laziness? Or the cunning of the recovering alkie who conveniently forgets the bottle of hooch taped inside the toilet tank?

She wasn't sure. She'd gone eight months without pulling the trigger on anybody. But tonight, negotiating with Kyle, she'd felt the old familiar frisson, the sense of danger, the lure of the forbidden.

Was it possible she actually *liked* killing people? That she didn't do it purely for expediency, but because, down deep, she got off on it? Was that why the habit was proving so goddamn hard to break?

She didn't care for that train of thought. It was pointing in a direction she didn't want to go. After all, it was one thing to be an outlaw like her namesake, the distaff half of Bonnie and Clyde, even if the real-life version wasn't half as glamorous as Faye Dunaway. Or to be a vigilante, taking the law into her own hands to help people who came to her in distress, people at the end of their string— she could live with that, if she had to.

But to kill for the sheer pleasure of killing ... To murder for fun ...

If that was her deal, she was no better than the people she'd gone up against. No better than Anton Streinikov, or Frank Lazzaro, or Ed and Edna Goodman of Palm Garden, Arizona.

Arizona again. She frowned. Why did she keep going back to that? She'd almost babbled about it to Sparky at the bar. It had been years since she'd thought of Palm Garden, with its biker bar and its crummy little diner, Ed at the counter slinging hamburgers, and Edna in the shop next door hawking sunscreen and Indian curios.

She had spent most of her teenage years on the street and then as the unofficial ward of Frank Kershaw, a hardware store proprietor and small-time forger in Philadelphia. Around the time she turned eighteen she'd grown bored with all that. A normal person would have gone back to school or looked for a regular job. But to her, school had always felt like a prison, and she'd been sure a nine-to-five stint in a cubicle would feel the same.

Instead she went all *Easy Rider*. She bought a zippy little rice-burner and headed off in no particular direction, bumming around, sleeping rough, earning money at odd jobs, and supplementing her income with occasional shoplifting and con jobs. Yeah, she'd been a grifter, pulling simple scams. *I lost all my money and I need bus fare to get home*—one of her favorites. Or she would talk some guy into ponying up fifty bucks for a blow job, then spook the john by spotting a nonexistent cop. By the time the guy realized there was no cop, she was gone, with her womanly virtue—such as it was—still intact.

In her backpack she carried a book about Bonnie and Clyde. She read it over and over and looked at the pictures. She felt an almost mystical connection with the historical Bonnie, the bony little waitress who'd gone from slinging hash to robbing banks, as though the same restless spirit was driving her to wander and take chances and shy away from well-traveled roads.

Good times. No responsibilities, no thoughts of the future. But after two years of it, she was no closer to figuring out who she was or what she wanted in life.

By then she was twenty years old, raw and windburnt, skinny from too many missed meals, and a little tired of spitting bugs out of her mouth. She wore a brown bomber jacket and a pair of faded blue jeans with holes in the knees. She hadn't bothered to patch the holes. She'd never been any good with a needle and thread. Besides, she had nice knees. She didn't mind showing them off.

Twenty miles east of Yuma, on a broiling July weekend, she blew into a flyspeck town called Palm Garden, a name that must have been chosen for irony. She ditched her Kawasaki outside the E&E Diner, feeling a little like a cowgirl tying up her horse at a saloon. She was half hoping the diner would feature a colorful character playing a rinky-dink piano, and a lady named Belle who invited the menfolk upstairs. Sadly, it was a hamburger joint like any other. Formica counter, row of stools, mist of grease. It was crowded enough. She had encountered the noontime rush.

She sat at the counter and scarfed down an overcooked hamburger served up by a paunchy fiftyish man in an apron. She had a feeling he'd done time. There was a tattoo in black ink on the side of his neck—a prison tat, she thought. A crude rendition of a spider, intermittently visible above his wilted shirt collar as he flipped burgers on the steam table.

A nursery rhyme came back to her:

The itsy bitsy spider
Climbed up the waterspout.
Down came the rain
And washed the spider out ...

The guy, who answered to the name of Ed, seemed to know nearly everybody in the place. Bonnie listened to him chat up the regulars about the prospect of rain—unlikely—and the day's heat—not too bad for July. Personally she thought the heat was brutal, like being hit in the face with a blast of air from an oven. But these desert rats were a different breed.

Attached to the E&E Diner was the E&E Variety Store. Through with lunch, Bonnie wandered the aisles, surveying prickly pear preserves, ironwood carvings, and ten-gallon hats. She liked the hats, but she couldn't afford one. She contented herself with a bag of trail mix for the road. She wasn't planning to spend the night in Palm Garden. She was kind of sorry she'd stopped there at all.

The frizzy-haired heavyset checkout lady had been watching her while chatting sotto voce on her giant cell phone. Worried about shoplifting, probably. There was a sign on the wall telling customers to leave their back-packs at the front counter, an instruction Bonnie had ignored. Didn't matter. There was nothing in this place worth stealing.

"Just passing through?" the lady asked as she rang up the purchases. It sounded like something she'd said many times.

"Yep." Since coming west, Bonnie had developed a talent for laconic, monosyllabic replies.

"Going anyplace special?"

"Nope."

"I might have work for you."

"Not looking for employment."

"I don't mean anything long-term. Just one night."

Sounded kinky. "Yeah?" Bonnie said warily.

"You came in from the diner. You know the man who served you? That's Ed. He's my husband."

"Okay." This was getting weird.

"I'm Edna. Yes, Ed and Edna—don't think people

haven't had their fun with that. We're the Goodmans. Lived in Palm Garden all our lives."

It didn't seem like something to be proud of. "So?"

"That'll be a dollar ninety. But it's on the house if you take the job. Plus another hundred for your trouble."

A hundred bucks was real money. "I'm listening."

"I trust Ed. I really do."

You really don't, Bonnie thought.

"I trust him, but lately there've been stories. See, every other night, he heads over to Sidewinder's. That's a bar, a local hangout. Not very nice. Bikers, mainly."

Bonnie was a biker, but she thought Edna Goodman already knew that. She could read the knowledge in the subtle malicious twist of the woman's mouth.

"Usually he shoots pool and hoists a few. Till about eleven. Then he toddles on home. I never go with him. It's not"—she coughed delicately—"my kind of place."

Bonnie thought that any place where people were having fun would not be Mrs. Goodman's kind of place.

"But I'm told—never mind by who, it's a small town, word gets around—I'm told that on Wednesday nights Ed leaves early, around nine. But he never gets home till after eleven. It got me to wondering just what he's up to."

"Okay," Bonnie said for the second time, still not sure where this was going.

"So, looking at you, I had a thought. Maybe you could help me out, one woman to another. Maybe you could go to Sidewinder's tonight and keep an eye on Ed. Today's Wednesday, as you know."

Bonnie hadn't known. At some point on the road she'd lost all track of the calendar. One day was like another.

"You could go there and just watch. No one would think anything of it. You'd fit right in." That nasty little smile again. Oh, she was a peach, was Edna. "And if he goes out before eleven, maybe you could, you know, follow him. At a distance, you know. Like a tail job—that's what they call it. You tail him, and tomorrow you report back to me."

"That's it? Just follow him?"

"Well, there could be one other thing. Do you have a camera?"

"No."

"Not even on your phone, the way some people do now?"

"I don't have a phone."

"Take this. She produced a disposable pocket camera from under the counter. "It doesn't have a flash, but that's just as well. You don't want a bright light giving you away." She wound the film to the first frame. "Try to get a picture of him and whoever he's with."

"You mean, like, through a window?"

"Well ..." Edna reddened slightly. She was uncomfortable, and Bonnie felt good about that.

"I'm not sure I want to be a peeping Tom." Bonnie was also pretty certain she disliked Edna.

"Come on. It'll be fun. Like you're a private eye. You ever watch private eye shows on TV?"

"Not really."

"*The Rockford Files*—that was a good one. You'll be like James Garner. Or one of Charlie's Angels."

"Isn't it illegal? Spying on people?"

"Oh, and you've never broken the law?" Edna said archly, her faded gray eyes fixing Bonnie with their stare.

"Maybe once or twice." She wasn't thinking of the little bit of shoplifting she'd done. She was thinking of a farmhouse in Ohio, the men who'd killed her parents— men she'd tracked down and executed at the age of fourteen.

"So a little snooping won't matter, will it?"

"Do I get the money now?"

"I'll pay fifty up front. The rest tomorrow. And I'll even throw in a little extra if you get a photo. Of course, I'll have to trust you not to run off with the down payment and the camera, and leave me in the lurch."

"I won't leave you in the lurch."

"That mean you'll do it?"

"I'll do it." She needed the money.

And she had to admit, Edna's stupid sales pitch had gotten to her. She liked the idea of sneaking around, going undercover, learning secrets. Anyway, it was only one night. No big deal.

What was the worst that could happen?

11

TWO BLOCKS AFTER crossing the railroad tracks into Brighton Cove, Bonnie saw a blue lightbar flashing in her rearview mirror.

Cop car. Of course.

The local constabulary had been riding her hard since February. In town she was always careful to obey the speed limit and to come to a complete stop at every stop sign. She'd spent enough hours in traffic school, and there were only so many videos of decapitated accident victims a girl could watch.

Oh, it was great being public enemy number one. Being harassed by every dipshit in uniform. Walking down the street and seeing strangers turn away. Hearing the remarks they made behind her back. Sometimes they left messages on her voicemail or chalked graffiti on the door of her duplex. Some asshole threw a rock through her living room window once. Pretty much the entire local population had turned against her. Halloween was coming up in two weeks, and she figured half the town would be dressed as her.

The cop blipped his siren to be sure he'd gotten her attention. Showoff. She guided the Jeep to the curb. Somewhere behind her, in the dark, Kyle must have parked also, waiting for the traffic stop to be over.

Studying the rearview mirror, she made out two figures in the front of the squad car. That in itself was unusual, since most Brighton Cove cops rode solo in the off-season. It wasn't as if they needed backup when investigating a stolen bicycle or a kitten up a tree.

74

But there was one time when two cops did ride together—when Dan Maguire, Brighton Cove's chief of police, was doing a performance review. A ride-along was part of the process.

Was that Danny Boy in the passenger seat? She squinted. Yep. Same square shoulders, same flat head.

The door on the driver's side swung open. She identified the driver by his stance and stride as soon as he emerged, even before she could see his face against the strobe of the lights. Oh, hell. It was Brad Walsh. The last person she wanted to see in a situation like this.

She rolled down her window as he walked up. "What now, Officer?" she asked, leaning out and putting a little extra sass in her tone. "More police harassment?"

Brad regarded her coldly. "Our department doesn't harass citizens. I pulled you over for a moving violation."

"Yeah, sure. How many tickets does this make since February? Three? Or is it four?"

"I didn't handle the previous stops."

"You're all in it together, pal. So what is it this time? I didn't slow down for a pothole? Forgot to give a squirrel the right of way?"

"Failure to use your directional signal."

Bonnie gaped at him, perhaps a shade too theatrically. "You have *got* to be shitting me."

"You took that last corner without signaling."

"The streets are deserted. Who the fuck would I be signaling to, my imaginary friends?"

"It's the law. We all need to follow the rules of the road. Though I know how much trouble you have following rules."

"Yeah, yeah. Save it."

"Where are you coming from?" he asked.

"Wonderland."

"Very funny."

"It's a real place, Walsh. The amusement park in Point Clement."

"Oh. Right." He seemed briefly embarrassed, but rallied. "Had anything to drink?"

"Not a drop," she lied.

"So you're a teetotaler now?"

"I'm dropping my bad habits."

"Not all of them, I'll bet."

Bonnie ground her teeth. "Oh, you're really pushing it," she muttered under her breath.

He held out his hand. "License, insurance, and registration."

She produced her driver's license from her wallet and the other documents from the glove compartment. He accepted them through the window.

"I'll be right back."

"Take your time. Absence makes the heart grow fonder."

He returned to his vehicle, where Dan waited, no doubt enjoying the show. Bonnie sat fuming. After a minute, she lit a cigarette so she could fume literally as well as figuratively.

It must have been Dan's idea to ticket her. The chief was a bully by nature, the kind of asshole who'd spent his formative years pouring salt on snails, and he never missed a chance to give her grief. There was no good reason for his fixation on her. She'd never done anything to him. Well, there was the time she'd poured a whole bunch of dog crap into his car, but that was just good fun.

Of course, it was possible Brad had come up with the idea on his own. Showing off for his boss, maybe. He might have wanted to prove his loyalty, and this bullshit citation was a way to do it.

If so, she couldn't really blame him. She knew he had to tread carefully around Dan, making sure he never suspected the truth. The one sin the chief would never tolerate was fraternizing with the enemy, and she and Brad had done their share of fraternizing, all right.

Yeah, they'd had a thing. And yeah, it had blown up in

her face, as her things had a tendency to do. As she had since admitted, it might just possibly have been her fault, seeing as how she had lied to him about her secret sideline and led him to believe she worked within the bounds of the law. Finding out otherwise had been hard on him. He'd said the chief had been right about her all along, and he'd told her they were through.

That was back in February. A lot had changed since then. For one thing, her insurance premiums had gone way up. For another, she'd quit the killing game, or so she'd told herself. And for another—

Both doors of the squad car opened in unison, and together Brad and Dan got out. She steeled herself for a face-to-face with the chief. It was never the highlight of her day.

Brad reached her first. He handed over the ticket, along with her ID and other papers.

"What's the damage?" she asked him.

"Eighty-five dollars."

"If it's not paid," Dan put in helpfully, "there'll be a warrant out on you." He leaned into the window, smiling. "And it *will* be enforced."

She blew a jet of smoke, getting him in the face. His eyes watered as he pulled back.

"So Danny Boy's babysitting you tonight?" she said to Brad.

"Don't call me Danny Boy," Dan growled, wiping his eyes.

Bonnie ignored him. She watched Brad. "Was it his idea to ticket me?"

"No," Brad said stiffly. "It was mine."

She couldn't tell if he was lying. "Well, I'm sure he'll give you a nice gold star. You can put it on the fridge."

"Just sign the ticket."

"What if I don't?"

"Then we're taking you in," Dan said, risking another approach to the window.

She met his gaze with a hard glare of her own. "Believe me, Danno, that is something you do not want to try."

"Is that a threat?"

"It's a statement of the friggin' obvious."

Brad pushed his way between them, ending the staring contest. "Sign the ticket, Miss Parker."

Miss? Jeez. He really knew how to hurt a girl. She gave in and signed.

"You seem to really be enjoying your role as Dan's butt-boy," she told Brad as she handed the ticket back.

"Zip it," Dan warned.

"Make me."

"Officer Walsh, wait in the car."

Brad hesitated a moment, then tore off Bonnie's copy of the ticket and handed it over. He walked away.

Dan eased closer to her, lowering his voice. "A little friendly advice."

"Right, because you and me have always been so friendly."

"You need to adjust your attitude."

"Oh, sure. I'll get right to work on that."

"You act as though you've got the upper hand here. You don't. Remember, I know the truth now. Everything I ever suspected about you has proved out. You fooled everyone else, but not me."

"You're a moron, Dan. If you were right about me, it was one of those blind-pig-acorn things."

"I was right," he said with stupidly obstinate pride. "And now everybody knows."

"Do they? There's supposed to be a confidentiality agreement."

"I don't mean they know the details. Your attorney protected you from that. But they know you're bad news. How are people treating you these days?"

"Hugs and kisses. Even from random strangers. It's embarrassing. I hear they're gonna throw me a parade."

"This town would sooner throw a parade for the Ebola virus."

"Yeah, well, I hear that was their second choice."

"You barely skated by in February. Next time you won't be so lucky. And every day brings you closer to your last mistake."

"You read that on one of those inspirational calendars, didn't you?"

"I've got your number, Parker. Never forget it."

She expelled another long plume of smoke into his face and was rewarded by his immediate departure. He got back into the squad car and sat talking with Brad for a minute—it wasn't hard to guess the topic of conversation—and then the car moved away. As it pulled past her Jeep, Dan gave her the old stink-eye out of the passenger window. She tipped her newsboy cap at him.

When the car was gone, she slumped in her seat, suddenly tired. It had been unexpectedly difficult, seeing Brad under those circumstances. His monotone and his cold stare had brought back the last time she'd ever been in his apartment, when he'd made it clear he wanted nothing to do with her, ever again. It had hurt her worse than she'd known it would. After so much time on her own, she hadn't imagined she could grow to need another human being—and certainly not Bradley Walsh, a small-town cop a few years her junior, whose own colleagues thought of him as a Boy Scout and a straight arrow.

Not her kind of man at all. Or so she'd told herself, even while they'd been together in the months leading up to February. It had been only a fling, meaningless, doomed.

And yet when it had ended—when he'd shown her the door, betrayal stamped on his face ...

She didn't like that memory.

As she finished the cigarette, Kyle's Hyundai eased alongside her. She noticed it only when the girl rolled down her side window and called out, "Are we going to get moving or not?"

"Right. Right." Bonnie crushed out the cig in the ashtray.

"What was that all about anyway?"

"Welcoming committee."

"You must be very popular around here."

"Yeah, like rat poison."

"What did you do to alienate the locals' affections?"

"They think I'm a bad element and I'm bringing in more bad elements and lowering everybody's property values."

"They might be right."

"Of course they're right. Doesn't mean I have to like it."

"You could relocate."

Bonnie shook her head, an abrupt, visceral reaction. "Not me. I'm staying put, whether Brighton Cove wants me here or not."

"Why? What's the point?"

"The point, Crocodile, is that I am a stubborn bitch. So fuck 'em all." She leaned out the window and raised her middle finger at the empty street. "Fuck. Them. All."

12

SHORTLY AFTER NINE, they arrived at the duplex on Windlass Court, half of which Bonnie called home. She punched in the six-digit code to disarm her security system, then led Kyle inside.

"So this is your place?" Kyle said, looking around.

"This is it."

"I guess being a PI doesn't pay as well as I thought."

"Yeah, yeah. The comedy stylings of a drug runner on the lam."

Bonnie herself thought her digs looked pretty sharp. Her half of the duplex had gone through a drastic remodeling job—an unfortunate necessity after the place had been shot to pieces by Anton Streinikov's crew. Every mirror and window had been replaced; for some reason, bad guys just loved shooting out panes of glass. The walls had been re-plastered, the carpets replaced once it became clear that no amount of vacuuming would ever remove every last splinter of glass.

Her next-door neighbor, the septuagenarian or possibly octogenarian Mrs. Biggs, had put her side of the duplex on the market. No offers had been made. Nobody wanted to live under the same roof as a notorious bullet magnet. As a result, Mrs. Biggs was still there, but she wasn't happy about it, a fact she made no effort to conceal. Too bad. She'd been friendly enough before the whole shitstorm had gone down.

"You have anything to eat here?" Kyle asked.

"Didn't you get dinner?"

"I didn't even get lunch."

"You could have eaten at the Sand Bar."

"Are you kidding? That wasn't *food*."

Bonnie suspected her own definition of food was different from Kyle's.

"Check out the fridge," she said without much optimism.

She wasn't exactly accustomed to entertaining. Brad had never stayed over at her place. They'd always used his apartment in Algonquin. They couldn't risk having his car spotted in her neighborhood; that was the kind of thing Chief Maguire would have been unduly interested in.

While Kyle explored the kitchen, Bonnie freed herself from the windbreaker and cap, but kept her purse on her shoulder. It didn't seem like a good idea to leave a loaded gun within Kyle Ridley's reach.

There was something about the girl—just, you know, *something*. She was crocodilian in more ways than mere cold-bloodedness. Bonnie had a feeling that most of her was submerged, hidden, and maybe waiting for an unwary passerby to make a mistake.

She lit another cigarette—the twelfth of the day, not that she was counting—and went into the bedroom. There were a half-dozen bullet holes in the headboard of her bed, which she hadn't tried to repair. She liked them.

Before February she'd stored her arsenal in a floor trap in the closet. Now she'd used a more secure hiding place. Given the increased scrutiny of the local authorities, she'd thought it wise to take additional precautions in case she was served with a search warrant.

The whole loose floorboard thing was pretty bush-league anyway. Her new hidey-hole was the air duct behind the bedroom wall. It could be accessed by unscrewing the aluminum vent cover concealed by her nightstand. She kept a small screwdriver in the nightstand drawer for just this purpose.

With the cover off, she reached in and snagged the strap of a gym bag. She hauled it out into the open, unzipped the bag, and started rummaging inside.

Behind her, Kyle entered the room, snacking on a banana. She was still wearing the damn coat. She looked like a polyester flag.

The girl regarded Bonnie's cigarette with disapproval. "Must you smoke?"

"Yeah. I must."

"You should switch to a vape pen. Much healthier."

"Health is overrated."

"You clearly think so. This was the only fruit I could find. And no veggies whatsoever. How can you not have any vegetables in the house?"

"I have popcorn. Popcorn is a vegetable."

"Everything in there is heavily processed and loaded with sugar and salt. There's nothing organic. How can you eat like that?"

"Who are you, the food police?"

"I try to make sensible lifestyle choices."

"Like hauling heroin for the Albanian mob?"

Kyle, unfazed, took another bite. "Do you even work out?"

"Lately? No. I was a gym rat for a while, but not so much now."

"What changed?"

Bonnie hesitated. "Well, it was back when I was dating a younger man. And it, um, didn't work out."

"That shouldn't make any difference. You don't want your identity defined by a romantic partner."

"Thanks, Dear Abby. Anyway, these days my idea of cardio is a bubble bath and a vibrator."

"Seriously?"

"Nah. I don't take bubble baths."

Kyle finished the banana. "*I* work out. Free weights, crunches, and kickboxing."

"Kickboxing? You studying to be a kangaroo?"

"It's good cardio."

And not so bad for self-defense, Bonnie thought. It was just something to keep in mind. She liked to know her adversary's strengths and weaknesses. Kyle Ridley was a client, of course, not an adversary. But that situation could change. It had happened before.

She wanted a .22 pistol, the kind of gun that worked best for a hit. There were three to choose from. She rejected the Beretta 948 because it was a 1952 model, a virtual antique which she'd picked up from her supplier, Mama Blessing of Maritime, for a special discount. That left a Walther P22 with a Gemtech Outback suppressor, and, for good measure, a two-shot Cobra derringer that fired .22LR ammo. She elected to take them both. The Cobra was small enough to be concealed in her palm. It never hurt to carry a backup gun, even one no bigger than a toy.

"Lemme just put this gear together," she said as she slid the gym bag back into the vent, "and we'll head to the motel."

"You have a place in mind?"

"The Crappy Mariner."

"Excuse me?"

"Well, technically it's the Happy Mariner"—Bonnie screwed the vent cover back on—"but since it's a shit hole, I renamed it in the interest of accuracy."

"Where is this place?"

"Maritime. Couple towns north of here."

"And how do you know about it?"

"Been there."

"You stayed at a motel you call the Crappy Mariner?"

"Didn't stay. Just snooped around on a job. Another unfaithful spouse."

"No wonder you're cynical. You see only the seamy side of life."

"Yeah, I ought to hang out with a higher class of people.

Like the Dragushas, right?"

"You're a real pain in the ass."

"That's my rep," Bonnie said cheerfully.

She carried the items from the gym bag into the dining room and arranged them on the table. It was a new table, the old one having been drilled with a few too many bullets to be salvageable. She'd selected two ten-round magazines for the Walther. She snapped one into place.

Kyle disappeared into the kitchen, returning with another banana. She seemed amused by the derringer. "What's that? The prize in a box of Cracker Jack?"

"I wish. I never got anything better than a whistle."

"Where do you get your hardware?"

"Guns R Us," Bonnie said without looking up.

"It has to be someplace off the radar screen."

"Yeah, once you go black market, you never go back."

"So who's your supplier?"

"The bluebird of happiness."

"I take it you don't trust me?"

"I don't trust anybody. You shouldn't, either."

"Not even you?"

"Especially not me. For all you know, I dropped a dime on you already. Could've made the call from my car on the way up here."

"At one point it did look as if you were making a call."

"Well, there ya go."

"This isn't very funny."

"It's not meant to be. You took a chance, approaching me. You don't know what kind of player I am. I might be the type who'd turn you in for a commission."

"Are you?"

"Nope." Bonnie screwed the suppressor onto the Walther's internally threaded barrel, testing it just to be sure it would go on smoothly. "Then again, that's just what you'd expect me to say."

The eyelids behind the square lenses closed halfway.

"You know what? I don't like you. But don't take it personally. I don't particularly like anyone."

"Not even Tom Hanks? They say he's the nicest guy in showbiz." She unscrewed the suppressor and slipped it into her purse with the Walther and the spare mag. "So what are your plans when this is over? Going back to school?"

"That's my intention."

"Still wanna be a shrink?"

Kyle pushed the last of the banana into her mouth, speaking around it. "You sound skeptical."

"I'm guessing not too many mental health professionals have a background in drug trafficking."

"It isn't something I'll put on my CV. What are you really asking?"

"You told me this was gonna be your last run. I wonder."

Bonnie loaded two .22LR rounds into the derringer, leaving the safety off and the gun uncocked. The cocking action took a fair amount of strength. There was no chance the little gun would go off by accident.

"Wonder what?" Kyle asked.

"If you're serious about going straight, or if you'll just resume your criminal activities in a new locale."

"What's it to you?"

"Curiosity. I'm a people person." She shrugged on the windbreaker, then put the derringer in the pocket. She didn't like the way it made the jacket sag. Instead, she hiked up one leg of her jeans and concealed the gun in her tube sock.

"I don't know what I'll do," Kyle said. "I intend to go legit. But you know what they say. The best laid plans *gang aft agley.*"

"Yeah, I say that all the time."

"It's Robert Burns."

"The rich guy on *The Simpsons*?"

Kyle did an exaggerated eye roll. "Never mind. My point

is, I want to walk away for good, but I'm not sure I can make it stick. Probably I can't. Is that honest enough?"

"Yeah. I guess so."

It was a little too honest, Bonnie thought. In her experience, when people were overly forthcoming about themselves, they were usually hiding something. It was the ones who pretended to be an open book who had the most secrets. She was pretty sure Kyle Ridley was stuffed chock-full of secrets.

"Okay." She smoothed out her pants leg and picked up her purse. "Let's book." She stuck the newsboy cap back on her head. With the jacket zipped up, she was a study in shades of dark blue—blue denim hat, navy windbreaker, jeans, sneaks. Even the purse was blue-black.

Dressed for wet work, she thought, wishing the idea didn't please her quite so much.

At the door Kyle gave her a quizzical sidelong glance. "May I ask *you* a question?"

"Shoot."

"How did you get into your—you know, your sideline?"

"I had a client who couldn't be kept safe any other way."

"So you simply decided to turn assassin?"

"You know what they say. Necessity is a mother." She shut the door behind them and turned to the alarm keypad.

"And ... did you like it?" Kyle asked.

"Did I like what?"

"Pulling the trigger on someone?"

Bonnie wasn't exactly thrilled by the question. It tracked her own thoughts a little too closely.

"Sometimes." She armed the security system. "When it's them or me. They go down, I stay upright. I win, they lose. It's a rush."

"And you always win? Every time?"

Bonnie turned to the small girl in the big coat and gave her a long steady look. "I'm still standing, Crocodile."

13

BRADLEY WALSH WASN'T entirely pleased with the way he'd handled the traffic stop. That citation was pretty bogus. Anyone else would have been let off with a warning, if he'd bothered to pull them over at all. He didn't like being unprofessional just to prove a point.

It had been his choice, too, just as he'd said. He wasn't much good at lying and did it only when he had to. He really had seen the Jeep first, noticed the illegal turn, and called the play before Dan Maguire could say a word. And he had done it entirely for the chief's benefit. He wasn't proud of that fact, but there it was.

"You're thinking about our girl, aren't you?" Dan Maguire said from the passenger seat.

"Yeah, I guess." He never had to ask who *our girl* was. Other than his wife, Chief Dan Maguire had only one female on his mind. And he liked talking to Brad about her, because Brad was the only one of his men who knew the full story of what had happened in February, when Bonnie had escaped a long-term prison sentence by the narrowest of margins.

"You don't really like giving her the business."

"The traffic stop was my idea," Brad said defensively.

"Yeah, I know. You still don't like it, though. You're a Boy Scout, Walsh."

"Maybe I am."

"Me, I enjoy our little encounters. Tonight's was the second one this week. I saw her last Wednesday, I think it was. In the morning. She was showing up for work. I stopped her in the parking lot by her office."

"What for?"

"Nothing, really. There wasn't anything I could cite her for. I just wanted her to know I'm keeping an eye on her."

"She knows."

"You bet she does. Got a little worked up about it, too. Says she's seen my guys running the tags of all the vehicles that park in the lot."

"Did you deny it?"

"Nope. Told her I just want to know who her clients are, in case anyone close to them should come to harm." He chuckled. "She called it harassment. Said she ought to sic the ACLU on me."

"Maybe she will."

"Not a chance. Those shitheads are too busy chasing manger displays out of public parks. Besides, they wouldn't take her as a client."

"We don't know she's still ... doing what she does."

Dan surprised him. "I don't think she is. Not right now. No fatalities in the area that would match up with what we know about her. She's keeping her nose clean for the time being."

"Okay," Brad said warily. It wasn't like the chief to ever cut Bonnie a break.

"But it won't last," Dan said. "She'll revert to form. They always do."

"It could be she's not as bad as we think."

"She's not. She's worse. That's why we need to keep after her. Either she gets so tired of it she leaves town, or she gets rattled and makes a mistake."

"You think she's feeling the heat?"

"I know she is," Dan said complacently.

Brad wasn't so sure about that. In his experience, Bonnie Parker didn't exactly wilt under pressure.

He turned the black-and-white Chevy Tahoe east on Birch and kept going till he hit Ocean Drive. Slowly he cruised north, past rows of Victorian mansions on the left and the boardwalk to the right. Some kids were bicycling on the boardwalk—breaking the law, but in the off-season no one bothered too much about enforcement. A sea breeze blew a breath of mist over the windshield; he ticked the wipers a few times to clean the glass.

"She's had three moving violations this year, prior to this one," Dan said, picking up the conversation as if there had been no interruption. "And her business has fallen off. You can tell by the number of clients she gets."

"Okay." Brad really didn't want to talk about this.

"Some people say I'm a little bit obsessed with her. My wife, for one. Maybe you think so, too."

"No." Yes, Brad thought.

"What those people don't understand is that it's my job to keep this town clean. That means scrubbing out the dirt. It means spraying the roaches. Parker is a fucking tumor, and she has to be excised."

He seemed to have mixed his metaphors there. "Harsh, Chief," Brad murmured.

"No more than she deserves." Dan studied him with a cool, squinty gaze. "You're feeling awfully chivalrous tonight."

Brad shifted in his seat. "Not really."

"You don't need to defend her. It's not like she's your girlfriend. Or is she?"

The question caught him off guard. He felt his gut tighten. "What?"

"You and her are about the same age. You could've hooked up." Dan was smiling.

"Come off it," Brad said with a nervous shrug.

"Why not? Some people might say she's a sweet little slice."

"She's a criminal."

"Maybe you like bad girls."

Brad blinked. Bonnie's voice came back to him, a teasing whisper: *Don't kid yourself, Walsh. I'm a bad, bad girl ...*

She'd said that to him in February, just before everything between them had fallen apart. At the time he'd taken it as a joke. Then he'd found out just how true it was. The reality had struck him like a slap. She'd made a fool out of him. She'd lied straight to his face. And he'd hated her for it.

He still did. He always would. And yet ...

Even hating her, he hadn't been able to forget her.

He'd met some girls, of course—he was always meeting girls—but somehow they just hadn't done it for him the way she had. They'd been ... ordinary. They'd held regular jobs. The biggest risk they took was navigating the traffic circle on 35.

Bonnie, on the other hand ... her whole life was a risk. All she did was take chances. She lived for danger, and she was dangerous herself, and though he knew it was crazy, there was something about her that he just couldn't shake free of.

And now here was his boss, making cracks about her being, you know, his girlfriend.

But Dan couldn't know anything about that. No one did. Right?

When Brad let his gaze slide sideways to the passenger seat, he saw a sly smirk puckering the corner of Dan Maguire's mouth.

14

THE HAPPY MARINER was a rambling one-story motel dating to the early 1960s, laid out in a horseshoe shape embracing a courtyard parking lot. The lot was nearly empty, and Bonnie was happy about that. She didn't want a lot of people around.

She ditched her Jeep at the rear of the complex, behind a disorderly row of trash bins, where it wouldn't be seen. Before leaving, she opened the glove box and removed a roll of duct tape, useful for patching rips in the seat cushions, and stuck it in her purse.

In the courtyard she reconnoitered with Kyle, advising her to park her Hyundai out in the open where Shaban would see it. "After that, check in. Get a room on the end. Pay cash. Don't use your real name."

"What if they ask for ID?"

"Take a hike, and we'll find a less classy establishment."

Bonnie waited outside, smoking yet another cigarette and watching the traffic on Route 35.

"They cleaned me out," Kyle said, returning with a room key. "Eighty-five dollars, cash in advance."

"Which room?"

"One-oh-one. Over there."

She pointed to a corner unit. The windows next door were dark, and no vehicle was parked in the space out front. Most likely they had no neighbors. Good.

Bonnie took the key and opened up the room. It had been a couple of years since she'd been inside the motel she knew as the Crappy Mariner, but the decor had not improved. There were still the same dead bugs on the carpet, the same cobwebs in the corners, the same aroma of cat pee and puke. In short, it was her kind of place.

"Believe it or not, the desk clerk told me this was a nonsmoking room," Kyle said, regarding the cigarette in Bonnie's mouth with disapproval.

Given the cigarette burns plainly visible on the bedspread, Bonnie was pretty sure this policy wasn't enforced. More to the point, she didn't give a rat's ass. "My body, my rules."

She checked out the rest of the unit. Small bathroom, barred window. Sliding door that opened on a patio by a drained swimming pool. She fiddled with the door for a minute, then closed the drapes to cover it.

"You know what's funny?" Kyle was saying. "People say, I have a body. When logically they should say, I *am* a body. Because that's all they are, just flesh and bone."

"Yeah, that's hilarious. You should do stand-up."

"I meant funny in a thought-provoking sense."

"So you don't believe in a soul, anything like that?"

Kyle made a disparaging grunt. "Superstition. No intelligent person buys that Cartesian dualistic crap."

Bonnie didn't know what Cartesian meant. She thought it had something to do with wells. "Guy I was talking to tonight is into it. He's a ghost hunter."

"I suppose you believe that nonsense."

"What makes you suppose that?"

"You said you'd never been to college."

Bonnie wondered what exactly they'd taught this kid at school. How to be a bitch, apparently. She found it strange that anyone would pay money to learn that skill. On the street she'd picked it up for free.

"As far as ghosts go," she said, "I have no opinion." She unscrewed the bulb from one of the two lamps on the bureau, cutting the light in the room by half. "You could be right about us being meat puppets. Or Sparky—that's my ghost-hunter friend—he could be right about the

Great Beyond." She shrugged. "That kind of stuff is above my pay grade."

"It shouldn't be. Everybody needs to cultivate a philosophy."

"I've been too busy just staying alive. You ever planning to take off that coat?"

Kyle hugged herself. "I'm still cold."

"Of course you are. Okay, time to make the call. You know what to say?"

"Naturally."

Bonnie didn't ask if she could be convincing. Kyle Ridley was a girl of many talents, and lying was definitely one of them.

Kyle seated herself on the sofa and used the room phone, dialing her handler's cell from memory.

"Shaban? It's me. Don't talk, all right? Just listen. I made a mistake today. It was stupid of me, really stupid. I don't know what I was thinking. I want to make it right."

Faintly, a male voice buzzed like a hornet. Bonnie couldn't make out the words.

"I know, I know," Kyle said. "But I've got the stuff. I put it someplace safe. I can take you to it. Come on, I'm taking a big chance, reaching out to you like this."

More buzzing. Shaban was not appeased. Finally Kyle broke in.

"Do you want the product or not? ... Then come and meet me. I'm at a motel, the Cra—I mean, the Happy Mariner on Route 35 in Maritime. Room one-oh-one. How long will it take you to get here? ... All right. I'll be waiting." She hung up. "He bought it."

"Probably."

"Of course he did. I was totally persuasive."

"Yeah, you're a regular Sandra Bernhard."

"I think you mean Sarah Bernhardt."

"Whatever. The Oscar goes to you." Bonnie circled around behind her and shut the curtains over the front windows.

"So where do you want me to be when this goes down?" Kyle rose from the sofa. "Can I watch it happen, or do you want me in the bathroom?"

"I don't want you here at all."

"Well, I'm staying. I need to be part of it."

"You're already part of it. You just shouldn't be here when the Shinola hits the fan."

"It's nonnegotiable. I'm not going anywhere."

"Then at least take off the damn coat."

"I told you—"

"Yeah, you're cold. What are you, ninety? You got some serious circulation problems, kid."

Kyle made a bored noise and turned away. "My circulation is fine."

"Not for long," Bonnie said, and she seized the girl from behind, throwing her right arm around her neck, wedging her throat in the crook of an elbow.

And squeezing. Squeezing hard.

Kyle was quick. Instinctively she tucked her chin and flung up both hands to grab Bonnie's arm. It was the right countermove to a rear chokehold. But it wouldn't save her.

Pressure on her carotids would cut off the blood flow to her brain, inducing unconsciousness in less than ten seconds.

Her right leg jerked backward. She struggled to hook her foot around Bonnie's ankle. Another smart move. If it worked, she could pivot and throw down her assailant, breaking the hold.

She hadn't lied about her training. But she also hadn't learned to fight dirty.

Bonnie slammed a sneaker down on Kyle's foot, pinning it to the floor.

The girl made a final effort to break free, jabbing blindly behind her but missing her target. Then she sagged, a hundred pounds of dead weight.

The faint wouldn't last long. Bonnie yanked the coat off the girl's body and threw it aside, then stripped off a pillowcase, stuffed it into her mouth, and used the duct tape to hogtie her wrists and ankles. Already the girl's eyelids were fluttering. Bonnie sealed her mouth with another strip of tape, then dragged her to the connecting door to the next room, leaving her on the floor.

By now Kyle was awake, her face red, eyes glaring. She looked angry, not scared, and Bonnie respected her for that.

"Keep cool, Croc. Everything will be okay."

Bonnie retrieved a set of picklocks from her purse and got the connecting door open. The adjacent room was indeed unoccupied. She would have to hope it remained that way for the next hour or so. In a dump like this, there was always the chance of a late-night check-in.

Lifting Kyle by her feet, she dragged the girl into the other room, a mirror image of the first. With effort, she heaved her facedown onto the bed.

Kyle jerked and writhed like a landed trout. Bonnie lifted the wallet from her back pocket. "No worries, okay? I just need you outta the picture while I deal with Shaban." She checked the other pockets for anything sharp. She didn't want the girl cutting herself free. "You can bang the headboard on the wall and make some noise, but I wouldn't recommend it." She found a key set, the vape pen, and some coins. She took the keys. "Anyone who hears you will just figure the neighbors are doing the nasty. And if the desk clerk does come to investigate, he'll probably call the cops, which wouldn't be good for either of us. *Capisce?*"

Kyle grunted unintelligible syllables behind the gag. Some salty language, most likely. But she did stop thrashing.

Bonnie stepped away from the bed. "Now just lie still and save your breath. If everything goes according to plan, you'll be untied as soon as Shaban's been taken care of. If things don't go as planned, and he takes me out—well, either he'll find you in here and kill you, or the cops will find you and arrest you. So let's hope it doesn't play out that way."

She left, shutting the door. Back in the first room, she went through the wallet's contents. According to the driver's license, Kyle Ridley was her real name, a fact confirmed by a student ID card, bank debit card, and Visa card. That was a little surprising. It had sounded like an alias. Then again, so did Bonnie Parker.

Her address on the driver's license was an apartment in Bayonne. She was carrying only four dollars in cash—she hadn't lied when she said that paying the room had cleaned her out—and a parking stub from Newark International Airport.

There were three keys on the chain—a car key, an apartment key, and a small key to a safe deposit box. That was another little surprise. Bonnie had assumed the story about the safe deposit box was a lie.

The red, white, and blue coat lay on the floor where she'd tossed it. She studied the lining in the light of a table lamp. It took her only a few moments to find the new stitching. A nice job. She'd read somewhere that the Turks were known for their stitching—rugs, towels, that kind of stuff.

She'd noticed right away that Kyle's jacket was too big for her and too heavy for this mild weather. And the girl had kept it on in the bar. Even here, she hadn't wanted to part with it.

Carefully she undid some of the stitches, peeled back a corner of the lining, and reached inside to finger the plastic pouches concealed within. Bags of heroin, sewn into the coat. Probably sprayed with special chemicals to mask the smell of the drugs.

Nobody had mugged Kyle at the airport. The only

person who'd stolen Shaban Dragusha's shipment was Kyle Ridley herself. She was no victim of circumstance. She'd planned the whole thing, knowing all along that she would need a hitter to eliminate her handler, the only member of the Dragusha organization who knew her name. Yeah, it was all very neat.

Bonnie hid the wallet and its contents in a drawer of the bureau, leaving the coat in plain sight. Then she took out the Walther, screwed in the suppressor, and settled down in the room's one armchair, facing the front door.

She didn't think she'd have long to wait.

15

SHABAN SLOWED AS the Happy Mariner came into view. He pulled into an alley alongside the motel, hiding the Porsche there. One disadvantage of driving a luxury sports car was that it was easily recognized and remembered.

He checked his phone, but there had been no further alerts in the last half hour. The ones he'd received were consistent with Kyle's story of holing up here.

It was a lucky break that she'd called him. Otherwise he might have been chasing her all night.

He left the car and prowled along the U-shaped building until he was close to room 101. It lay on the end, well away from the office. Most of the rooms he passed were dark and, if he could judge by the number of empty spaces in the lot, unoccupied.

The light in 101 was on. It glowed behind the heavy curtains drawn over the front windows, with narrow stripes of light bleeding through at the edges.

She was probably in there. Waiting, hoping to return the shipment and beg his forgiveness. But it was just possible she had some mischief in mind.

He had never known Kyle Ridley to carry a gun. But then he knew very little about her. She might have lured him here with the intention of silencing him before she left New Jersey for good.

His safest strategy would be to shoot her as soon as she opened the door. But suppose she did not have the product with her. On the phone she'd said she had put it someplace safe and would take him to it. This might have been a lie. But he couldn't be sure.

Frowning, he made his way around the building to the rear. A swimming pool was back there, empty of water. It faced a line of concrete patios. Each patio had its own sliding glass door.

The door to room 101 gave him an idea. Kyle Ridley would be watching the front door. She would not expect him to enter from the rear.

He approached the door and tested the handle. Locked, naturally. But the lock was nothing. It was not even keyed, just a simple latch. There was a chain on the inside, but it hung down uselessly, unattached. He saw no obstacles on the track—no plywood plank or security pin that would arrest the door's movement once it was unlatched.

Even for an amateur like himself, a lock like this would pose no obstacle.

Defeat the latch, slide open the door, enter through the thick drapery. If he could do this with sufficient stealth, he could surprise Kyle Ridley from behind and take control of her at gunpoint before she had a chance to react.

Such precautions might well prove unnecessary, but he was a cautious man.

Kneeling by the door, he set to work.

BONNIE SAT IN the armchair, watching the front door, her hand on the Walther. She had no idea when Shaban Dragusha would arrive. He might come in an hour or in ten minutes. He could be here already.

Only an hour ago, in the Sand Bar, she'd told Kyle that Shaban might enter shooting. Kyle had insisted he wouldn't. That was probably true. But you never knew about these things. If he did plan on making a dramatic entrance, she would have only a fraction of a second to react. It could go either way.

Oh, hell. It would probably work out okay. She wished it hadn't had to take place in a motel room, though. Motel rooms always had been unlucky for her. There was the motel in Pennsylvania where her parents had been killed by Lucas Hatch and his gang while she hid in the bathroom, hearing every sound. The motel in Brighton Cove where Pascal had tried to make her talk. The motel in Ridgefield where Streinikov's crew had nearly finished her off.

Yeah, motels had never been lucky for her. Motels ... or mobile homes.

She remembered a mobile home in Arizona. The heat and the closeness and the vinyl record spinning on a turntable ...

Her cell phone rang, startling her out of the memory. The screen displayed the name G Mitter. Gloria, Bill's wife. Bonnie answered. "Parker."

"Well?" a peremptory voice demanded.

"Huh?"

"Did you follow him? What did you find out?"

"You mean he's not home yet?"

"No, he's not home yet. Shouldn't you know that? Aren't you with him?"

She wanted Bill to be the one to break the news. "Sorry, no. I lost him."

"What you mean, you lost him?"

"I had him, and then I didn't have him anymore."

"How could that happen?"

"There was a lot of traffic. I got stuck at a red light. Redboarded, as it's known in the biz. By the time the light turned green, he was gone. Them's the breaks."

"You sound awfully insouciant about it."

Bonnie didn't know what insouciant meant. "I won't lose him next time."

"I'm very disappointed in you, Miss Parker."

"Yeah, I get that a lot."

She clicked off, bored with the conversation. It was bad enough that she had to sit and wait for a guest who might or might not try to shoot her on sight. She wasn't going to add insult to injury by taking a bunch of abuse for a purely imaginary screwup.

SHABAN HAD NO lock-picking tools, but he did carry a pocket knife with multiple functions—a Swiss Army knife, he believed it was called, though he didn't know why. Surely no army would be outfitted with such minuscule equipment.

One of the knife's extensions was a flathead screwdriver. Carefully he inserted the tip between the door and the frame, then raised it along the frame until it made contact with the latch. He pressed upward on the lever. Once or twice the screwdriver slipped and made a small scratching noise, but he was sure it wasn't loud enough to be heard from inside.

He shifted the screwdriver's position experimentally until the lever disengaged. With his other hand, he again tested the handle. This time the door yielded, sliding open a half inch.

It glided noiselessly on the track. There was no breeze to stir the draperies.

All right. Inside.

He drew the FEG 9, his *American Gangster* gun, from his shoulder holster. He had not used the gun on Todd Patterson in the church. He would use it on Kyle Ridley tonight. But first he and the girl would have a talk about loyalty and honor and the foolishness of crossing a man like him.

Standing, he eased the door open another few inches, then a few inches more, until he'd made a gap just wide enough to slip through. It would be impossible to enter without disturbing the drapes. Best, then, to shove them aside and go in fast. She would surely be facing the other direction. In the time it took for her to turn, he would see if she held a gun in her hand. If she did, he would fire. Hesitation was what got men killed.

He took a breath, put his fate in the hands of the saints, and brushed the draperies back as he plunged through the opening into the room.

There was just enough time for him to see that the space before him was empty, and then a gun's muzzle kissed the side of his face.

She had anticipated his move, had hidden alongside the glass door. She had him—what was the expression?—dead to rights.

His eyes tracked sideways, and he saw the woman holding the gun. Not Kyle Ridley.

"Parker?" he breathed.

"Hey, Shabby," Bonnie Parker said. "Long time, no see."

16

BONNIE THOUGHT IT was funny, the way Shaban gaped at her, slack-jawed.

"Kinda unfriendly," she said, "sneaking in the back way like this."

"It appears I did not sneak so well."

"Yeah, I heard you scratching around back there. I knew there was a fair chance you'd try that route. That's why I unhooked the chain."

"You unhooked it?" He shut his eyes briefly. "I have been outplayed. And now—what?"

His expression was calm, his eyes clear. She admired him for that.

"Now we sit and talk. But first—drop your piece."

He straightened his shoulders, and his Adam's apple bobbed once. She recognized the body language. He was thinking of trying something.

"Don't be a hero," she added in her most reasonable tone. "I don't want to shoot you, but you know I'm capable of it."

He hesitated a moment longer. Then his fingers opened, and the pistol fell to the floor.

"Kick it away." He did. "Good boy."

She studied him. A year had passed since she'd seen him, but he was still a hawk-nosed, sharp-eyed badass, lean and fit, and, unlike most of his colleagues in the Albanian mob, clean-shaven. He was a snazzy dresser—she pegged his suit as Giorgio Armani—and he didn't show off a lot of bling, though she remembered he wore two gold wristwatches, one set to local time and the other to Albanian time. He had showed them to her, the last time they met.

"Got any other weapons on you?" she asked. "Another gun, a blade, that Swiss Army knife you used to carry?"

"No."

"That's probably a lie. Reach for anything, and you'll regret it."

"I will not reach."

"Okay. Take a seat over there." She pointed to a straight-backed chair tucked into a kneehole in a bureau.

He crossed the carpet in quick jerky strides. He was young—early twenties—and still had an adolescent's gangly frame and clumsy coltish way of walking. He spun the chair around and sat. She resumed her place in the armchair, turning it slightly to face him.

"May I ask what the hell is going on?" His tone was polite, but his eyes burned. He didn't like being held at gunpoint. Well, hell. Nobody did.

"Yeah," Bonnie said, "you may ask. This was supposed to be a setup. Kyle wanted me to take you out."

"The girl hired you?"

Bonnie nodded. "Gotta say, you really hit the jackpot when you hooked up with her."

"She has proved untrustworthy," Shaban said mildly.

"No kidding. She told me she got ripped off at the airport and lost her stash. Since you'd never believe that story, it was my job to put you out of action before you could put the kibosh on her. She would lure you here with a phone call, and when you walked in, it'd be wham-bam, bye-bye Shaban."

Silence hummed in the room for a long moment. "And yet I am alive," Shaban said finally.

"Noticed that, did you? Yeah, I never intended to go through with the hit."

"Why not?"

"Because I knew she was bullshitting me."

MICHAEL PRESCOTT

"Then why do you work for her at all? For money?"

"This is turning out to be kind of a pro bono assignment."

"If no money, then why?"

"I don't know. She reminds me of someone."

"Who?"

"Me, I guess. When I was younger. But only in some ways. Unlike me, she's book smart, not people smart. And she's in way over her head. She could never have outmaneuvered you."

"I am flattered."

"Statement of fact. For instance, you got here in under half an hour. You couldn't have made it all the way from Hoboken that fast."

"I had already crossed the Millstone County line when I got her call."

"So you tracked her that far on your own. Color me not surprised."

His right hand drifted toward his belt buckle. There could be a blade inside. She wagged the gun at him.

"Nuh-uh, silly rabbit. Tricks are for kids."

His hand retreated. It would bear watching. By the rules he played by, he was entitled to take her out if he could.

"Where is the girl?" Shaban asked too casually.

"Around."

"I would like to see her."

"I don't think so. You might do something you'd regret. More to the point, you might oblige me to do something I'd regret."

He gave her a shrewd look. "Would you indeed regret it?"

"I'm not interested in killing anybody. I don't do that sort of work anymore."

"No? You have gone straight?"

"Absolutely. You're looking at friggin' Mother Teresa here."

"What, then, is your purpose?"

"In life?"

"In holding this meeting."

"Oh. I intend to broker a deal."

"Deal," he said quietly. He smacked his lips as if tasting the word.

"Why not? I did it once before, and there were no complaints, were there?"

"This situation is different."

"Every situation is different, but I think we can work this one out and walk away friends. Okay, not friends. But we can all walk away, at least. Like last time."

A year ago the head of a local chain of office supply stores had come to her with a problem. He'd purchased a shipment of high-tech gear at a bargain price from some freelancers. Sure, the deal had seemed shady, but you had to cut a few corners to make a buck, what with the economy and all. He'd done it before.

Trouble was, this particular shipment had been stolen from a truck owned by the Albanian mob, and they were looking for it. If they traced it to him, he would be in their crosshairs, and everyone knew the Albanians were not people you could afford to piss off. He wanted to make things right, but he was afraid to approach them on his own.

Bonnie had brokered the deal. Her negotiating partner had been Shaban Dragusha, the big boss's grandson. Shaban had struck her as a rare find among mobsters—a guy who actually believed in honoring his word.

"You wish to strike a bargain, is that it?" Shaban asked, measuring her with his gaze. "You negotiate on her behalf?"

"That's about the size of it."

"Does she know you do this?"

"Not a clue."

"She will be unhappy when she finds out."

"Yeah, I'm guessing I'm off her Christmas card list."

"You lose a client, you make no money. There is nothing in it for you, Bonnie Parker. But there can be." He leaned forward, the chair creaking under him. "Here is the deal I offer. You and me share all profits from the product. No pro bono bullshit. Street value is two hundred twenty or more. You get half, I get half. This is good money for you. More than you make for a hit."

"Used to make. I'm out of the business, remember? And anyway, how would you know my price?"

"People talk. I know your reputation. You have killed, sure, yes, but only when you feel it is justified. And you have never tortured."

"Right." Though as far as torture was concerned, she admitted to some doubt about Frank Lazzaro's sendoff.

Shaban nodded in approval. "Torture is for fools and sick perverts. I like a quick kill, no pain. To make the man dead is all that matters. You know this. You are smart. Professional."

"Aw, stop. You'll make me blush." She leaned forward. "I take it you're telling me this to convince me we can work together."

"Is an idea."

"If you and me go halfsies, won't your superiors miss their cut?"

"Let me worry about them."

"And in exchange for this windfall, I also give you Kyle?"

He spread his hands. "Is only fair."

It was fair, in its way. But it wasn't the deal she had in mind.

She sat back in the chair again. "That's not how we're gonna play it, Shabby. We're gonna come to a different agreement."

He crossed his legs and folded his arms, a study in sales resistance. "What agreement?"

"See the American flag coat on the bed?" She knew he

had. She'd noticed his eyes tick toward it more than once since he'd sat down. "As I'm sure you're aware, your latest shipment of Turkish delight is sewn into the lining. You'll take it and let me and Kyle skate. No retaliation, no retribution, now or later."

"This is bullshit."

"It's the deal that's on the table."

"Is crap deal."

"Not really. You get the shipment. No need to split any profits with me. All you give up is the opportunity to take revenge on a dumb kid who doesn't matter anyway."

He shook his head fiercely. "She betrayed my trust. For this she must pay."

"Yeah, I get that." She lifted the Walther a tad. "But you're not in a position of strength in this negotiation."

"You expect me to agree to your terms under duress?"

"Duress. Nice use of the lingo. Your English has come a long way. Yeah, you're gonna sign on."

"And what makes me keep this agreement? Why do I not go after her later?" His eyes narrowed, and the light in them turned cold. "And go after you too, Parker?"

"You're going to give me your word."

"So you count on my sense of honor."

"I do. As a matter of fact, that's the only reason we're having this conversation. When I heard you were involved, I saw a way to play it. A nice nonviolent way that would pull Kyle's bacon out of the fire without the need for bloodshed. But it had to be you. I wouldn't trust anyone else to play fair."

"Maybe you trust me too much."

"I don't think so. You're a straight shooter. And you know I am, too."

He spun his chair halfway around, fidgeting like a trapped animal. "I do not like it."

"But you'll do it."

"You seem very sure of this."

"That's 'cause I'm the one holding the gun."

"I always liked you, Parker. I am disappointed now."

"You never liked me. And I never liked you. We did business together, that's all. Let's not make a whole big thing out of it."

He shut his eyes, inhaled slowly, and released the breath with a hiss. "Give me the coat."

"Give me your word."

"I will meet your terms. No harm comes to you or the girl."

"On your honor?"

"On my honor."

"Pinky swear? Only kidding."

For the first time, she thought she just might get away with this gamble. Before this moment, he had been within his rights to make a move on her. In principle, at least, that option had now been foreclosed.

She walked to the bed, collected the jacket, and tossed it to him.

"There you go. Two kilos of junk all wrapped up in the red, white, and blue."

He inspected the lining and nodded. "I take your word that it is all here."

"What, like I'm gonna rip you off?" She couldn't suppress a twitch of irritation. "I don't want your fucking dope. How do you sell that shit to kids and still live with yourself?"

"I do not sell to kids. I sell to dealers. What they do with it is not my trouble."

"That's a pretty questionable way of looking at it."

"Also I confess my sins very often. I get absolution."

This was news to her. It hadn't come up in their previous business dealings. "You a Christian, Shabby?"

"I talk to Saint Bessus sometimes."

"Who's he?"

"Patron saint of men in war."

"Is that what you are?"

"I am a soldier on the field of battle, sure, yes."

"And you've got this Saint Bejesus looking out for you?"

"Saint Bessus," he corrected.

"So you're in the clear with the powers that be, no matter what you do?"

"Fate of my soul is God's will, not mine. But I think I am okay."

"Even if I'd gone through with the hit?"

He shrugged. "You shoot me, I go to heaven maybe, which is better than here. Or to hell, which is about the same."

"Yeah, the distinction between hell and Jersey is pretty thin. But I don't think you're that cool about getting aced. No one is."

"Is a dangerous life. I know this from day one. Odds are, I die from a bullet. If it is tonight, is tonight. If not tonight, is later. Different night, different bullet, same result. Why should I not be, as you say, cool?"

"I dunno, but if you ain't shining me on, you're a very different breed of cat. Okay, we're done here."

He stood, facing her. "May I collect my handgun?"

"Knock yourself out." Under the circumstances there was little additional risk in letting him retrieve his weapon. Either he would honor their agreement or he wouldn't. If he chose not to, then he would sic the whole Dragusha mob on her, and she would be dead in short order anyway. And from what she understood, his colleagues didn't share his reservations about torture or his preference for a quick kill.

"You can leave by the front door," she said as she holstered her gun. "It's more civilized that way."

"Sure, yes."

"Incidentally, how much did you pay Kyle per run?"

"Fifteen hundred."

"She said ten grand. Did you help her set up a bank

account with a safe deposit box?"

"I did not help her do nothing. What do I care where she puts her money?"

"Yeah, I hear you. I'm betting you and her never hooked up, either."

"She tells you this?"

"Said you two did the dance with no pants at your apartment. Probably she's never even been there."

"Once she was there, for a party. She came with a friend. Is where we met. But there was no dance. I do not fuck any goddamn courier."

"Not even a swallower?"

"What?"

"Never mind. Our Kylie's just a little liar, isn't she?"

"And yet she lives," Shaban said bitterly.

"A deal's a deal. And Kyle's life is possibly worth saving."

"This I doubt."

"You know me. I try to believe the best about people."

"Except for the ones you have killed."

"Right. Except for them."

"You are a strange one, Parker."

"Yeah, I'm one of a kind."

His gaze drilled into her from a yard away. The muscles of his face were taut, his mouth a bloodless line like a paper cut.

"Someday," he said, "we may meet under circumstances where I have the upper hand, and when I am not bound by honor."

She returned his stare without blinking. "Looking forward to it, Shabby. Don't take any wooden kopeks."

He turned away, breaking eye contact. "Currency in Albania is not the kopek. Is the lek."

"Well, don't take any wooden ones of those, either."

He didn't answer. He opened the front door and stalked off into the night. Slowly she shut the door.

Only then did she allow herself to relax. Remarkably

enough, the encounter had gone smoothly. This was the first time in a long while that a visit to a motel had worked out well for her. Maybe her luck was changing.

Of course, there was still Kyle Ridley to deal with. And man, was she gonna be pissed.

17

"YOU *BITCH*, YOU *BITCH*!"

As expected, Kyle was not taking it well.

It had been easy enough to cut her loose. When the tape over her mouth came off and she spat out the gag, she was suddenly free to express her feelings. Evidently she'd heard everything through the closed door and the paper-thin wall.

"You gave him the heroin," she wailed. "Just *gave* it to him."

Her fists came up, driving at Bonnie's face. Bonnie seized her by the wrists and held her down on the bed.

"That's right," she said evenly.

"God damn it, you *played* me."

"We played each other. I was just better at it."

"You've ruined everything!"

"*Au contraire.* I just saved your life, kid."

Kyle made a noise like a strangled scream. Her wrists jerked wildly in Bonnie's grip. "You never even *intended* to do the hit!"

"I told you I'd reformed."

"Everything you agreed to—it was all bullshit."

"Not all problems can be solved with violence, Crocodile." Bonnie was getting tired of the drama. "I said you were taking a chance, coming to me. It's always risky to depend on the kindness of strangers."

Kyle groaned. Her hands opened. Her head drooped over the side of the bed.

"You think you're so smart," she said behind a dark fall of hair, "but you fucked it all up."

"Yeah, all your pretty plans."

"If you weren't going to go through with it, why take the job at all?"

"I only took it because I wouldn't *have* to go through with it. When you name-dropped Shaban, I realized I could make a deal with him. I wouldn't be killing anybody. That's how I play it now. I'm on the wagon, remember?"

"Yeah, yeah, so you said." She raised her head. "What makes you think he won't still hunt me down? Just because he made you a *promise*?"

"That's about the size of it. He's young, but he's old-school. He's all about honor."

"So I should trust him?"

"It's not so crazy. He's an honest guy, in his way. Gotta respect that."

"Are you telling me you actually *like* Shaban?"

"I wouldn't call him likable. But I don't hate him. He's smarter than the average mobbed-up asshole, and I don't think he's exactly evil."

"If he's not evil, then what is he?"

"I don't know. Complicated. Like me."

She released the girl's wrists and watched her climb slowly off the bed. Kyle adjusted her glasses, riding crooked on her nose, then stripped away the last of the tape. She winced as it tore the small hairs on her arms. "You don't understand a goddamn thing about it," she whispered.

"I understand that ninety percent of what you told me was crapola. I'm surprised you even gave me your real name."

"I had to. If you were any kind of PI, you could run my plate number."

It was actually pretty hard for a civilian to match a name to a vehicle's tag, but Bonnie didn't enlighten her. "I also understood that you were a user."

"You're wrong. I told you, I never touch the product."

"I don't mean it that way. I mean you're a manipulator. You use people and then you throw them away. Once I got rid of Shaban for you, you were gonna duck out on me, sell the heroin, and run. Right?"

Kyle shrugged, setting her mouth in a pout. "You wouldn't have wanted drug money anyway. You have moral objections." She pronounced the last two words with distaste.

"That's not why you would've done it. You wanted all the cash because you always want it all. You're greedy, which can be a good thing, but you're also impatient, which is usually a bad thing, and you overestimate yourself and underestimate everyone else, which is a really bad thing."

The girl stomped past her, through the connecting doorway. "All right, all right. Lecture delivered."

Delivered, Bonnie thought, but not received. Kyle hadn't heard her, because no one could teach her anything.

She followed the kid into the other room, where Kyle was jerking open the bureau drawers in search of her pocket litter.

"You need to grow up, Crocodile."

"Don't tell me what to do. You can't run my life for me."

"Somebody has to. Because you're doing a piss-poor job of running it yourself."

"Fuck you." She found the wallet and her other stuff and crammed them back into her pants.

"By the way, what's your safe deposit box key for?"

"A safe deposit box. What else?"

"There's no fifty grand in the bank. Shaban told me."

"Shaban doesn't know everything." Kyle opened the door to the parking lot. "And neither do you."

She marched off into the dark. Bonnie stared after her. Slowly she shook her head.

This whole reform business was a pain in the ass. Maybe it was easier to just shoot people.

18

IT TOOK BONNIE a few minutes to clean up after herself in the motel. She made sure the connecting door was locked again. There was duct tape to be disposed of, and the sliding door to be locked and chained. And because being a private eye wasn't all glamor, she took a whizz.

She retrieved her Jeep and headed out on 35, going south for no particular reason. She'd covered less than a mile when she spotted Kyle's white Hyundai Accent in the nearly empty parking lot of an all-night eatery with the unlikely name of Clown Burger. The building's conical roof in red and white stripes gave it a passing resemblance to a circus tent. Overhead loomed a giant neon clown with a flashing red nose.

It didn't seem like Kyle Ridley's kind of place. Either she was hungrier than she let on, or she was really falling apart. Bonnie decided to find out. She steered the Jeep into the lot and locked it.

As expected, a place that called itself Clown Burger would not be giving Tavern on the Green any serious competition. In a corner booth a homeless guy lounged, asleep. At the counter a sallow-faced girl flipped through a tabloid magazine with an expression that suggested she was contemplating suicide. A staffer guided a floor waxing machine across the tiles—red and white striped tiles, like the roof. The machine droned like a lawnmower, occasionally cutting out for a few seconds, its drone replaced by rinky-tink circus music from speakers in the ceiling. The music fit in all too well with the clown-themed plastic placemats and the clown cartoons on the walls.

Yeah, the atmosphere sucked. It was like a bus terminal decorated by carnies.

Kyle Ridley sat in a booth near the counter, backgrounded by the flash of lights on the highway. As Bonnie approached, the girl looked up from her burger and winced. "Jesus Christ."

Bonnie slid into the booth. "Nah, it's just me."

"What the fuck are you doing here?"

"And hello to you too. You calm down yet?"

"I'm calm. Get lost."

"We ought to talk."

"I'm eating."

"Multitask."

Bonnie lit a cigarette. It was illegal to smoke in a restaurant, but she didn't see anybody who was likely to make an issue out of it.

"What's there to talk about?" Kyle said.

"We could swap recipes." Bonnie drew in a long, healing drag. "You know, I wouldn't have thought you ate fast food."

"I don't."

"You're eating it now."

"Only because I'm starving. Haven't eaten anything all day except a banana at your place."

"Two bananas, but who's counting?"

Kyle tore off a bite of the burger like a starving dog. "I'd heard you were reliable."

"Most of my clients have been satisfied."

"Yeah, well, you can expect a blistering Yelp review from me."

Bonnie expelled a jet of smoke. "That's good, Kyle. Humor is good. If you can find the humor in the situation, you're halfway home."

"Oh, shut the fuck up."

"You were so friggin' impressed with how brilliant you are. You figured it would be a snap to put one over on a small-town PI."

She took another angry bite. "Maybe I underestimated you."

"Ya think? It wasn't hard to see through you. You're as transparent as the lenses of those phony smart-girl glasses you wear."

"They're not phony."

"Then they're the only thing about you that isn't."

"How about you? All your self-righteous crap about school kids and playgrounds, and then you let Shaban Dragusha walk out with two kilos."

"Two kilos is a drop in the bucket in the grand scheme of things. The Dragushas move maybe a thousand kilos a year. They're surfing a money tsunami, and little old me ain't gonna stop it."

"So you're a hypocrite."

"I'm not a martyr. When I took this piece-of-shit case, I had two objectives. One was to keep you alive, because maybe there's something in you worth saving. The other was not to make a dime off of drug money. I don't need that on my conscience."

"Your conscience." Kyle shook her head. "You're a fucking assassin for hire."

"Not anymore," Bonnie reminded her. "Shaban was going to get his product back one way or the other. He was always going to win this game, and you were always going to lose. The only question was if you'd end up dead or keep breathing. Congratulations. You still got a carbon footprint."

The bitter twist of her mouth was ugly to see. "Hurrah for me."

The floor waxing guy finally finished his job and wheeled the contraption out of sight. Now it was circus music all the time. Not an improvement.

"You never should've gone to work for Shaban and company in the first place," Bonnie said. "It was a really dumb move."

"What was I supposed to do? I needed money."

"You could have gotten a regular job."

"Flipping burgers in a shit hole like this? I don't think so."

The counter girl heard her and frowned.

"People work their way through college," Bonnie said. "It's been done."

"It wasn't just college. I was tired of it, that's all."

"Tired of ...?"

"Cutting corners. Counting pennies. It's ridiculous for someone like me to have to nickel-and-dime it when there's money out there—a money tsunami, like you said. More than I could ever spend, and it's just waiting to be taken."

"Except the people who have it don't like other people trying to take it away."

"Whatever. I took a shot. What was the alternative? Work as a sales clerk? Or in a fucking cubicle? That's no life. There's no meaning, nothing to look forward to. It's just an endless run on a hamster wheel. Life in a Skinner box. Perform on cue and win a food pellet. No, thanks."

"You could try being a motivational speaker, maybe. This stuff is gold."

"Don't get me wrong. That kind of life might be all right for most people. They have nothing better to aspire to. Or they're content to wait their turn and climb the ladder one rung at the time. Not me. I'm not going to be defined by arbitrary rules. I make my own rules."

"Uh-huh. How's that working out for you?"

"It would have worked. It *should* have." The eyes behind the chunky square-framed glasses were big and scared. "You just don't get it. You don't understand."

Bonnie returned her gaze steadily. "You said this was your last run. I'm hoping that's true. Not that the Dragushas would hire you again, obviously, but someone else might. If you take that road, it's only a matter of time till you're caught. Everybody slips up eventually. The big boys know it. That's why they only have you carry a couple kilos at a time. If you get made, they don't lose that much. Cost of doing business."

"I'm done with the drug trade. I just wanted to go out in style. I wanted to keep a nice little retainer."

"Well, instead you get to retain your life. It's up to you what you do with it. Personally I think you need to go back to school and try living a normal, crime-free life."

"You're one to talk."

"Yeah, I am. Because I know I fucked up my life choices. You've still got a chance to get it right."

"What is this, an after-school special? I hired you to do one job, and you didn't come through."

"Hey, the best-laid plans go all ugly."

"*Gang aft agley*. It's Middle English."

"Yeah, like Shakespeare, right?"

Another one of her patented eye rolls. "Shakespeare wrote in modern English."

"Didn't sound so modern to me."

"You've read Shakespeare?" Kyle asked skeptically.

"Sure."

"Which one?"

"The one where Leo DiCaprio guns down Chi-Chi Rodriguez."

"Oh, my God."

Bonnie let it go. "Look, I'm sorry your little scheme went all to shit. But it wasn't a very good scheme. Too many uncontrollable variables."

"Like what?"

"Like me, Crocodile."

"Stop calling me that."

"Why should I? Everything you told me was a crock, Croc. Even that bit about you and Shaban hooking up. He says it never happened."

"It didn't."

"Why'd you lie?"

"It made a better story."

"Or maybe you would've liked to do the nasty with him. That it? You got a thing for bad boys?"

"I don't have a thing for anybody."

"What's that supposed to mean?"

"I'm not exactly a party girl."

"No? Well, maybe that's your problem right there. When's the last time you got laid?"

"Never."

"Seriously?"

"Yes." She sucked furiously at the straw in her soda glass. "I've never had sex, all right?"

"How old are you again?"

"Twenty. Yes, I know it's unusual."

"Holding out for the right guy?"

"Not really."

"Right gal?"

"You wish."

"No, I don't, sugarplum. Even if I did swing that way, you are definitely not my type."

"I'm cut to the quick."

"Maybe you'd have more luck in the dating game if you didn't say stuff like that."

"I don't play the dating game. I'm just not interested."

"Not even in a little solo action? You know, taking matters into your own hands?"

"Once or twice. But it didn't mean anything."

"It's not supposed to mean something. It's supposed to curl your toes."

"So I'm told. I never felt much of anything."

"Oh."

Kyle looked up sharply. "Don't say it like that."

"Like what?"

"Like you're feeling sorry for me. I'm not your kid sister, and you don't have to concern yourself with my well-being."

"So having zero sex life doesn't bother you?"

"No, it doesn't."

"What did you major in, again?"

"You think I took up psychology to figure myself out? And possibly fix myself?"

"It's a theory."

"A stupid theory. I'm not broken and I don't need fixing."

"Okay."

"And I don't need pity."

"Okay."

"And I *certainly* don't need the armchair analysis of a high school dropout who kills people for a living."

"Used to kill," Bonnie corrected. "And it was more of a sideline."

"I don't care if it was a religious calling. I didn't come to you for therapy."

"It's sort of a free bonus."

"Well, I don't want it or need it."

"Fair enough." Bonnie couldn't keep an undertone of sympathy out of her voice.

Kyle heard it. She stood, her slight body shaking. Without the polyester coat, she looked awfully small and very young.

"You know what, bitch? Fuck you. Just stay away from me and—and *fuck you*!"

She stormed out of the restaurant. The counter girl gaped at her, and even the homeless guy blinked awake. Bonnie looked at them and smiled.

"Kid knows how to make an exit," she said, helping herself to the last of the burger. "Gotta give her that."

19

AT THE 7-ELEVEN in Miramar, a few blocks north of Brighton Cove on Ocean Drive, Brad fetched two cups of coffee. His shift ran until midnight, and he and Dan needed the caffeine.

He stood by the magazine rack, filling a second extra-large cup from the dark roast spigot. Another long night on patrol. Except for his encounter with Bonnie, it had all been pretty routine. Other traffic tickets, a silent alarm that had gone off accidentally, an elderly man who was having trouble breathing and required paramedics.

He'd imagined police work to be different. Sometimes he hardly felt like a cop at all. He wore a uniform, sure, but patrolling Brighton Cove wasn't exactly like running SWAT raids in Camden. Some days, his biggest challenge was shepherding ducks across the street. He'd never fired his service pistol on duty. Self-defense was seldom necessary when the worst lawbreakers you encountered were jaywalking waterfowl.

Of course, there had been that night in February when a crew of mobsters blew through town, shooting off machine guns. That had been exciting enough, even if he had gotten to the scene only after the fact.

Since then … nothing but ducks.

Coffee overflowed the cup. His mind had wandered, and he'd overfilled it. He grabbed some paper napkins. He was cleaning up the mess when two other customers wandered in. Young guys, scruffy looking, with long hair and beard stubble covering their chins and their necks. They wore a lot of bling and spoke too loudly in a foreign language that sounded like something out of Eastern Europe.

Brad watched them from behind the row of coffee-makers. He was thinking of last February, the hit squad that had come to town. They had been Russians.

The pair in the store hadn't noticed him. They went straight to the counter and asked for cigarettes. Their English was imperfect, but they got the idea across. They bought four packs of Marlboros, paying cash.

When they left, Brad's gaze followed them to their car. Big black Hummer, showroom new. Two other guys waiting in the front seats. They'd parked out front, while he'd parked around the side. Probably they hadn't spotted the cruiser. He wondered if they would have come in if they'd known cops were around.

The Hummer pulled out of the lot and headed south, in the direction of Brighton Cove. He didn't like that. He paid for the coffee and returned to his ride, moving a little faster than usual.

"Took you long enough," Dan said as he accepted his cup.

Brad got behind the wheel. "You see the Hummer?"

"What about it?"

"Four guys. I think they might be Russians."

Dan frowned. "They went south."

"I know."

"You get the tag?"

Brad rattled it off.

"I'll call it in."

The Hummer wasn't in sight by the time Brad pulled onto Ocean Drive, but it shouldn't be too far ahead. He retraced his route, the boardwalk gliding by on his left this time. If his suspicions were right, the Hummer wouldn't stay by the beach. It would be headed inland—downtown, maybe, to Bonnie's office, or farther west to her home.

Those were the locations the gunmen had gone after last time.

The idea was crazy. There was nothing to suggest a replay of February. Plenty of people came from Eastern Europe. They weren't all hitmen, for God's sake. He was just getting antsy, looking for something to liven up his night—something more exciting than ducks.

The license plate came back clean. "Doesn't mean much," Dan said. "If they're pros, they wouldn't use a plate that would draw a red flag."

"You really think there could be something to this?"

"Where our girl's concerned, there can always be something to it. Even if she's been keeping her head down, she might still be on somebody's hit list."

"I guess it would simplify things for us," Brad said tentatively, "if we just let it work out that way."

"Nobody's getting murdered in my town, Walsh. Not if I can help it. Not even her."

Brad was glad to hear it. Sometimes he wasn't quite sure how far the chief might be willing to go.

"There." Dan nodded to their left.

The Hummer was slant-parked on the street, headlights off, facing the boardwalk. The vehicle's interior was a blue fog. All four occupants had lit up, it seemed.

Brad drove past without slowing noticeably. From the car came laughter mingled with hip-hop on the radio.

Weird how they were just sitting there. It didn't seem like the kind of thing a crew of professionals would do.

Slowly he turned the patrol car around and circled back. He parked a few spaces away from the Hummer and watched with Dan as someone struck a lighter, firing up a fresh cigarette.

"Not doing anything illegal," Brad said.

"Nope. It's not a crime to park at the beach. But ..."

"It feels wrong."

Dan nodded. "Let's say we have a talk with them."

"Both of us?"

"Yeah. Both of us."

Brad got on the radio and reported the stop. "What's our excuse?" he asked the chief.

One of men in the Hummer tossed a spent butt out the window onto the verge of grass that lined the curb.

"Littering," Dan said.

Brad nodded. He and Dan slipped out of the squad car and approached the Hummer. Faces turned toward them as they drew near.

Dan stayed back a couple of feet while Brad rapped on the driver's window. Grudgingly the window slid down halfway and the music clicked off. The driver had two gold chains around his neck, dangling down on his black turtleneck under a sport jacket.

"Yes, Officer?" he said with a heavy accent and exaggerated politeness. "There is problem?"

Brad studied him. Lean face. Black beard, a white streak running through it like a badger's stripe. The other three were equally young. Every one of them a smoker, and every one dressed in black.

They watched him and Dan warily. The one in the passenger seat was scowling. The two in the rear showed no expression. The driver wore a frozen smile.

"May I see some identification?" Brad asked the driver.

The man dug in his pocket and extracted a laminated card from his wallet. Brad took a look. His name was Raco Prifti. Hoboken address.

"From out of town, I see," he said.

"Yes. North Jersey. I do something wrong?"

He ignored the question. "How about your friends? They have ID?"

Reluctantly the other three handed over their driver's licenses. Two more Hoboken addresses, and one in Jersey City.

Brad memorized all the names before giving back the

cards. The four watched him expectantly. No one was smiling now.

"Okay," he said. "We happened to see one of you guys toss a cigarette butt out the window. It would be better if you didn't do that."

The driver seemed to relax a little. "Is littering?"

"That's right. Also a fire risk. The weather's been dry lately, and the dead grass along the curb is like tinder."

"I make apology."

"I'm not going to write you up, but from now on, please dispose of your used cigarettes in the ashtray."

"Of course." He showed a cool, unfriendly grin. "We do this."

The man's words were fine, but his smile was an insult, and the small dark eyes were mocking him.

"Great. Thanks for your cooperation."

Dan leaned in to ask a question. "You fellows staying for the weekend?"

"No. Just take a drive. Pleasure drive."

One of the pair in the back snickered.

"Seeing the sights?" Dan asked.

"The sights, yes." The driver gestured vaguely at the windshield. "See water."

They couldn't see anything from this spot except the boardwalk and an occasional jogger flitting in and out of the pale cones of light thrown by the streetlamps.

"Well," Brad said, "drive safe."

He and Dan walked away. "What do you think?" Brad asked when they were back in the squad car.

"Let's keep an eye on them," Dan said. "Just in case."

RACO PRIFTI DROVE away from the boardwalk, lifting his phone from his pocket, and placed a call to his employer.

"Is a problem," he said in his native language when his

boss answered. "The local police spotted us."

"How did this happen?"

"We were parked. A patrol car pulled up. There was nothing we could do."

"Parked, why? You were told to circle the neighborhood."

"It was early. She could not be here so soon."

"So?"

Raco licked his lips, which were strangely dry. "We stopped for a smoke."

"A smoke. *Rrot kari.*" The man took a moment to compose himself. "It may be okay. Even if they ran your plate, it would come back clean. It cannot be traced to us. We got it from Sali."

Sali was an auto dealer in Bergen County who supplied the organization with vehicles as needed. The Hummer could be reported stolen and made to disappear.

"There is more than that, *Xhaxhi,*" Raco said unhappily.

"Speak."

"They ... they talked to me. They checked our ID. All four of us."

The man released a long sigh. "You are a fool, Prifti. Maybe you were better off in Shqipëria. Maybe soon you go back there to live with your grandmother. Go back for good. You would like this?"

Raco's chief memory of his grandmother was of a mist of greasy stink rising from a pot of lamb stew. "No, *Xhaxhi.*"

"Very well. Your assignment is off. We will handle it some other way. Come north. Visit me at the pier where the ship is loading. The *Mazeppa.*"

"*Mazeppa,*" Raco breathed. He had heard stories of the cargo sometimes carried by that ship.

"Bring your men. I may have some use for you yet."

The call was over. Raco pocketed the phone with

sweaty fingers.

He didn't like it. Didn't like the talk of returning to the old country. Didn't like going to the pier. Didn't like hearing of the *Mazeppa*.

He hadn't argued, though. Nobody argued with *Ujku*—Arian Dragusha, the Wolf.

Nobody who wanted to live.

20

AN UNWELCOME SURPRISE was waiting for Bonnie when she emerged from Clown Burger. Her Jeep was in even worse condition than before.

One headlight had been kicked in, the front window on the driver's side smashed. The front seats had been attacked with something sharp—a key, probably—the cushions grooved with jagged gashes spelling out *F. U.*

She looked around for Kyle's Hyundai, but it was long gone, of course. With a sigh she opened the door. Her glove box had been pried open, its contents distributed everywhere. Kyle had been looking for something. A gun, probably. If she'd found one, she might have gone back inside Clown Burger with more serious trouble in mind.

"Crocodile, Crocodile ..." Bonnie shook her head sadly. If you couldn't trust a renegade drug mule, who could you trust?

She settled behind the wheel and put the Jeep into gear. The night air through the broken window was cold on her face. At least it wasn't raining. You had to look on the bright side.

She headed south for a mile or two, then cut over toward the ocean. She went through Brighton Cove and kept going. No particular reason. She was edgy, that's all. Something was nagging at her, some stray thought or memory she couldn't quite bring into focus.

Shitty night anyway. The tail job hadn't worked out the way she'd hoped. And she'd gotten another ticket. And yes, she'd saved Kyle Ridley's life—but she was starting to wonder if that had been such a great idea.

Maybe she should have stifled her good Samaritan impulse and let nature take its course.

But no. Even after the little bitch trashed her ride, Bonnie still couldn't help feeling sorry for her. Sure, she'd done a stupid thing, but Bonnie herself had done some stupid things when she was that age.

Like working for Edna Goodman ...

And boom, just like that, she was back in the past, reliving her summer night in Palm Garden.

The bar called Sidewinder's was just as classy an establishment as she'd expected. Above the entrance a flashing neon sign spelled out the name and an animated rattlesnake lashed its tail. Motorcycles and pickup trucks crowded the parking lot.

Inside there was a long bar, four pool tables, and smoke everywhere. Back then it was still legal to light up in a restaurant, at least in Arizona. She sat at the bar and ignited one of her Parliament Whites. She'd been a smoker since she was fifteen.

The bartender delivered her order, a Jack & Coke, her beverage of choice when she could get it. Though she was a hair under twenty-one, the guy didn't ask to see her ID. Sidewinder's wasn't that kind of place. Anyway, her time on the road had made her look older than she was. Something about the squint of her eyes, she thought.

She nursed the drink, making it last. She wasn't planning to order another. She needed to stay sharp.

Now and then she brushed off come-ons from random barflies. It was just possible the come-ons were encouraged by the words printed in big letters on her T-shirt: *If You're Hard, I'm Easy.* It was a joke, but some of these dirt farmers and tarantula wranglers seemed to take it a little too seriously.

Most of the time, she just sat back and took in the atmosphere—the slap of pool cues, the roll of balls into the pockets, the grudging handovers of cash, the occasional near-fights, with the contenders puffing themselves up like toads and challenging each other, but always backing down. Not a violent place. Not like some of the dives she'd seen, where people would cut you with a switchblade for an offending glance.

The pool tables were arranged under suspended lights, where money for wagers was deposited. Spectators occupied highback chairs along the rear wall. Railbirds, they were called. They murmured appreciatively after the better shots.

Bonnie had played some pool back in Philly, and there was a good chance she could have hustled these rubes, but she resisted the temptation. She had to stay low-profile, like a real private eye.

A jukebox stood in the corner, playing everything from Buddy Holly to Tim McGraw. One guy kept slugging in coins and selecting *Bad Moon Rising*, the Creedence tune. He must have played it half a dozen times until a pal got hold of him and escorted him away from the jukebox. Bonnie hadn't minded. She liked that song.

Mainly, she watched Ed Goodman. He shot some pool—not badly, but not well enough to elicit any murmurs from the railbirds—and he played a couple of numbers on the jukebox. He downed a single beer, straight from the bottle, and joshed with the waitresses, giggly gals ranging in age from twenty to sixty, all of them showing a lot of tit in varying degrees of pertness. Nothing too suspicious. Bonnie was beginning to think the assignment was going to be a washout.

Around nine o'clock, she caught Ed sneaking glances at his wristwatch. Shortly afterward, he sauntered out of the bar.

Bonnie followed, abandoning the melting ice that was all she had left of her Jack & Coke. By the time she got outside, Ed's Mustang was already pulling away. She hopped on her Kawasaki and got going. She'd never tailed anybody before, and she hoped she was doing it right.

He surprised her by driving out of town. She shadowed him down a stretch of two-lane highway. The sky was fully dark and the road was empty. The asphalt hummed under her tires in its steady, reassuring drone. The song of the road—that was how she thought of it. She'd heard that song in many different keys throughout the past two years.

She'd often wished she could have afforded a Harley rather than the beat-up secondhand Kawasaki, but tonight she was grateful for the soft burr of the Japanese motor. A Harley's angry growl would have echoed through the desert like the mating call of a T-Rex.

At a turnoff marked Rattlesnake Junction, Ed left the highway. First Sidewinder's, now this. Bonnie wondered what it was about rattlers that made them worthy of so much signage. If she lived in a place infested with venomous reptiles, she didn't think she would want to advertise the fact.

The Mustang went off road, plowing up a wide wake of dust. It headed into a box canyon with sculpted sandstone walls. The floor of the canyon was flat and sandy and tufted with prickly pear cactus. Saguaros clustered near the entryway, sentinels standing watch. The sky was a spread of deep purple embroidered with impossibly bright stars.

In the middle of the canyon sat a solitary motorhome. Lights glowed behind venetian blinds. Low music throbbed from within.

Ed Goodman's secret love nest? Could be.

Bonnie parked the chopper just inside the canyon's narrow gateway, killing the ignition before Ed's car came to a stop alongside the mobile home. She didn't want him hearing her motor when the Mustang fell silent.

On foot she made her way down a gravelly incline,

hugging the canyon wall. Her progress was slow and precarious, the loose stones slip-sliding under her feet like a hill of marbles. It was hot in the canyon, hotter than it had been in town, probably because no wind reached here. Somewhere an owl hooted. Horned owl, probably. Bird of prey.

Hearing that cry, she felt a little like a field mouse herself. Some part of her sensed that there was death in this canyon. But she kept going. She hadn't learned to trust her instincts. She was young.

The Mustang's door swung open and thumped shut. Ed stood there for a moment. He seemed to be surveying the area. She shrank back against the rock wall, wishing there was more cover. She wasn't sure just what would happen if Ed spotted her. He didn't seem like the violent type, but you never knew about people.

Truth was, she almost felt sorry for old Ed. Being married to a harpy like Edna couldn't be any treat. If he wanted to sneak off and have his fun with some lady friend whose eyes weren't so faded and whose mouth didn't shape itself into that bitter grin, who could blame him?

She wondered if she ought to turn back, return what was left of the money, and call the whole thing off. Or more plausibly, just get back on her bike and ride out of here, keeping the money and the camera, and let Ed keep his secrets.

But she wasn't going to do that. She'd made a bargain with Edna Goodman, and she was just honest enough to want to see it through.

Ed walked to the motorhome and rapped on the door. It opened, and a female silhouette appeared in the dim lamplight. Ed's voice was clear in the stillness. "Hey, sweetie."

The woman said something in reply, but her voice didn't carry. He went in, and the door shut behind him.

Bonnie crept closer. The music seemed louder now. Some guy was crooning about the way you look tonight. She hated that shit. Give her some good head-banging balls-to-the-wall rock 'n roll over that sappy-crappy mood music any time.

She reached the side of the mobile home and listened. Voices from within, but no distinguishable words. Murmurs. Lovers' coos.

The vehicle was sheathed in aluminum siding, dented in many places, ribboned in dark dust. The two windows on the near side were screened by blinds. She couldn't see inside.

She circled around to the other side of the mo-torhome, doing her best to make no sound. Her boots weren't made for stealth; they made soft crackling noises as they sank into dirt and loose stones. But with the music playing, she didn't think anyone could hear.

The RV rocked slightly, as if weight had shifted inside. Were the lovebirds getting it on already? It seemed like a good bet. Ed didn't strike her as the sort who'd be real big on foreplay.

The blinds were shut on this side, as well, but in the nearest window one of the slats was broken, allowing a stripe of lamplight to bleed through. She thought she could see through that opening—probably take a picture through it, too.

Stalking Edna's hubby was bad enough, but taking a snapshot of him in the throes of passion was even worse. Again she thought about turning back. But there was that bargain she'd made. And the extra money Edna had promised as a reward for a photo.

It was the money that decided things. She would snap the photo if she could.

The voices were silent now. Only the song went on, building to a big finish.

Pressing herself against the side panels, Bonnie stood

on tiptoe and looked through the gap.

She saw a record spinning on an old-fashioned turn-table, a couple of chintzy lamps with soiled shades, a collection of porcelain figurines. There was no bed. There were only two chairs, facing each other. One was empty, and in the other, knitting contentedly, sat Edna Goodman.

Shit.

Ed hadn't strayed, after all. At least not tonight. He'd gone straight home to his wife.

At that moment she realized her earlier qualms hadn't been real. The truth was, she had wanted to catch him in the act and supply Edna with photographic proof. Not out of vindictiveness or greed or any personal motive, but because—well, just because it made a more interesting story.

The song on the record player ended. There was a beat of silence as the phonograph needle slid lazily to the next track.

As she turned away from the window, it occurred to her to wonder where Ed had gone.

That was her last thought before something slammed her in the back, hard and stunning between the shoulder blades, and she went down.

BONNIE CAME UP short at a red light in Point Clement, not far from the amusement area. And suddenly she knew why her *Easy Rider* days had been on her mind tonight, why she'd kept circling back to the same unwanted memories ever since she'd glanced in the direction of the shooting gallery, and why her restlessness had brought her back, without conscious intention, to the vicinity of Wonderland.

She wasn't sure. But it could be him. It really could.

Eleven years older. Different part of the country.

But it was possible.

The man who ran the shooting gallery just might be Ed Goodman of Palm Garden, Arizona.

21

BONNIE PARKED THE Jeep a half block from Wonderland and sat there thinking it through.

She remembered noticing the carny just before she'd gone into Mulligan's to have her talk with Bill Mitter. Then in her conversation with Walt Churchland, she'd found herself talking about Arizona. And thinking about it on the ride to her house.

Subconsciously she must have recognized him right away. The fact that she'd been tailing an errant husband probably helped. It was the same job she'd taken in Palm Garden.

Even so, it hadn't registered until just now. She still found it hard to believe.

Ed Goodman, two thousand miles from his old haunt. Was Edna still with him? And were they still playing their little game?

She had to confirm the sighting. She was ninety percent certain, but ninety percent wasn't good enough.

Wonderland was still open. She could do it now. But if it really was Ed Goodman and she could recognize him after eleven years, there was an equal chance he would recognize her.

She pulled up the hood of her windbreaker, bunching her hair underneath. It helped, but it wouldn't be enough. In the litter of crap Kyle had tossed from the glove box she found a pair of sunglasses. She popped out the lenses and snugged the frames over her ears. In the rearview mirror she checked out her disguise. She was dismayed to see that the glasses really did make her look smarter.

In Wonderland the crowds had thinned considerably. The place would close for the night only about only fifteen minutes from now. Some booths were already shutting down. Luckily, the shooting gallery wasn't one of them.

No one was playing the game, but the carny was still there, sullenly eyeing the passersby as if they had personally offended him. He didn't seem interested in attracting new business.

Most of these midway types kept up a brisk patter. Not this guy. He was almost antisocial. That wasn't like Ed Goodman. She remembered how he'd chatted up the customers in his diner. But years had passed. He could have changed. Turned taciturn and grumpy. If he was still married to Edna, he had plenty to be grumpy about.

Bonnie had been hoping for a crowd—it was less likely she would be recognized that way—but with time running out, she would have to play solo if she wanted to play at all.

As she approached the shooting gallery, she felt her heart pumping a little harder. There was a slow slide of nausea in her belly and a weakness in her knees. She wasn't overly concerned about being identified. It was simply the prospect of seeing Ed Goodman again, coming face to face with the man who ...

Don't think about it. Let it go. Center yourself, be in the moment, all that Deepak Chopra crap.

Good advice, but tough to follow. The memory of her last encounter with Ed and Edna was etched too deeply in her brain. Mere proximity to Ed—if it really was Ed—was enough to start shorting out her neurons.

"Try your luck, little lady?" the man who might or might not be Ed Goodman asked without particular interest. He was a big guy, graying and unkempt. Probably in his early sixties, which would be just right for Ed.

"I might be," she said. "I'm not too bad with a gun."

"I'm sure you're a regular Annie Oakley. What's your name, honey?"

"Alice." She was in Wonderland, after all. And if this guy really was Ed, she'd gone through the looking glass for sure.

"Nice name," he said with all the sincerity of a viper. "Real pretty."

"How much do you charge?"

"Five bucks a play."

She paid with a twenty. As she handed it over, she took a close look at the right side of his neck. But his coat collar was turned up high; she couldn't tell if there was a tattoo or not.

"Gotta get change." He disappeared into a back room and emerged half a minute later, shaking his head. "Sorry, darling. This bill's counterfeit."

He showed it to her. A black stripe covered Andrew Jackson's face.

"When the iodine in the pen reacts like that," he said, "it means the currency's fake."

"Wow, that's never happened to me before. You sure about that pen?"

"Afraid so."

"Can I have the money back?"

"Sorry. Gotta confiscate it. Can't have counterfeit bills in circulation. That's the law."

Yes, it was the law. It was also a scam. He kept a counterfeit twenty on ice in the back room and switched it with a customer's bill whenever he got the chance.

"Aw, shit," she said.

"Sorry." He didn't sound sorry at all. "Still want to try your luck?"

She pretended to think it over. "What the hell, I'm already down twenty, right?"

She forked over another bill.

"That's the spirit." He barely troubled to conceal his contempt.

He did his disappearing act again. This time he returned with the correct change. No way would he have the balls to pull the same scam twice in a row.

"Been at this long?" she asked him as she lined up the rifle.

"Long enough."

Not a very helpful answer. Bonnie allowed herself a sidewise glance at the man. He was large and paunchy, with squinty cynical eyes and a puckered smile that was nearly a scowl. The eyes were right for Ed. The smile too, maybe. But she couldn't be sure.

She took potshots at the ducks, not having much success, probably because the game was gaffed in some way. The electronic sound effects were pretty good, but the rifle lacked the recoil of the real thing.

Finished, she set down the gun, having scored only four hits. "Guess my aim is off today."

"Want to give it another go? You came close. Almost won a plush."

Standard patter, delivered listlessly.

She didn't care about a plush. But she still hadn't made the guy as Ed Goodman.

He was the right age, and his face had the right shape. The voice, too, was the slightly high-pitched, slightly raspy one she remembered from the motorhome. Like that old-time cowboy actor. What was his name? Andy Devine.

She was ninety-five percent certain. But she needed more.

"Try your luck again?" he pressed.

"Why not?" She plucked a five from her pocket—part of the change he'd given her. "In for a dime, in for a dollar."

"That's the spirit," he said, almost sneering. He'd made her as a rube, all right. First she'd fallen for the counterfeit con without making a fuss, and now she was throwing good money after bad in a chase for an unwinnable prize.

As she handed over the five, she let the bill slip from her hand before he could grab it. It fluttered to the floor behind the counter. Grunting, he stooped to retrieve it from the floor of the booth. The movement tugged back his coat collar just enough to expose the right side of his neck. And there it was. A prison tat in black ink.

The itsy bitsy spider
Climbed up the waterspout ...

Bonnie's reactions were quick. She'd always been fast on her feet, and years on the job had only honed her skills. So she didn't freeze up, didn't stare, didn't react at all, even though the sight of the tattoo hit her like a fist in the base of her stomach. Feelings and images and tactile sensations came flooding back, and for a moment she was there again, in the stifling heat of the motorhome, while Mozart tinkled from the phonograph and Edna sat in a rocking chair, knitting a sweater.

She merely picked up the rifle and lowered her head. She took a slow, calming breath. By the time she took aim, the feelings had passed.

She fired off a full complement of shots, lighting up six targets. Her performance was good enough to win her a shitty little prize.

"Not enough points for a plush," Ed Goodman told her, "but you scored this bangle."

He handed her a loop of flexible blue plastic, tooth-pick-thin. It had to be worth all of four cents, retail.

"Lucky me." She slipped it onto her wrist. When she looked up, she saw a gun in his hand and a fierce, gloating smile on his face.

"I don't think so, biker girl. I think your luck just ran out."

22

BONNIE STARED AT the gun. A single-action Colt .45 revolver, pretty old, but probably serviceable enough. Ed held it low, just above the counter, invisible to any passersby. Not that anyone actually was passing by. The boardwalk behind her was deserted.

"You're on to me, huh?" she said. "Guess my disguise wasn't as good as I thought."

"Your disguise is okay. It was the way you handled the gun. Like you knew what you were doing. Made me wonder if you were a cop or something."

"Not a cop."

"Maybe not, but it got me looking at you in a new way. And then I saw it. It's your mouth. You've got very pretty mouth."

"Thanks."

He smirked at her. She remembered that fucking smirk. It was the same as it had been eleven years ago, as was the cold light in his eyes. She wondered how she ever could have doubted.

"I don't see any weapon printing through that jacket," he said. "If you're carrying, the gun will be in your purse."

"I'm not carrying," she lied.

"Hand it over anyway."

She thought about resisting. If she ducked down fast, using the counter as cover, how long would it take her to get her hand on the Walther?

Too long, she decided. He only had to lean over the counter and fire straight down. He would kill her before she could wrap her finger around the trigger. Then he'd claim self-defense against an armed assailant and, given what the police knew about her, probably get away with it.

Slowly she unslung the purse from her shoulder and set it down on the counter. He snatched it by the strap.

"Now you're coming with me into the back room."

"What's in there?"

"Puppies and baby chicks. You'll love it. Move."

She couldn't argue. He lifted the hinged corner of the countertop and waved her over to the open door.

"You made another mistake," he said as she paused in the doorway. "You didn't make a fuss about the counterfeit bill scam. Most people get pissed. They holler. They say they'll call the police. You just stood there and took it. Like you had something more important on your mind."

"Good point. I'll remember it for next time."

"Biker girl, you're all out of next times."

He gave her a light tap between the shoulder blades, urging her into the room. They entered together. He reached for a wall switch bearing three large buttons. He punched one, and an electric motor drive came alive with a grinding noise as metal security shutters rolled down over the front of the booth. The trickle of neon glare from the midway was cut off.

She looked around. The room's only light was now the pale glow of a pull-chain lamp with a water-spotted shade. It rested on an apple crate near a garage-sale filing cabinet. A folding chair sat at a card table. There was no other furniture, and the walls were bare.

"Doesn't look like you do a lot of entertaining," she said, and then his hand closed over her arm, and with surprising strength he flung her into a corner.

She fell sprawling. Her glasses came off, but since they had no lenses anyway, she didn't bother to retrieve them. With a grimace she hauled herself to a sitting position against the wall.

"Shit," she hissed. "Think I twisted my ankle."

Ed was unsympathetic. "It won't trouble you for long. I got plans for you."

"Gonna hunt me for sport?"

"Nothing that dramatic." He unclasped her purse and checked the contents, while keeping his gun—and one eye—trained on her. "Well, what do we have here? Looks like a sweet little twenty-two and a silencer. You a pro, biker girl?"

She leaned forward and massaged her ankle. "I'm not a biker anymore."

"You'll always be a biker girl to me. I've thought about you a lot over the years. You're the one that got away." He squinted at her, his eyes cold. "You messed up everything for us."

"How inconsiderate of me."

"It truly was. You didn't have the good grace to die when you should have. So what's the deal? You been tracking us?"

"Nope. Dumb luck, that's all."

"I don't believe you. Not when you come here toting this gear."

"That wasn't meant for you."

"Oh, yes, it was. First me, then Edna." His squint narrowed. "Unless you took care of her first."

"I didn't take care of anybody. How is Edna, anyway? She ever get that knitting needle out of her neck?"

"She pulled through. She's a tough old bird. She'll outlive us all."

"Well, they say only the good die young." She pulled her leg closer, tugging at the sock. "I read about Lily."

His mouth twisted. "Don't you talk about her."

There was unhealed grief in his voice. She looked at him, a shambling stoop-shouldered man with a sagging belly and gray hair, and she felt almost sorry for him.

"Did you keep doing it?" she asked in a quieter voice.

"I'm guessing it's a hard habit to break."

"I kept my hand in. Not so much these days. You'll be the first in over a year. I'll throw your body in the woods, let the animals at it."

"And pray over me?"

"I don't do so much praying anymore. These days it don't seem to do much good."

"You sound all worn out, Ed."

"I'm tired. Honest to God, I am. But I still got a few years left in me. Which is more than you've got." He drew back the hammer on the revolver with a sharp click. "Now I'm gonna do a little target shooting of my own."

"Maybe you'll have better luck than I did. I couldn't hit those ducks for shit."

"Don't blame yourself, biker girl. That game's rigged."

"So's this one," Bonnie said.

The derringer from her sock fit neatly in the palm of her hand. She brought her arm up fast and fired twice, recocking the little pistol between shots.

The first shot caught Ed in the throat, spinning him sideways, and the second took off the side of his face in a mist of blood.

He hit the floor with a thump, the revolver skittering out of his hand.

"Asshole," Bonnie said, lowering the gun.

For Ed Goodman, it was as good an epitaph as any.

She remembered what she'd told Kyle about situations like this. *They go down, I stay upright. I win, they lose. It's a rush.*

She hadn't lied.

23

THERE WAS NOTHING wrong with her ankle, of course. She stood up and listened for any indication of a commotion outside. She heard nothing. Probably no one had heard the shots through the security shutters.

Her purse was trapped underneath Ed's body. She had to lift him up, straining at the weight—dead weight, literally—in order to retrieve it.

In the purse she kept a pair of gloves. She pulled them on and wiped down every surface she'd touched, including the rifle from the game. She recovered the sunglass frames, took Ed's wallet and his wristwatch, but left his revolver. Let the police think it was a holdup gone wrong. Ed fought back and lost.

When the crime scene had been properly sanitized, she left via a back door that opened on an alleyway. No one saw her return to the Jeep. In the glow of the dome light she went through Ed's wallet, pocketing the cash. She noted with satisfaction that she'd gotten her twenty bucks back. Finally she studied his driver's license.

He was calling himself Roger Coverdell now. His address was someplace on Devil's Hook Island, a barrier island south of Brighton Cove. Bonnie knew Devil's Hook pretty well. She'd killed three men there during Hurricane Sandy. Only one was a hit; the other two had been strictly self-defense.

On her way home, she stopped at a public park on the Crab River Inlet. She tossed the gloves into a dump bin, along with her windbreaker—she'd gotten blood on it when she reached under Ed's body to recover her purse—and Ed's wallet. She'd already memorized his address.

The derringer went into the water. It was never a good idea to hold on to a murder gun.

She noticed the plastic bangle on her wrist and thought about tossing it, too. She decided against it. Hell, maybe it had brought her luck. She left it on.

Then she took a few moments to process what had happened. As usual, the period immediately after the action had passed in something like a sleepwalker's trance. There was the initial euphoria, then the calm professionalism of a programmed routine. Now she could unwind a little and allow herself to feel again.

Had she been scared when she sat in the corner, tugging at her sock and trying to work the derringer loose without letting Ed see? She thought she probably had been. Honestly, she couldn't remember. But she'd known he might snap off a round at any moment. He'd done some talking, but not much. All he'd really wanted to know was if she'd tracked him down deliberately. Probably he'd been afraid she'd left a trail that could lead to him.

Once he'd been satisfied on that score, he had been ready to shoot. Hadn't wasted any time, either. If she hadn't been carrying the derringer, she would have been all out of options. There would have been nothing she could do except die.

But she hadn't died. She'd outplayed the son of a bitch. And, for better or worse, she'd enjoyed it. It was more satisfying than firing a fake rifle at fake targets at five dollars a pop. More satisfying than tailing a closeted gay hubby, or negotiating a deal with a low-level mobster, or pretty much anything else she'd done lately.

For the second time that night, she asked herself if she actually liked killing people. She hoped not. It seemed like the kind of sentiment Hannibal Lecter would relate to. She didn't want to be Hannibal Lecter. That facemask thing they'd put him in would do absolutely nothing for her.

Finally she gave up thinking about it. She'd never been any damn good at psychoanalyzing herself. Introspection was not her forte. What she needed to do was get drunk. Well, there was booze at home, among the many other unhealthy foodstuffs Kyle Ridley disapproved of.

She crossed into Brighton Cove and was approaching her duplex when she caught sight of a squad car prowling the neighborhood.

Brad and Dan again, most likely. And here she was, driving a vandalized vehicle with one dead headlight. Another writeup for sure, if Dan had anything to say about it. Shit.

Prudently she detoured to her office, figuring she'd lie low there for a little while. She parked in the gravel lot and checked the time. Midnight exactly. She must have lingered at the inlet a little longer than she'd thought.

The offices of Last Resort were housed on the second floor of a 1920s brick building next door to an upscale shoe store called Oxford's, whose snooty proprietor always treated Bonnie like she was patient zero in the zombie apocalypse. She couldn't blame him. Only eight months ago Streinikov's gang had shot up her office with automatic weapons, and a few stray rounds had drilled through Oxford's wall. From what she understood, a pair of Italian leather pumps had been the only casualties.

She unlocked the lobby door and made her way up

the steep, narrow staircase. After the Streinikov incident, she'd installed a top-of-the-line Schlage lock on her office door. It wouldn't stop another crew from blasting their way in, but at least it earned her a rebate on her insurance premium.

The office didn't amount to much, just two rooms with unreliable heat in the winter and no AC in the summer. Still, she'd had to fight to hold on to it. Her landlord had tried to get her out of her lease. Apparently he didn't like having his building shot up. The other tenants weren't exactly overjoyed about it either. They gave her cold stares in the hallway.

But she'd stubbornly refused to vacate, and eventually the landlord had surrendered. She wasn't optimistic about the prospects of renewing the lease next month, but she'd learned not to look that far ahead. What the hell, by next month she could be dead. It might not be the outcome she was hoping for, but she had to admit it would solve a lot of problems.

The office had been totally redecorated—a necessity, inasmuch as the original decor had been blown to shit. In place of her yard-sale furnishings, she'd sprung for some decent stuff from a local office supply store. Got a good price on it, too; the proprietor was the same guy who'd needed her help in making things right with the Dragushas last year, and he'd given her the employee discount.

As a result, she was able to sit at a smart contemporary desk with a commodious knee hole in which to conceal a loaded .44—a precaution in case the next shooters who came after her happened to drop by during business hours. The new computer on the desk—her old one had resembled an exploded hand grenade—was a no-name box out of South Korea, but it ran Windows okay. Her screensaver was a photo of the historical Bonnie Parker, looking mean and young, but mostly young. There had been a pic of old Bonnie on her wall, but the gunmen had turned it into so much confetti; now she displayed dismayingly anodyne seascapes from Art Attack, a nearby print shop.

Yeah, that's right—generic desk, generic computer, generic art. Her new office had all the personality of an Egg McMuffin. But with her rep in town at an all-time low, she felt obliged to make a bid for respectability.

She Googled Roger Coverdell's address and discovered that it was part of the Locust Hill RV Park. It seemed that Ed and Edna were still grooving on the mobile home lifestyle. She checked the location on a map, zeroing in on 63 Red Hawk Lane, their assigned slot. Campers on either side of theirs; not much space between them. Hardly the perfect place for a hit, but it could be managed ...

Sure. Anything could be managed. Question was, did she intend to go that route?

She sat back in the desk chair, thinking it over.

Every living part of her wanted to take care of Edna Goodman personally. The woman was trash, she was a killer, and Bonnie couldn't forget how she'd just sat there knitting.

Knitting ...

She shook off the thought. Yes. The woman deserved to die. That much was certain. Still ...

Shooting Ed in self-defense was one thing. Kill or be killed—no choice about it. But a straight-up hit was something else. She could call it an execution, street justice, but it was premeditated murder just the same.

A year ago, she wouldn't have hesitated. But these days she was coloring inside the lines, right? Turning over a new leaf—though what leaves had to do with it, she couldn't imagine. Anyway, the point was that she'd promised herself she was through with all that. She was on the wagon. And she guessed she had to keep it that way.

She shook her head, pissed off at herself for having so goddamn much integrity. All right, all right. She would play by the rules. Wait a few days so the connection with the midway shooting wasn't obvious, then call the police. Trust the authorities not to screw it up. It would be hard. Her whole life was based on not trusting anyone. But that, too, had to change.

Admittedly it would be nowhere near as satisfying as doing the job herself, up close and personal.

Of course, it was possible Edna would suspect the truth about her husband's demise. She might find it just a little too convenient that Ed Goodman, of all people, should meet with foul play in a town as normally crime-free as Point Clement. But that didn't matter. Edna wouldn't run. Even if she knew justice was on the way ... even then, she wouldn't run. Bonnie was certain of that.

She erased her browsing history—a habitual caution—then shut down the PC and locked up the office. By now the prowl car must have left her neighborhood.

It had. Unfortunately, it was parked outside her office, and Brad was standing by her Jeep.

She put her newsboy cap on her head and strode up to him while Dan looked on from inside the squad car, amused.

"This really *is* fucking harassment, Walsh."

Brad raised a placating hand. "Calm down. I'm not here to ticket you. Though I did notice your headlight is broken ..."

"Don't even. I swear I will physically hurt you."

"It was just an observation."

"Be sure it stays that way."

"Your Jeep *is* pretty trashed, though. What've you been up to tonight?"

"Murder and mayhem."

"I wish I could be sure you were kidding around."

"I wish you could, too. Why the fuck are you here?"

"Just wanted to pass on some information. About an hour ago, Dan and I ran into a car full of questionable characters. Four young males, Eastern European types. They were driving a black Hummer and they had a lot of attitude."

"Eastern European," she said slowly.

"Russians, maybe. I don't know. I got their names." He recited a list beginning with Raco Prifti and continuing with other unfamiliar combinations of syllables. "Mean anything?"

"It's Greek to me." More like Albanian, she thought.

"The driver had a beard with a white stripe in it. Pretty distinctive."

"Doesn't ring a bell. They live locally?"

"Hoboken and Jersey City."

Dragusha territory. "Why were they paying us a visit?"

"Just out for a drive, they said."

"Doesn't sound like they were being completely truthful."

"Is anybody ever completely truthful?"

She was pretty sure that was a dig, but she let it pass. No point getting into an argument. Dan was listening, after all.

"The chief and I," Brad went on, "have been going back and forth between your house and your office in case they come back. But they seem to be gone for good."

"Yeah. You made 'em, so they had to call off the party. If there was a party."

"They may still be looking for you."

"For their sake, they better hope they don't find me."

He studied her with a mistrustful gaze. "You really don't know what's happening?"

"I really don't. But I'd like to find out."

"Well, anyway, we just thought you ought to know."

"We? As in you and Danno?"

"Yes. Both of us." Brad lowered his voice. "Whatever you may think, he doesn't want you dead."

"Just in jail."

"Right."

She took a step back, hands on hips. "You probably think that's where I belong, too."

"Maybe I do."

She watched him climb back into the squad car. It pulled off, and she was left leaning on the Jeep, thinking about the crew in the Hummer and feeling plenty steamed.

She'd done the right thing tonight. She'd kept Shaban alive, and Kyle too. And all the same, it looked like she'd ended up with a bull's-eye on her back. What good was coloring inside the lines if the other guy had an eraser?

One thing was for sure. She and Shabby were gonna have a little talk about this.

Right now.

24

Shaban was tired and ready for sleep, but there was unfinished business to attend to. His grandfather had asked to see him at Port Newark, where the container ship was being loaded for tomorrow's voyage.

It was late—nearly midnight—but Shaban knew Arian Dragusha had never required more than three hours' sleep. And he did like to watch as his cargo was hoisted aboard the ship. Shaban himself took no pleasure in it. He rarely visited the docks.

His connection with the Dragusha family got him through the gate at the port. He left his car in a parking lot that would be crowded with trucks during the day, but which was nearly empty now, long past the 6 PM cutoff for deliveries.

The ship, the six-hundred-foot bluewater freighter *Mazeppa* out of Liberia, had sailed into Newark Bay via the Kill Van Kull and stopped overnight to discharge some five hundred containers of cargo, while taking on a few hundred more. Tomorrow, the automobiles now parked in the vast floodlit lot would be driven on board. The cars had no connection with his family, but among the new containers were two hundred from an import-export concern that was one of Arian Dragusha's shell companies. The merchandise was entirely legal—textiles, leather goods, and tobacco coming in; tanned hides, medicines, and factory equipment going out. The Dragusha syndicate had been diversifying into legitimate businesses for years.

The *Mazeppa* was an odd-looking beast, nothing like

Shaban's idea of a proper ship. It looked more like drawings he had seen of Noah's Ark—a great squarish crate, a floating box, with so little of its hull submerged that the whole vessel appeared curiously top-heavy. The seven-story deckhouse, positioned aft, broke the stark monotony of its profile. The flags of several nations fluttered from the flying bridge above the wheelhouse.

Panamax gantry cranes loomed over the cargo on the dock. Spreader jaws, like giant mandibles, bit down on each twenty-ton steel box and lifted it high into the air before depositing it in the freighter's hold, first centering it inside a vertical shaft, then lowering it gently between the shaft's steel rails. Tall vehicles called straddle carriers lugged fresh containers from the storage depot to the dockside. At the freighter's stern, a ramp had descended onto the quay, providing access for vehicles that would be driven aboard in the morning and stowed as cargo. Giant wharf lights blazed over the scene.

Few human beings were involved. A dozen or so longshoremen were in sight, reduced to insignificance by the immense moving structures that towered over them. Nearly all the work was done by gleaming automatons, giant insects in a humming mechanized hive.

There was something unsettling about it, something alien, inhuman. But that in itself wasn't why Shaban so seldom came here. It was his knowledge of one particular container that was always stowed at the bottom of the stack in one of the forward holds. A container that carried no cargo—or at least no cargo of the ordinary kind.

Reflexively, he crossed himself.

He knew where to find his grandfather. He took an elevator to the top floor of an administrative building, where, in an air-conditioned aerie, controllers worked the night watch, following the progress of the containers on banks of computer screens.

Seated in a corner of the room was Arian Dragusha. He gazed out at the panorama framed in floor-to-ceiling windows, watching the show—the pendulous swings of the cranes, the lift and fall of containers, the multiplying boxes in their geometrical arrays.

Shaban approached. "Grandfather?" he said.

The old man started. He turned in his seat, looking up at Shaban, and blinked several times.

Bowing, Shaban kissed him ritually on each gray-bearded cheek, then took a chair opposite him. "I am told you wanted to see me."

"Yes. Yes ..." Arian looked away, his gaze returning to the windows. The silver-handled cane lay on his lap, gripped by both hands. "The man Patterson, the one who stole from me—he was found tonight."

"Sure, yes," Shaban said.

"And you attended to him?"

"I did."

"He is dead, then?"

Shaban hesitated, but he knew the truth could be withheld no longer. "No, Grandfather. It was—I thought it was not needed to kill him. The other two men are dead, and so I thought—"

"Yes, you thought. You *thought.*" Arian spat the word. "You do much thinking."

Shaban watched him. Slowly he said, "You knew already."

"I know much more than you think. I am not so old that I can be tricked and fooled."

"There was no trick."

"It is easy to snip the dead wolf's tail, eh?" A proverb from the old country.

"I had no such thought," Shaban said stiffly.

Arian waved him silent. "By good fortune, Ahmeti arrived at Saint Astius soon after you left. He saw Luan and Jozef put Patterson in a car. He saw them dump the man near the Jacobi Medical Center. You told them to do this?"

Shaban nodded. "Was done on my orders."

"Because you had chosen to leave Patterson alive?"

"Yes, Grandfather."

"This was not your choice to make. You do not run the show, boy. You are not hired by me to think. You are hired to do as you are told. To follow orders. To obey."

"In this case, I did not see the need—"

"It is not you who decides about the need. If I say a man is to die, he dies."

Shaban knew his safest move was to apologize and agree. But there was pride in him. He could not bring himself to do it.

"I took care of the two others," he said carefully. "I left Patterson a cripple. It should have been enough."

"So *you* say. But *I* say it was not enough. That is why, when Ahmeti called with the news, I had Patterson picked up and brought to me at the bakery."

He removed a cell phone from his pocket and brought up the photo gallery, then passed it to Shaban. Framed in the bezel was a flash photo of Todd Patterson sprawled across a tiled tabletop. Shaban recognized those tiles. It was the table in the back room of the bakery where he had sat with his grandfather nearly a year ago.

The tiles were discolored now, stained by a bright red plume. Patterson's brains had been blown out the top of his head.

Shaban did not flinch. "Who shot him?" he asked.

"I did."

"You?"

"Yes. Me. You are surprised? You think I am an old woman who faints at the sight of blood?"

Arian snatched up the phone. It went back into his pocket.

"Ahmeti told me none of this when I was with him,"

Shaban said. "He told me only that you wished to see me here."

"It was not his place to tell you. So you have seen him, have you? Yet all day you avoided his calls."

"I was ... busy."

"He went looking for you. This is why he visited the church. He knows you are there so often." Arian, no churchgoer himself, put a faint contemptuous emphasis on the last words. "You wasted his time."

"This was not my intention. It is only that I knew why he was calling. There was a delay in the latest shipment. But it was my problem. It is taken care of now."

"*You* took care of it."

"Sure, yes."

"Just as you took care of Patterson—on your own, without consulting anyone, without authorization."

"However it was," Shaban said with calm stubbornness, "I delivered the package."

Arian's hands on the walking stick curled into fists. His voice sank lower, the hiss of a fuse. "The package is nothing. One shipment out of hundreds. A few dollars. Unimportant. What matters is discipline. What matters is organization. What matters is respect."

"I respect you, *baba*."

The use of the honorific left his grandfather unmoved. "You are too sure of yourself," Arian said coldly. "Too proud, rebellious. You have the *inat*, the dangerous pride. Like your father, you think and you plan and you scheme—" He stopped himself.

"What about my father?"

Arian's age-spotted hand rose and fell in a dismissive gesture. "He was like you in many ways."

Shaban lifted his chin. "I am glad to know this."

He let a moment pass, daring the old man to speak. Arian said nothing.

"Is this all, Grandfather?"

"Yes. It is all." Arian's cold, staring eyes flicked over him. "You are a clever boy."

His attention refocused on the window. He did not speak again.

Shaban stood. He bowed once more and walked slowly out of the room.

He was not thinking of Todd Patterson or of Ahmeti. He was remembering the moment when the Wolf had first laid eyes on him. The way he had started. His brief uncertainty.

He had looked—it was not possible—but Shaban could almost swear that his grandfather had looked afraid.

25

BONNIE DROVE ONLY two blocks from her office, then parked at the curb and pulled out her cell. She hadn't wanted to hang around in case Brad and Dan came back with more questions. But she needed to make a call, and at the moment she was too pissed off to talk and drive at the same time.

She'd gotten Shaban's cell number last year, when she was representing the office supplies impresario. The number was still on her phone, and with any luck it was still current.

She tried it. After three rings Shaban picked up.

"It's Parker," she said. "Hit's off. Your boys got made."

"What is this you say?" He sounded like he was in a moving car.

"I have to admit, I never took you for a welsher. All that bullshit about honor and the old country really had me going."

"Why do you insult my honor?"

"'Cause you sent a crew of *West Side Story* rejects to my town, gunning for me. I'd call that a breach of friggin' promise, compadre."

"I sent nobody."

"Yeah, right."

"This I swear. I do not like you, Parker. Do not like Kyle Ridley, either. Would kill both of you if I could. It would be worth the penance I must pay. But I gave you my *besa*."

"Your *besa* doesn't mean jack shit."

"If you believe this, you should have killed me at motel."

162

"That's what people keep telling me."

"You are wrong about me. I have not betrayed you."

"Then what were a bunch of Albanian lowlifes doing in my hometown tonight?"

"I do not know."

He sounded honestly puzzled. She thought it was just possible he was telling the truth.

"Anyone else know about me and Kyle?" she asked.

"No ..." he said slowly, with an odd note of dawning realization.

"Wanna try again? That last take didn't really sell it."

"There is ... perhaps ... someone. Maybe."

"Who?"

"I cannot say this until I know for sure."

"Well, while you're figuring it out, there's a good chance some other crew is gunning for Kyle. She's my only connection to you guys, other than you. If they're after me, they're probably after her."

"This troubles you? She lied to you as well as me."

"She's a pain in the ass, but I'm sorta committed to keeping her alive."

"Why?"

"I got this hero complex. If you're on the level, help me locate her."

"In what way do I do this?"

"First, give me her phone number. You've gotta have it."

"I am texting it to you now."

"Second, you told me you tracked her movements as far as Millstone County before she called from the motel. How'd you trace her?"

"Her car, it has the E-ZPass."

"So?"

"I have a friend in the Transportation Authority. He sends E-ZPass alerts to my phone. These tell me what exit she uses on the parkway, what traffic lights she has driven past."

"Can you forward the alerts to my phone?"

"I can do this. You will get all the alerts I have received so far, and any new ones in real time."

"Do it. I need to find her fast. Right now she's a sitting duck."

"Duck?"

"An easy target."

"Oh. Sure, yes. A duck that sits. I am forwarding the messages right this minute."

"Okay, Shabby. Maybe you're not the lying scumbag I thought you were."

"You have bad manners, Parker. You are not civil."

"Yeah, well, life's a bitch and so am I. Now you might want to get going on whatever theory you've got in mind. And try praying to Saint Whosis while you're at it."

"Saint Bessus," Shaban said stiffly.

"Him, yeah. 'Cause if that girl ends up dead, it's gonna put me in a very bad mood."

She clicked off, checked the text message to learn Kyle's number, then found a disposable cell phone in the litter of debris from the glove compartment. She didn't want a call to Kyle to be traceable to her phone. If the girl died—or if she was dead already—it would be better if Bonnie herself had no known connection to her.

After four rings, the call bounced to voicemail. She left an anonymous message. "Kiddo, it's your new friend. Call me pronto. Looks like shit's gone sideways for both of us. I'm not fucking around."

She thought that would get her attention, if she re-trieved the message. Kyle had said she'd ditched her cell at home so she couldn't be tracked. Most of what she'd said was a lie, but that part could have been true. She wouldn't have wanted Shaban catching up with her too soon, and she had no way of knowing what resources he might have at his disposal.

Back on her regular phone, she reviewed the Turnpike

Authority alerts. The system had snagged Kyle's license plate when she jumped onto the parkway, heading north. The latest alert, ten minutes old, showed her switching over to the turnpike.

Bonnie had seen the address on her driver's license. An apartment on Avenue E in Bayonne. She didn't know exactly where Avenue E was, but Sammy would help her find it. The only question was whether she would get there in time.

She gunned the engine and pulled out of town.

26

BRAD'S SHIFT SHOULD have ended at midnight. He'd extended it by a half hour, waiting for Bonnie to show up. Kind of a long night, more eventful than most.

He changed out of his uniform in the locker room, then stopped by the chief's office on his way out. Dan Maguire sat at his desk eating an Egg McMuffin, which he'd insisted on picking up on their return.

"Good work tonight," Dan said. "You might have saved your girlfriend's life."

Brad took a slow breath, then approached the desk. "Is there some reason you keep calling her my girlfriend?"

"Matter of fact, there is." Dan put down the sandwich and licked a cheesy finger. "I know about it, Walsh."

"About what?" The words came out flat and oddly hollow.

"About you and her."

Brad phrased his next question carefully. "What is it you think you know?"

"I know you had a relationship. And I know it's over."

"Is that so?"

"Yeah. That's so. One of your neighbors was paying a little more attention than you realized. I got it from that individual. But not until after the fact. After you had stopped seeing her."

Mentally Brad scrolled through a list of his neighbors, hunting for the likely snitch, settling on Mr. Burgundy directly below him. A gossipy old man who probably could hear too much through his ceiling.

"How do you know I stopped?" he asked evenly.

"I kept tabs on you."

"You followed me around? You watched my place?"

"For a while. Until I was sure."

He took this in. The chief had tailed him, waiting for a new transgression.

"What if I had kept seeing her?" he asked, already knowing the answer.

"You'd have been out of this department."

"Why didn't you kick me loose anyway?"

"I thought about it. But see, at least you'd had sense enough to end it. And I decided it probably wasn't your fault."

"What's that supposed to mean?"

"It means Parker's the type who can work on a kid like you. Twist you around her little finger, play to your vanity, pump you for info."

"I never gave her any info."

"Not even about Ohio? I always wondered how she tumbled to that."

"I wasn't seeing her then."

"That's what your neighbor said, too. Her visits to your place started later. Still, you might have told her."

"I didn't," Brad lied.

"Not even to make a good impression? A man will do a lot of dumb things when he's trying to get into a lady's pants."

"I didn't tell her," he said again, hoping the words carried conviction.

Dan watched him for a long moment, then picked up the Egg McMuffin again. "I believe you. If I didn't, I'd shitcan your sorry ass right now."

"Even when we were together, she never asked me for information."

"Maybe not. But you can bet she expected to find a way to use you in the future. She's like that. She's crafty and sly, and she has no conscience. She's a sociopath. I've always said so."

"Yes. You have."

"She's not capable of normal human feeling. Whatever she pretended to feel about you, it was all an act. You were just one more rube to be conned." Dan smiled at him. Given his choice of meal, it could be literally described as a cheese-eating grin. "But at least, when you found out the truth about her after that bullshit legal deal, you had the brains to walk away."

"Why'd you keep all this to yourself? Did you still distrust me?"

"A little bit. I couldn't be sure you wouldn't backslide."

"Then why are you being so open with me now?"

"Because you proved yourself tonight, kid. I saw the way you interacted with our girl. No love lost there. And really, why would there be? I should've realized you've got at least as good a reason to hate Parker as I do."

"You said I was being suspiciously chivalrous."

Dan waved away the comment. "I was just ribbing you."

"Good one," Brad murmured.

The chief didn't hear. "No, you're not being fooled anymore. We both know what she is."

"What she was, anyway. You told me she's been keeping her head down since February. There's a chance she might really have ..."

"Reformed? Don't kid yourself. She can't be civilized. She can't be tamed. It's not in her nature. You know what she's like? Those hybrid dogs."

"Dogs?"

"Part dog, part wolf. Some people raise them as pets. This wolf-dog, I guess you call it, lives with you, eats your food, acts just like a regular dog. He loves you. He's affectionate. He wants his belly rubbed. And then one day, for no reason, that wolf-dog of yours just up and tears out your throat. Or your heart, right?" Dan nodded, a thin smile riding his lips. "Or your heart."

Brad swallowed. "I can't disagree with anything you've said."

"Make sure you remember it."

"It's not something I can forget."

"That's good. Because I'm allowing you this one mistake. You won't get another."

Brad felt Dan's eyes on him as he left the office and made his way down the hall.

27

AT 1 AM, BONNIE was charging hard up the Jersey Turnpike, closing in on exit 13, which would take her to the Bayonne Bridge. It was the same route Kyle Ridley had followed less than an hour earlier. A toll plaza camera had flagged the Hyundai on the bridge as Kyle headed north into Bayonne.

Since then, she'd been off the radar. Probably she'd gone to her apartment. Not a good move. It was the first place the bad guys were likely to look.

Which once again raised the question Bonnie had pondered as she'd traveled along the parkway and turnpike, lighting a new succession of Parliament Whites: Just who *were* the bad guys?

Shaban had denied sending the hitters. He'd sounded sincere, and breaking his word would be out of character. Anyway, she pegged him as the type who would do his own dirty work, not farm it out to a crew.

But if Shaban wasn't behind it, who the hell was?

Throughout the drive, the girl's voice had kept coming back to her. *You fucked it all up ...*

Fucked all of what up, exactly? Kyle's plans—or somebody else's?

Fencing two kilos of H wasn't the easiest thing to do, especially if word was out that the Dragushas were looking for a rogue drug mule. Anyone Kyle had approached might have been willing to turn her in to the syndicate in exchange for a cut of the action and a little goodwill. That was assuming she knew anybody in a position to move that much weight in the first place.

But suppose absconding with the heroin had been only a ruse to lure Shaban to the motel. Suppose Kyle had never intended to sell the stuff. Suppose she'd been working for someone else the whole time, someone who would know how to unload the heroin and who would reward her in cash.

Bonnie thought of the safe-deposit key the girl had been carrying. Kyle hadn't earned fifty thousand bucks from her courier job. But she could have been paid that much by someone who wanted Shaban Dragusha out of the way.

"Yeah, but then they'd just hit Shabby themselves," she said aloud as she fired up another cigarette. It was more of a question than a statement. She really wasn't sure.

There could be valid reasons for somebody to hire Kyle Ridley as a cutout. That way, the hit could never be traced back to the person who'd ordered it.

And if the plan failed—well, then Kyle would be looking at some pretty serious consequences. Somebody would be gunning for her. No wonder she'd gotten all panicky and wild.

A sign for exit 13 slid into view. She was easing into the right-hand lane when her phone chimed with a new alert.

The Hyundai was on the move. It had been pinged on I-78, heading west out of Bayonne.

Okay, forget the exit. New plan. I-78 was only five miles away. No traffic at this time of night. Bonnie stomped the gas pedal. With any luck, she could catch up with the Hyundai once it pulled onto the turnpike.

Assuming, of course, that it did pull onto the turnpike. The other option was to shoot over to US 9 and swing into Newark International, the airport she'd used in her travels to Turkey. Not too many planes were taking off at this hour, but she might be hoping to hole up there until morning.

Two minutes later she received another alert. The Hyundai had just passed through a toll plaza, taking the Port Street exit.

Which made no sense at all. Port Street didn't go to either the airport or the turnpike. It didn't really go anywhere. It looped around and made a beeline for the water. Nothing was out that way except Port Newark. The docks.

Bonnie steered the Jeep onto I-78, speeding west. The Port Street exit came up immediately. She took it, letting the road carry her in a half circle that turned her eastward. She kept pushing the Jeep hard. She had to be moving faster than Kyle. The girl ought to be close.

Port Street was a four-lane divided highway bordered by giant shipping containers on the right and ramshackle fenced-in compounds on the left. The long, straight road was nearly empty of traffic, but far ahead, a pair of taillights shimmered.

Kyle's Hyundai.

Bonnie narrowed the gap between them, but held back a couple hundred feet. At some point during the chase, she realized, she'd killed the Jeep's one working headlight. She'd wanted to be invisible, because all of a sudden she had a not-so-great feeling about this.

For the first time, she was wondering if Kyle was the one driving the car.

28

AT MARLIN STREET, the Hyundai hooked right. Bonnie copied the move in time to see the car turn left onto Distribution Street. The Hyundai pulled into a driveway guarded by a small gray gatehouse. Bonnie stayed well back, idling at the curb, as a distant sentry raised the gate and the Hyundai slipped through.

There appeared to be only one person in the car, but she couldn't tell if it was Kyle. All she knew was that whoever was behind the wheel had just been admitted to a secure shipping facility in the middle of the night.

She put the Jeep into reverse and backed down Distribution Street, away from the guardhouse. At the corner she went right, prowling along the fence, looking for a way in.

The fence was high and topped with a triple row of razor wire, but it wasn't electrified, and there didn't seem to be any guard dogs or surveillance cameras. She could cut her way through, but she'd prefer an easier approach.

She found one—a padlocked gate, unguarded. Perfect.

Parking in front of the gate, she grabbed a pair of bolt cutters from a bag of crap she kept in the rear of the Jeep. It took only a few seconds to slice through the padlock chain. She pushed the gate open and drove through, undeterred by the red octagonal DO NOT ENTER sign.

Easy peasy. No wonder the terrorists were winning.

To get her bearings, she rattled over a rough service road until she found Marlin Street again. She retraced the route for a few hundred yards, then went off-road, paralleling Distribution Street as she headed east. The stink of brackish river water wafted through her busted window.

She drove slowly past a disorderly collection of buildings, most of them low and long—utilitarian one-story structures of brick or wood, the roofs festooned with lines from utility poles. Offices and supply depots, she guessed. The land was flat and almost featureless, with a few sad spindly trees standing here and there amid drifts of dead brown grass littered with wastepaper and soda cans.

Through breaks in the buildings around her, she could see the glare of giant wharf lights and the slow movements of immense cranes, and she could hear the echoing clang of metal on metal. Couldn't see the ship, though. It was lost in the foggy darkness.

Sammy, in her pocket, startled her by belting out "I Will Survive." She was really getting tired of that tune.

The number on the display belonged to Shaban. He was receiving the alerts, too. He had to know Kyle had gone to the port.

"There is a problem," he said when she answered.

Bonnie thought there were a whole lot of problems. "You think she's meeting with her employer?"

"So you have already figured out that someone hired her."

"I may be slow, but you can count on me to cross the finish line eventually."

"Is possible there is a meeting, but is more possible she has been taken."

"Same thing occurred to me. But why bring her here?"

There was a beat of silence. "What do you know of *Mazeppa*?" Shaban asked.

"Never heard of the guy."

"Not a guy. Is a container ship used by several companies controlled by our family. Tonight it is moored in berth seventeen of the Port Newark auto terminal, being loaded with heavy-lift cargo."

"Okay ..."

"Ship is used for another purpose sometimes. People are put on board. They are made to disappear."

"Burial at sea?"

"Sure, yes. But only after many weeks in the cargo hold. The victim endures much torture." Shaban's voice lowered. "I have told you, I do not like torture."

"I'm not real big on it myself. You think they plan to ship Kyle overseas?"

"Her car will be driven aboard the freighter, with her in the trunk. This way no one on the pier sees her, and the car can be disposed of in a foreign port."

"How soon will they put her on board?"

"Maybe right away. But probably they wait a while. Stevedore crews show up at seven, start moving cars. Probably they wait till then so her car goes on with the others and does not stand out."

"You sound pretty familiar with the routine."

"All know of it. It is his way of dealing with enemies."

"Whose way?"

"*Ujku.*"

"Talk English."

"My grandfather, Arian Dragusha. The Wolf."

Bonnie paused in the act of lighting a cigarette. "You're saying Big Bad is behind all this? He paid Kyle to have you killed?"

"It must be so. It explains why he is afraid when he sees me tonight. Like he has seen a ghost. He thought I was already dead."

"Why the hell would your grandpa want you six feet under?"

"This I do not know."

"Shit. Kind of a kick in the nuts for you, huh?"

"As you say, a kick."

"Maybe you should've stayed in Albania."

"My mother said this to me many times. I thought she feared for my soul. Now I think she feared for my life also."

Overhead a plane screamed by—coming into Newark very late. Somebody's flight had been seriously delayed, Bonnie thought irrelevantly. Even so, they were having a better night than she was.

"If Arian sent a crew after me," she said, "he's gotta know Kyle hired me to do the hit."

"Possibly the girl told him. Possibly he learned of it some other way."

"I'm hoping it's the second thing. 'Cause if she knew I was on Arian's hit list and she didn't tell me ... Well, that's the kind of thing that could really sour our relationship."

"You owe her nothing in any case."

"True. But it looks like I'm gonna save her ass anyway."

"Why?"

She didn't have a good answer. "I guess because I still think of her as a dumb kid who's in too deep."

"Then wait for me. We go together."

Bonnie was amused. "What is this, chivalry? You hate Kyle Ridley way more than I do."

"Is my mess. I help clean it up."

"Sweet of you, but no. I don't play well with others, and if I ever do get a sidekick, it'll be some hot Asian chick who knows kung fu."

"You make jokes. This is serious."

"I'm being serious. I'm already inside the compound. Just tell me where to find the auto yard."

"There is more than one outdoor lot, and warehouses, too. But I think they will leave her outdoors for just a couple hours. Probably as close to the wharf as they can get. Find Doremus Avenue and go toward the ship. You will see the main lot on your left. Very big, holds twelve thousand cars. All lit up. You cannot miss it."

"I think I'm coming up on Doremus now."

As she rounded the corner, she saw a distant bluish mist of luminescence from huge floodlights encircling an unfenced lot. Beyond it loomed the cargo ship, rising high over the water, its outline defined by rising stacks of containers and by the tall superstructure near the stern.

"I see it now," she said. "And the *Mazurka*, too."

"*Mazeppa*. I do not like you doing this on your own."

"You don't get a vote. Just sit tight, Shabby. You and me will have a drink together when this thing is over."

"We are not friends, Parker."

"Yeah, but at least we're not trying to kill each other. That's gotta count for something."

She clicked off and switched Sammy to vibrate mode. Couldn't have him bursting impetuously into song while she was sneaking around behind enemy lines.

The auto yard was close now. She thought about parking there, but the Jeep was too beat up to be concealed in the rows of shiny new exports. But since she'd seen other ramshackle vehicles scattered throughout the complex, she figured the Jeep could be ditched almost anywhere.

She chose a spot near a row of giant containers, slotting the Jeep in behind them. Before getting out, she finished her cig, then bunched up her hair under her newsboy cap, hoping to look as masculine as possible from a distance. Even in these days of shattered glass ceilings, most longshoremen were probably male, and she preferred not to stand out. Her tits might give her away, but there was nothing she could do about that. The windbreaker would have helped cover her up, but she'd left it in a trash bin by the Crab River Inlet.

With her purse wedged under her arm to minimize its visibility, she crept between two of the containers, down a narrow passageway bordered by corrugated steel walls. A wet breeze blew off the river, and she shivered.

Something brushed her ankle. She heard small skittering noises.

Rats. Fuck.

She hated rats. Hated rodents of all kinds. Never really got the whole Mickey Mouse thing.

It was dark between the containers, but the light of the car lot beckoned from the far end. Sort of like one of those near-death experiences—the tunnel and the light, all that spooky shit. Even so, she definitely didn't expect to meet her dead parents at the other end. If she did, she would have some harsh words for them about her upbringing.

The passage opened up into a floodlit acre of cars. With any luck, Kyle's Hyundai was still here, and not already lashed down inside the *Bazooka*, or whatever the hell it was called.

Finding one car wouldn't be easy among the thousands of vehicles, but she was guessing it had been left close to the entrance. She started with the first few rows, moving quickly down the center aisles.

Things were starting to make sense. Kyle had probably been an ordinary drug runner until Arian had made her a proposition. He'd wanted her to take out Shaban. She had regular access to him, and she couldn't be connected with anyone else in the organization.

She'd outsourced the hit to a local PI with a reputation in that line. Naturally she'd lost her shit when the PI double-crossed her and kept Shaban alive.

The big question was why Kyle was here. Had she really been kidnapped, or had she come of her own free will? Maybe she'd arranged a meeting. She could be doing a face-to-face with old Arian Dragusha right now, trying to explain how things had gone wrong. The kid just might have enough misplaced moxie to believe she could talk her way out of this jam.

If so, she would have parked by the ship, not here with

the prospective cargo. So the mystery would be solved if and when Bonnie found the car.

And right on cue, there it was. The white Hyundai four-door, easy to spot because it stuck out at an angle, indifferently parked.

Bonnie sidled up next to the car and rapped on the trunk lid. "Crocodile? You in there?"

Frantic thumps answered her.

The trunk was locked, and the key wasn't in the ignition. But that was okay. The lock on a car trunk was no big deal. With her pick set Bonnie got it open in less than a minute.

The lid lifted. Kyle lay curled up, mouth taped, hands tied behind her back with a twist of rope. The girl kicked again—another thump—and made angry mewling noises behind the gag.

Bonnie leaned over. For the second time that night, she stripped tape off the girl's mouth. She did it fast this time, with one hard jerk, intending it to hurt. What the hell, the kid deserved it.

Kyle winced. "Shit."

"Not exactly a thank-you, but I'll take it. Incidentally, you can open a car trunk from inside with the safety latch."

"Don't you think I know that? They disabled the mechanism. Obviously."

"Wow. Even when you're being rescued, you're obnoxious." Bonnie helped her to sit up inside the trunk. "Let's get a look at those knots."

"Can you find my glasses?"

They'd fallen off. Bonnie retrieved them from the trunk and set them gently on the bridge of Kyle's nose.

"I can't believe you showed up," the girl said in a lower voice. "I'm almost sorry I fucked up your Jeep."

Bonnie lifted an eyebrow. "Almost?"

"I'll pay for the damage. I really do have money in a safe deposit box."

"Arian Dragusha's money."

"You know about him?"

"I know about a lot of things." She went to work on the rope, undoing the knots. "But I still can't figure out why he's doing it."

"He's King Lear, only smarter."

"King Lear—that's from Shakespeare, right?"

"Good guess. How'd you find me?"

"Tracked your car. I'll explain later." She set to work on the last of the knots. "You shouldn't have gone home."

"I had to get my stuff."

"Rookie error. You never risk your life for anything you can replace. Did you know Arian sent a crew after me?"

"A crew? He's not even supposed to know about you."

"So you had no idea?"

"Of course not."

"I'd like to believe that, I really would. What'd you mean about King Lear?"

The rope fell away, and Kyle's hands were free. Rubbing her wrists, she climbed out the trunk. "Lear was an old man who let the younger generation take over. It didn't end well for him. Arian isn't going to make that mistake."

"Yeah, well, there's a reason they call him the Wolf and not, say, the Panda Bear."

"How did you learn he was behind it?"

"Shaban told me. He's been sorta like my cheat sheet. Between him and me, we worked out the whole plot. All three facts. Or is it four?"

"Five." Kyle reached into her pocket. "Shakespeare's plays have five acts."

Her hand flashed forward. Bonnie had time to see something small and metallic wedged in her fingers, and then steel prongs bit into her ribs. Voltage crackled. There was white light everywhere and pain and her muscles going taut.

From a lengthening distance Kyle Ridley's voice chased her down into the dark:

"You'd know that, if you'd gone to college."

29

AWARENESS CAME BACK to her in bits and pieces. Throbbing pain between her shoulder blades. Dry heat, stifling and close. Hands on her body. A man's hands, patting her down.

She almost opened her eyes. Some instinct restrained her.

"She still out?" Edna Goodman's voice, coming from a few feet away. "How hard did you clock her?"

"What difference does it make?" That was Ed. It was his hands she could feel all over her, turning her pockets inside out. "Damn girl stinks. Don't she ever bathe?"

Ed had brought her into the motorhome and set her down in one of the straightback chairs she'd seen through the window. Her hands were tied to the back rail of the chair. Bound with twine, she thought. It was stiff and bristly against her wrists.

"She's only got thirty-six dollars on her," Ed said, stepping away.

"I gave her fifty."

"Must've spent some."

She had. She'd needed gasoline for her chopper. And there'd been the Jack & Coke at Sidewinder's.

"We're down fourteen dollars on the deal," Ed groused. "She's not worth fourteen dollars, goddamn little tramp."

"Well, someone's in a fine mood."

"You know how I get when I'm up close and personal with them. How I always get."

They were running some kind of crazy scam. Paying

her to tail Ed to the middle of nowhere, then taking her prisoner. And she wasn't their first. The way they talked about it so casually, she might not even be their tenth.

The question was, what was the endgame here? Some kind of sex play, torture play? Or something more permanent? It almost had to be permanent. Otherwise, the previous victims would've talked, right? Even if they'd been drifters like her, disinclined to go to the police, some of them would have talked.

But maybe not. Maybe there was some angle she wasn't seeing. She needed time to get herself together. Her one advantage was that they thought she was still unconscious. They might hold off on whatever they were planning until they knew she was awake.

"See what she wears on her body," Ed was saying. "How she parades her own shame."

He'd read the risqué catchphrase on her T-shirt. She heard him smack his lips in a way intended to convey disapproval. A sloppy, hungry sound.

"Yes." Edna's voice had a sympathetic tremor. "I knew she was a lost one, all right. Could see it in her eyes. Wary and mistrustful."

"And greedy," Ed said. There was the sound of something being dragged out of storage. Something heavy, metallic, scraping the floor. "She's the type who would sell her soul for a dollar. I'll bet she never so much flinched at the dirty job you offered. You feed her the line about *The Rockford Files*?"

"Surely did. That one never gets old."

Near Bonnie's feet, the thunk-thunk of two latches snapping open.

She risked opening her eyes a fraction. Through a scrim of eyelashes she looked down at Ed as he bent over a trunk. Inside was something like a gas mask, along with a couple of long plastic hoses and a canister. There was a label on the canister. She couldn't quite make out the words ...

"You see that?" Edna said sharply. "I could swear her eyelid twitched."

Crap.

"You're forever seeing things." Ed sounded bored. He leaned in close, and Bonnie felt his hot breath on her face. "She's out like a light. You fret too damn much."

"I just don't think it's smart, doing another one so soon. I told you so, when I got your call."

Bonnie remembered how the woman had been talking on her cell phone in the shop. Talking to Ed.

"It's worth the risk," Ed said. "She was meant for us. It's plain as day. I sized her up as a ripe prospect soon as she sat down at the counter. Young and on her own."

"Young ..." Edna's voice was low and sad. "About the same age our Lily would have been."

"Now, Mother. Don't go down that road."

"It just makes me sorry, that's all."

"What should make you sorry is the unfairness of it— Lily being gone and a filthy vagabond animal like this one still breathing."

"Well," Edna said quietly, "she won't be breathing much longer, will she?"

"No, indeed. You can comfort yourself with that."

So there it was. Final confirmation. They were a pair of serial killers, a husband-and-wife team, and they had lured her inside their mobile home to do what serial killers did.

More noises from below, Ed unpacking the trunk. "What are you knitting, Mother?"

"Something useful."

A straitjacket, Bonnie thought.

"A sweater, I'll bet," Ed said.

"Indeed it is. Winter's coming, and your old one's nearly worn through."

"My dear, you are a treasure. You're the pearl of great price."

Bonnie's heart was pumping fast and hard. It sounded like a jackhammer in her ears. She was sure the Goodmans would hear it too—hear it and know she'd come to. She had been scared at other times in her life, but never quite like this. Not when she'd huddled in the bathroom of a motel room while her parents were executed a few feet away. Not even when she'd broken into a farmhouse in Ohio to take revenge on the men who'd done it.

"What name does our young friend go by?" Ed asked.

"She didn't say and I didn't ask. Just look at her license."

"Didn't find one on her." That was because she kept her driver's license in a rucksack tied to the rear of her chopper. "I'd like to know her name before she goes in the ground. So I can say some words, you know."

"You do say the nicest words. I think that's the part you like best. Putting 'em in the earth."

"Dust to dust, Mother. The way of all fleshly things. Some might think I'd have trouble squaring God's good word with what goes on in here. But do you think Torquemada or Cortes or Pizarro had any problem with it?"

Bonnie didn't know who any of those people were. Other crazy assholes, probably.

"I'll remove this evil raiment from her person before I perform the interment. Naked came she into the world, and naked shall she depart."

Edna served up a halfhearted amen.

Bonnie felt something go over her face. The gas mask. Had to be. Involuntarily she opened her eyes a little. It was only for an instant. Ed, preoccupied with fastening the mask's Velcro tabs behind her head, didn't notice.

His wife did.

"Her eyelids twitched again. I saw it. She's shamming, Ed. I know she is."

"I doubt it. But I'll check."

She had to keep fooling him. As long as he thought she was unconscious, there was a chance he wouldn't go ahead with—with what he meant to do.

His fingers found her left eyelid and tweezed it open. She did her best to keep her eyeball rolled up in the socket. She'd seen an unconscious man in Philly once, a street person like herself. When she'd examined him, his eyes had been like that.

It took an effort of will to hold the eye rigid and unfocused. She thought she was doing okay. She—

The flat of his hand caught her hard on the cheek. "Deceitful jezebel."

"She *was* shamming, wasn't she?"

"That she was." He slapped her again. "But you're wide awake now, aren't you, biker girl? You're not shamming now."

Another slap, and then he took a step back, mastering himself. He was breathing hard, his face flushed and sweaty. She met his gaze and held it, unblinking.

"Got your attention, did I? Good. Now we can start the show."

The mask covered her nose and mouth, but she hadn't been gagged. Ed seemed to expect her to talk. Ask questions, bargain, beg. He waited, watching her with a thin smile, while Edna sat peacefully in her chair, knitting.

Bonnie wouldn't talk. Wouldn't give these crazy fucks the satisfaction.

"Nothing to say?" Ed was clearly disappointed. "Well, we're not here for conversation anyway. We mean to put you down, girl. Put you down like a rutting stray, a mongrel bitch."

Still Bonnie didn't speak. She stared at them. Slowly something rose in her, brighter and harder than fear.

"She's a mean one, isn't she?" Edna breathed. "You can see the devil in her."

"You might not talk, girl," Ed whispered, "but you'll die, all right. You'll die real good." He smacked his lips again. "I see people like you come and go. Always passing through, never stopping anywhere. Locusts. That's what I call you. Swarms of locusts thick on the land."

"Amen," Edna said, more forcefully this time.

"Our whole country is running to seed, losing its way. No moral foundation. No rules to follow. Every Cain and Delilah doing what they like. It's the same as those lawless days when there was no king in Israel, and each man did what was right in his own eyes. Wherefore God has given them up to uncleanness and vile affections and a reprobate mind. The women go against nature, and likewise the men burn in lust, one toward another. And all are filled with unrighteousness, fornication, wickedness, and though they know the judgment of God, they commit things worthy of death, and take pleasure in it."

He paused, catching his breath. Edna knitted and bobbed her head.

"Now I don't put the blame on you personally, any more than I would blame any other vermin. You're a symptom, not a cause. The cause is the modern world itself, with all its false idols and sexual deviancy and concupiscence. The virus of modernity—that's what it is, a virus—and you're a carrier, you're Typhoid Mary. So ... you got to go."

The hard, bright thing in her grew bigger, gaining strength and purpose.

"But I won't make it too rough on you. This mask—see how snug it fits on your dirty face? Like it was made for you. Now I'll hook up the hoses, and after that, what's in this canister will make you just float away. See? Not so bad, is it? No pain, no pain at all. My yoke is easy and my burden is light."

He was smiling, a crooked yellow smile slanting across his fat face. When turned his head to address his wife,

Bonnie saw the spider tattoo on his neck again, the black prison ink.

"Put on the music, Mother."

"What do you want to hear? I brought Mozart and Bach."

"Mozart, I think. You know, by the time he was this one's age, Wolfgang Amadeus had written operas, violin concertos, piano concertos. Look what he made himself, and then look at her. No wonder the herd needs culling."

Edna set a new disk on the turntable. The needle dropped. Hisses and pops came over the cheap speaker, followed by a spray of piano notes like the tinkling of a music box.

"Lovely, isn't it?" Ed whispered. "The music of angels."

He knelt by the trunk again, attaching one of the hoses to the canister. Edna kept on knitting. She glanced up, feeling Bonnie's steady gaze.

"I know you think we're doing wrong," Edna Goodman said, sounding almost apologetic, "but if you think about it, you got no one but yourself to blame. We never could've got you here if you hadn't been an old snoopy-nose, now, could we?"

The words and the music blurred together, melting in the heat and closeness, the sweaty intimacy of the motorhome. Bonnie barely listened. She heard something else, a kind of distant roar, growing louder as the thing taking shape inside her began to flex itself and test its strength.

"As I guess you heard," Edna went on, talking compulsively with a faltering nervous smile, "I'm making Ed a sweater. Oh, I'm a great one for knitting."

Standing, Ed cracked a window and fed the other hose through. "She always knits when there's a show."

"I do." She nodded with an enthusiasm that was somehow artificial. "I'm like that one who sat knitting by the guillotine as the heads rolled. What was her name, Ed?"

"Madame Defarge."

"Ed's the reader in the family. You should see all the medical books he's got."

Ed stooped and retrieved the hose he'd connected to the canister.

"I'm not a doctor," he said, "but I play one in our RV."

Edna chortled a little too loudly. "Play one in our RV. Ed, you're a riot. Oh, now look what you made me do. I dropped a stitch."

The hose in Ed's hand came closer. Ed reached out tentatively, expecting her to jerk her head away, to put up a hopeless fight.

Bonnie didn't move. She let him push the hose into a socket in the mask.

And still the hard new thing inside her wasn't displaced by fear. It had taken on a life of its own. She recognized it as something almost familiar, something like anger. But not quite anger. Anger was a pale, timid thing compared to this. What she felt now—it was a hot knife, a burning brand, a war whoop. It was insanity, and it was alive and growing and she could hear its rising scream.

She shifted in the chair. The old wood creaked. The worn joints shivered.

Her hands were bound to the back support, but her feet were free. Both Ed and Edna were close.

Ed picked up the other hose, the one that ran out through the window, and attached it to a different socket in the mask. One line to feed her the gas, the other to carry off her exhaled breath.

"Guess we're about ready to begin," Ed said, searching her eyes above the mask for any confession of fear.

She stared back at him, seeing every pore in his fleshy face.

"She's still not talking." Edna paused in her knitting. She seemed perplexed. "Not squirming or struggling, the way they always do. It's a marvel. Maybe ... maybe she wants to die." She said it with a vaguely hopeful lilt.

Ed grunted. "If so, we can oblige her. So here's the story, little Miss No-Account. What I got for you is nitrous oxide. Not the watered-down brew your dentist might use. This is the real McCoy, one hundred percent pure, and when I open the valve, you're going to get real happy and real sleepy, and then you're going to get real dead."

Bonnie kept on watching him with cold, clinical intensity.

"See how blue her eyes are," Edna whispered. "Like Lily's."

Ed spun to face her. "Will you stop talking about Lily?" He made a sound like a choked sob. "Damn, Mother, you sure know how to take all the fun out of things."

"I'm sorry, Ed. I shouldn't have said it. I'll be still now. I'll sit and watch. You know how I like to see 'em stop breathing."

"Yeah. I know."

"That very last breath ... There's something fascinating about it. Something ... holy."

Ed nodded, mollified. "Let's get to it then. Time to die, biker girl."

He stooped, reaching for the valve on the canister, while the phonograph played and Edna knitted, and the thing building up inside Bonnie, the nameless thing that was more than anger, came fully awake.

They weren't going to kill her. Not these two, with their dirty fingernails and rodent brains. They didn't have a chance.

Bonnie threw herself to her feet, lifting the chair with her. She wheeled, using the chair lashed to her back as a weapon, smacking the armrest against Ed's face as, bent over, he turned in surprise.

The impact shivered through the chair. The armrest snapped off. Ed fell sideways, blood on his face. Edna gasped.

Bonnie pivoted again, slamming the chair into the wall and breaking it apart. Most of it fell away, but her hands were still tied to the vertical rail. She clawed at it until it dropped free, the twine unraveling.

Edna started to stand, her hands raised in a placating gesture. "Wait, girl, just wait a minute, will you just wait—"

Bonnie wasn't going to wait. She pounced on the woman and shoved her back into her chair, driving her backward against the phonograph. The needle ripped across the tracks and got stuck in a groove, skipping madly, recycling the same splinter of melody.

Edna's fists came up, flailing at the mask. Bonnie didn't even feel the blows. She was past feeling anything beyond the furious determination to go on living and to kill anything that got in her way.

From Edna's lap she plucked one of the knitting needles. She drove it into the woman's throat.

Edna's tongue clucked. She made a gagging noise. She pawed at the needle, her fingers slick and reddening with blood. Her eyes were big and startled and uncomprehending.

"How's *your* last breath?" Bonnie said from behind the mask.

The voice that had spoken those words wasn't hers. It was the voice of the thing inside her, the thing that refused to die.

She left them there—Ed unconscious on the floor, Edna struggling to breathe. She climbed out of the mobile home and walked across the canyon's flat expanse, not fleeing, simply leaving, her stride efficient and unhurried. At some point she must have ripped the mask from her face—the hoses had long since popped free—and let it fall to the ground, but she was unaware of doing so.

She retrieved her motorcycle and got the engine going and rode away. And thought of nothing. Nothing at all.

◉

IN EL PASO she bought a newspaper. Ed and Edna Goodman were on the front page.

According to the story, an anonymous phone call on Wednesday night had alerted the police to an attempted murder in the Goodmans' camper. The caller, a woman who spoke in a whisper, had given enough details to lead three squad cars of sheriff's deputies to the scene. Purgatory Canyon, the locale was called. It seemed appropriate.

By the time they got there, the motorhome was gone. It was found abandoned the next day. The Goodmans had disappeared, taking almost nothing with them. There was speculation that they'd hidden a car in the stables of a nearby horse farm, long closed, as a precaution if they should require a quick getaway.

Unspecified evidence uncovered in the motorhome confirmed that the Goodmans had made a hobby of killing drifters—loners who would be hard to trace and unlikely to be missed. Ground-penetrating radar was put to work in Purgatory Canyon, eventually making possible the recovery of fourteen bodies, some of which dated back two decades. It was believed that the death of the Goodmans' infant daughter had served as the trigger for their activities. Edna Goodman had no history of violence, while Ed had done time for aggravated battery in his youth.

The authorities expressed a hopeful interest in finding the nameless tipster who'd set them on the Goodmans' trail. So far the woman had declined to come forward. Bonnie had a feeling she never would.

She spent several days in El Paso, doing simple things. Drinking cold water. Eating rice and beans. Watching the progress of the sun across the sky. Being alive.

She hadn't expected to be alive. Probably she had no

right to be. She'd been shaving it pretty close for a long time. This last adventure could have—should have—ended with her as the fifteenth body in the ground.

If she had died in Purgatory Canyon, no one would have known or cared, and there would have been nothing to show for her existence on earth except the graves of the men she'd killed in Ohio.

There had to be more than that. But she wasn't going to find it buzzing around the country scrounging for day jobs. She was twenty years old. It was time to settle down.

She headed east. She was sick of the damn desert. She wanted to see water and trees, the Atlantic Ocean. Some little town with a boardwalk and a cutesy Main Street and a park with ducks.

During the long hours of travel, as she listened to the song of the road, she considered what she ought to do with her life. She didn't want to answer to a boss and she wasn't qualified to do much on her own. But there was that one idea—the idea that Edna Goodman, of all people, had put into her head.

She could be a private detective. No, seriously. It was a job that required street smarts, a knowledge of deception, and familiarity with criminals and the darker side of life. She had all that.

True, her initial foray into the world of PI work hadn't gone all that smoothly. But she was the stubborn type. Once a notion took hold of her, she wouldn't let it go. It might take her a while to work it all out, raise the necessary capital, establish herself. Even so, she began to think she could really do it.

Bonnie Parker, PI, she thought.

Had kind of a ring to it.

30

BONNIE CAME OUT of a haze of white light and found herself in the backseat of the Hyundai, heading toward the wharf, where the freighter languished in the glare of floodlights. A man she had never seen was driving, with another guy riding shotgun.

Her purse was gone, and the Walther with it. And of course she wasn't toting an ankle gun. She'd already played that card.

Her slow circling gaze came to rest on Kyle, seated beside her, a stun gun in her hand.

"Don't try anything," the girl said, "or I'll give you another jolt. Do you understand?"

"Yeah." Her voice was strangely hoarse, as though she'd been screaming, and her head ached. "Was I out long?"

"Couple of minutes. I take it you're sentient again."

"I'm okay. Everything's just a little"—she tried clearing her throat and coughed up a thread of mucus—"fruity in the loops."

"You do have the most creative street patois."

"Yeah. I bet you're gonna miss that about me."

Her cap must have come off when she'd been loaded into the car. She found it on the floor and put it back on. She didn't know why, really.

"So it looks like you didn't need rescuing," she said slowly.

"Of course not. I knew you'd fall for the damsel-in-distress routine. It fits in so perfectly with the atmospherics of your cherished pulp-fiction, film-noir mise-en-scene."

Bonnie shut her eyes against the slow throb in her skull. "Use smaller words."

"I can't help having a better vocabulary than someone with only a high school diploma."

"No diploma."

"What?"

"Never finished high school. Dropped out when I was fifteen."

"Jesus."

The guy in the passenger seat lit a strong-smelling cigarette. Turkish or something. Serious fumes.

Bonnie tried to focus. "You worked it out with the old man. Somehow you knew I could find you here ..."

"Arian knew. He's pretty paranoid. He had Shaban's car and apartment bugged. He heard your phone calls, knew exactly what you were up to."

"If you think handing me over to Arian solves your problem, you're wrong. You still messed up your assignment. You were hired get rid of Shaban."

"Shaban's not an issue anymore."

"What does that mean?"

"It means he's currently rounding up two of his friends, people he trusts. He intends to come here with them and confront his grandfather. We can hear his phone calls, remember? What he doesn't know is that the hit crew from Brighton Cove is already on board the ship, not to mention Zamir and Timir." She nodded at the men up front.

"Wow. You really are a psycho bitch." Bonnie sighed. "I thought that was my department."

On the pier, cranes were still filling up the cargo holds. Dockworkers strolled around. They couldn't all work for the Dragushas. But even if she yelled for help, no one would hear over the clamor of machinery. She thought of trying a combat roll out of the sedan, but it was hopeless; Kyle would zap her before she even got the door open.

"So Arian's going to do the job himself, with his own people?" She shook her head, then regretted that when her skull throbbed harder. "His only reason for hiring you must've been to avoid tipping his hand. Now he's gonna pop the kid right on the boat?"

"Ship," Kyle said. "It's a ship, not a boat. And your logic is valid, except now there's a new way to spin it. The story will be that Shaban hired you to kill his grandfather. Arian got wind of the plan, took care of you, then defended himself from Shaban when he and his accomplices arrived to do the job personally."

The freighter expanded in the windshield. A wide ramp descended from an opening in the stern, hanging out like a lolling tongue. The Hyundai turned onto the ramp, climbing.

"Who came up with that scenario?" Bonnie asked. "Him or you?"

"Mostly me. I stopped at a payphone after I left the burger place. I'd gotten myself together by then. As you may have noticed, I was a bit frazzled when I left."

"Yeah. Thanks again for trashing the shit outta my ride."

"I'm surprised you could tell the difference."

The Hyundai passed inside the ship, into a vast echoing cavern made of metal floors, steel columns, and a high ceiling studded with banks of fluorescent lights. It could have been an underground parking garage in the city.

"I had a phone conversation with the old man," Kyle said. "He told me the hit in Brighton Cove had just been canceled. I saw my chance and sold him on a new strategy. I said that once you found out about the hit crew, you'd feel duty-bound to find me. With me as bait, I could lead you right to him."

Bonnie studied the girl in the flicker of overhead lights streaking past. "You're a real piece of work, kiddo."

"Thank you."

"It wasn't a compliment."

The sedan's headlights flared on the rising surface of another ramp, this one leading to a higher level of the hold.

"I don't care what you think of me." Kyle shrugged. "I won, you lost. In a few hours I'll be in Honolulu. I'll remember you when I'm sipping a daiquiri on the lanai."

"Hawaii? That's the plan?"

"I've earned a vacation."

"Sure, you're crazy employee of the month."

The driver bypassed the next ramp, heading for a rear corner of the hold. It was darker here, most of the overhead lights extinguished. The Hyundai's high beams snapped on.

"So," Bonnie said, "you knew right from the start that Arian would put me out of the way."

"Sure. That was a given. Am I supposed to feel bad about it?"

"Some people would."

Kyle shrugged. "You chose a dangerous occupation. Your luck had to run out eventually."

"Sweet."

"Anyway, from what I know of you, your demise won't constitute much of a loss."

"At least I ain't gonna die a virgin."

The car slowed. Its single headlight lit up rows of vehicles parked four deep, lashed to holes in the flooring by orange cables. Exports picked up at some other shipping facility, already secured for their trip overseas.

"I got news for you, kiddo," Bonnie said. "You won't be getting any vacation. The old man will take care of you, just like he intends to take care of me."

"He won't kill me if I can be useful."

"Your usefulness is pretty much over at this point."

"You're wrong. There's one more thing I can do." She plucked the cap from Bonnie's head and put it on. "I can be you."

"It takes more than a hat to pull off that impersonation."

"I have more than a hat. I have your ID. I'll be traveling as Bonnie Parker. I'll use your credit card to book the flight. And I know how to breeze through airport checkpoints without drawing attention. All I need is to take off my specs and put on a wig. One blonde female looks enough like another."

"What's the point?"

"No matter how dumb they are, the police in your little hick town will connect your disappearance with the drive-by crew. The timing is too close to be a coincidence. They'll track down the hitters, and the hitters will lead them straight to Arian. Unless ..."

"Unless my last known whereabouts were somewhere in Hawaii."

"*Brava*. That way, suspicion can't fall on anyone local. So you see, Arian has a reason to keep me alive. I'm providing an alibi for him and his crew."

"And what about Kyle Ridley? What happens to her, officially?"

"My car will be shipped overseas and disposed of with no paper trail. I'll get a new ID in Hawaii. For all practical purposes, Kyle Ridley will simply cease to exist."

"You came up with that plan, too, I take it."

"*Naturellement.*"

"You always think you're the smartest one in the room."

"Only because I am."

The Hyundai pulled into a corner. The driver shifted into park, but left the engine idling, headlights on.

In the darkness beyond the lights, someone stood waiting. A small slender figure, narrow-shouldered, face invisible.

Bonnie had never seen Arian Dragusha, not even in a photo. She knew she was looking at him now.

The two men got out of the car.

"There's something I still don't get," Bonnie said. "Arian doesn't trust his own people. He doesn't trust his own flesh and blood. Why would he trust you?"

"That's exactly why. Because I'm not part of the organization. I'm an outsider. As you so eloquently put it"—Kyle snugged the cap tighter on her head—"I got no skin in the game."

The back door opened on Bonnie's side. The driver reached in. He was a big man with a stupid face and a bad smell. He grabbed hold of her with a meaty hand and hauled her out of the car.

Her legs were surprisingly wobbly. The stun gun had left her weaker than she'd realized. Both men propped her up, one on either side. The driver carried an appalling stench, the reek of some serious BO. He wore a short-sleeved tee with yellow pit stains and a knife sheathed to his arm. His companion chewed his foul-smelling cigarette and scratched himself. Both sported unkempt beards of black wiry hair, like Brillo pads.

A real classy duo. They made Ed Goodman look like Fred Astaire.

They marched her forward, into the spill of glare from the high beams.

"So which one of you is Zamir?" she inquired. "Timir?"

They ignored her.

"Not big talkers, huh?"

"They speak no English."

The voice, a smoker's rasp, came from outside the circle of light. Arian Dragusha advanced in slow shuffling steps punctuated by the tap of a cane. She waited, held by the men, as the headlights' glow mounted his body and reached his face. A fuzz of gray beard. Loose jowls, wattled neck. Dead eyes.

He stopped before her. Up close he seemed feeble and shaky, his limbs as spindly as the walking stick he leaned on, his black coat enfolding him like wings.

"They have come over from Albania," he said. "Speak only their native language."

"That's gotta be convenient for you. Hear no evil, and all that."

He looked her over without interest. "You are Parker?" His shoulders rose and fell. "Nothing special. Just a girl."

"And you're just a senile old fart. Looks like both of us are kind of a disappointment."

Unexpectedly he laughed—a series of low chuckles that shook his frail body like coughs.

"Brave woman, eh?" he said mildly. "But not for long."

His long-fingered hand gave a languid wave. The man on her right jerked her arms forward, holding them outstretched. The driver, on her left, produced a pair of steel handcuffs joined by a short welded chain.

She didn't like being helpless. When the locks clicked shut, a small involuntary shudder trembled through her.

Arian watched her with a thin smile. "No fear, Parker. You don't die right away."

"That's very comforting."

Kyle materialized in the light, carrying a purse Bonnie recognized as her own. "I wouldn't take too much reassurance from it," she said. "I really wouldn't."

Arian chuckled again. "Should listen to her, Parker. Smart girl, this one."

"Yeah, she's a peach."

"Will take you a long time to die," Arian said. "Is eighteen days before Malta, first port of call. Zamir and Timir will work on you. They have done this before. When they are through, you go into the North Atlantic. Splash."

Bonnie turned to Kyle. "You know, I'm only here because I was trying to save your life."

The girl rolled her eyes. "Well, cry me a river."

"When you told me you don't feel anything, you

SKIN IN THE GAME

weren't just talking about sex, were you? You don't feel anything at all. Ever."

"The technical term is alexithymia. And yes, I studied psychology to understand myself. But *not* to fix myself. I'm not broken. Quite the contrary. I really believe I represent a step forward. Humanity two point oh, so to speak. You know Gould's theory of punctuated equilibrium, the hopeful monster? Of course you don't. But I think it applies to me."

"The monster part does."

"Say whatever you want. I see things with a clarity of focus you'll never know. And I'm a survivor. I'm adaptable and resilient."

"So's a cockroach, but you don't hear him bragging about it."

Arian clapped his hands once. "*Marrë atë.*"

Zamir and Timir tightened their grip on her arms. Roughly she was escorted out of the light, her hands cuffed in front of her.

She looked over her shoulder and saw Kyle tip her cap. "Later, hater," the girl said cheerily.

Bonnie turned, facing forward. Her mouth barely moved.

"In a while, Crocodile."

31

THE AUTOMOBILE BAY was huge, and the walk to the far bulkhead seemed endless. Bonnie marched stolidly, her hands clasped over her belly.

She knew better than to struggle against the cuffs pinching her wrists. She was pretty familiar with handcuffs. She'd practiced getting out of them often enough. Cops were trained to double-lock a cuff, first clicking it shut and then locking the ratchet in the swing arm so it couldn't be inadvertently tightened as the prisoner struggled.

Out of stupidity or sadism, the driver hadn't bothered with that step. If she twisted her wrists or tugged against the chain, the cuffs would only clamp down harder.

Flanking her, Zamir and Timir kept up a vigorous dialogue in their native language. The word *kurvë* kept coming up. It seemed to have something to do with her. It didn't sound complimentary.

Senseless radio chatter boiled up once from the walkie-talkie in the driver's back pocket. He answered and clicked off. There was no other contact with the larger world, no reminder that other human beings existed. The emptiness of the vast space was unsettling. The three of them might have been ghosts on a ghost ship.

Not the most sophisticated ghosts, however. The guy who'd ridden shotgun apparently had some kind of digestive disorder. Every so often he would crack off a volley of noxious farts almost loud enough to rip his trousers. Whenever this happened, the driver greeted the event with appreciative chortles.

In addition to the knife on his arm and the radio in his back pocket, the driver had a Glock .44 snugged into his waistband, Mexican-style. Not a great idea. A Glock's safety was part of the trigger mechanism. Toting it around in your pants was a good way to shoot off your own genitals. On the other hand, it probably wouldn't be any tragedy if a professional torturer with weapons-grade BO was unable to reproduce.

She'd glimpsed a gun tucked into the other man's belt, too, but because it was on his right side, she couldn't get a good look. Not that it mattered. One firearm was as good as any other at this range.

She still didn't know which one was Zamir and which was Timir, but she had to call them something. The smelly one, she decided, was Elvis. The farty one with the bad-smelling cig sticking out of his beard was Ringo. She'd made friends with a couple of mangy stray cats in the days when she lived on the street, and those were the names she'd given them. These two were even mangier, and probably a lot less intelligent.

Finally they reached a door that opened on a basement corridor lit by overhead rails of fluorescent light. The hallway took them out of the hold and past the engine room.

An elevator approached. Ringo pressed the button.

On the fly she came up with a plan. She didn't do a lot of thinking about it. Her philosophy was that thinking was highly overrated.

In the elevator, she would stun Ringo with a knee to the nads. The pain would force him to release her. Then all she had to do was snatch Elvis's Glock out of his waistband, and she could make some noise. Even with her hands manacled, she could point and shoot, and in the confined space she wouldn't need to aim. She would take care of Ringo before he could fire, then finish off Elvis with his own weapon.

A lot of things could go wrong. Ringo could be quicker on the draw than she expected, or Elvis could wrestle the gun out of her hand. But with any luck she could take out at least one of them, maybe both. The worst that could happen was she would end up getting shot, and that was still better than playing torture games without a safety word.

The door opened. They hustled her inside. Ringo pressed a button labeled Main Deck. He did not heed the No Smoking sign. The stench from his cigarette was even more headache-inducing in a closed space.

She waited. The elevator shuddered into motion, climbing. Neither man was looking at her. Neither suspected an attack.

Now.

She pivoted and rammed her knee into Ringo's groin.

He winced, but his hold on her arm didn't weaken. He didn't double over, didn't collapse, didn't do any of the things he was supposed to do.

"*Te qifsha, kurvë,*" he muttered, and delivered a backhanded slap across her face.

She staggered, almost falling against Elvis. He smiled down at her and dragged his finger slowly across his throat.

Fuck.

She wasn't fighting her way out of this. What this pair lacked in social graces, they made up for in animal strength.

She turned away, tasting a warm trickle from her

lip. She'd drawn blood, at least. The bad news was that it was her own.

Behind her, Ringo once again broke wind, eliciting new chuckles from his partner. Between the stink from his cigarette and the odor from his blood, the guy was a walking compost heap.

The elevator opened on a different kind of corridor, one with white walls and short nap carpet. It could have been part of a hospital wing. She guessed it belonged to the high superstructure that dominated the freighter's profile near the stern.

The hallway was narrow, not wide enough for two people to walk side by side. Elvis led her, with Ringo at her back. They passed a stairwell and what looked like a kitchen—a galley, she guessed it was called—before emerging via a side door onto the open deck.

The deck was slick with river water blown by the wind. A mountain of containers sat on the closed lid of the nearest hold—big steel boxes, red, green, orange, gray, some with manufacturers' names stenciled across them in huge letters. Building blocks for a giant child.

To her left was the shore, still busy with activity as more crates were lifted aboard the ship. There were people around, but they couldn't help her. In the darkness she would never be seen, and in the racket made by the giant gantries stacking the containers, she wouldn't be heard.

Roughly the two men pulled her in the opposite direction, toward the starboard side of the freighter, where she was hidden from sight behind the deckside containers. A walkway lined by a steel railing edged the ship's perimeter. Beyond the railing was the river, a spread of black water. The air was chilly, and for the second time she wished she still had the windbreaker.

She considered her options. If she broke free of her captors, she might be able to vault the railing and dive into the drink. It would be a long drop, a hard splash, and swimming with her hands cuffed wouldn't be easy. Probably she would drown—unless Elvis or Ringo managed to shoot her first.

Even so, it would be a better exit than what they had planned for her. She was tempted. But she couldn't bring herself to do it. Her whole being rebelled against it. For her, there was always a way out. Always.

They led her forward, past a giant hold with an open lid, still being loaded with towers of steel crates. The next bay was closed, and more crates were being piled on the cover. Alongside the bay ran an elevated walkway accessible by a short ladder. Elvis climbed the ladder, and she and Ringo followed. Kneeling, Elvis spun off a pair of twist locks that secured a hatch lid in the floor. With a grunt he lifted the heavy lid out of the way.

The open lid exposed a vertical shaft plunging into darkness. A series of yellow rungs embedded in a wall of the shaft led down.

Elvis pointed. He was ordering her to climb down the shaft.

This was not something she wanted to do. She had a fair idea of what lay at the bottom, and she was in no hurry to get there.

Seeing her hesitate, the two men lost their composure. Elvis leaned into her face, screaming. Ringo slapped the back of her head nearly hard enough to knock her over.

"Okay, okay." She gave in, raising her hands. "I'm going."

She knelt by the hatchway and swung her legs into

the shaft, her feet finding the rungs. Before descending, she took a last breath of the breeze off the river—a fresh breeze, cold but clean. Then she lowered herself into the airless dark.

Down the rabbit hole, she thought. This time for real.

32

IN A ROOM off the bridge, Arian Dragusha prepared a pot of oatmeal. He had brought the steel-cut oats with him, in a Ziploc bag in his pocket, not trusting the *Mazeppa* to stock his brand.

He mixed water and oats, then set the pot on the stove, stirring with a long spoon. At the other end of the room, Kyle Ridley sat at a small table with a checkered vinyl tablecloth, waiting restlessly for her money.

The young were always impatient. As a young man, he too had been in a hurry to obtain the things he wanted. From the start, he had been indifferent to the methods he used or the victims he left in his trail. He had been ruthless, desperate, driven by the urgency of one who had known hunger and privation. He had scratched and clawed, had bared his teeth at all those who opposed him, and had not hesitated to kill. *Ujku*, they called him, as if he were something inhuman. He hadn't minded. He had liked the name and reputation he had won.

In his middle years, having acquired his hoard of treasure, he had settled in for a long period of watchfulness, knowing that what he had taken from others could all too easily be taken from him. To win one's fortune, he had discovered, was not so difficult. To preserve it against the jackals and carrion birds—that was a harder task. He had passed the prime of his life in constant vigilance, a sentry in a tower, defending the ramparts, repelling all attacks.

Curiously, he did not make much use of his money. He lived modestly. He never traveled. It had been many years since there had been a woman in his life. He supported only such charitable causes as were necessary to maintain his respectability in the community. To him, money was not to spend but to have. He liked the thought of it, the sheer fact of its existence. He liked to read the columns of figures. Sometimes he visualized them as he nodded off to sleep.

It was a warm and comforting feeling to have money. Without it, a man was as naked and unprotected as a beast in the wild. An old man was a frail creature, one who felt the cold too readily. Money was his only buffer against the vast incalculable cruelty of the world.

The mixture in the pot steamed and bubbled as it thickened into a glutinous sludge. Arian ate oatmeal three times a day, and he always prepared it himself.

He detested the stuff. It was peasant fare, flavorless and cheap. But he knew his stomach would rebel at more sumptuous nourishment. A little coffee he could tolerate—he liked to sip a good macchiato—and some fresh fruit and boiled potatoes, but little else. His digestion was failing. Everything was failing. His hands shook. His eyes were dim. He wore two hearing aids. Sometimes to his great shame he soiled himself. He forgot things, very recent things, and yet he remembered the days of his youth with arresting clarity. When he looked in the mirror, he saw a stranger's face, wrinkled, age-spotted, sagging.

Still he hung on to life, even if it was a life he despised, the life of a half-crippled old man slurping porridge from a bowl. The Wolf was elderly and lame, but not helpless, and he would lead his pack until the end.

He poured out the oatmeal, placed the bowl on the table, and sat, shoulders hunched, head lowered. For a long time his only action was the slow rise and fall of the arm holding the spoon.

Across from him, Kyle adjusted the newsboy cap at

different angles, studying her reflection in the table's stainless steel surface. She seemed amused by the sight, smiling as if at a private joke.

At length Arian finished his oatmeal, pushing the bowl aside. "Now I guess you want your pay."

Kyle nodded. Her cool gaze never left his face.

"Is a lot of money. Much cash."

"So?"

"Lot of money," Arian said again.

"Perhaps you're thinking you could put me in the container with Parker and keep the cash."

"Me? How could I think a thing so unworthy?" He spoke the words lightly, smiling his cold lupine smile.

"You know you can't. Not if you want Parker's trail to dead-end in Hawaii, as we discussed."

"Yes, your clever plan. Your blonde wig and stolen identity."

"A hundred grand is a bargain for an airtight alibi. You don't want the police sniffing around your crew. Someone may talk."

"As I have said, a smart girl."

"Am I getting my money or not?"

He sighed and pushed himself to his feet. "You get it."

Cane in hand, he tapped his way to a footlocker. He opened the padlock and retrieved a briefcase. It had two latches, each secured by a separate combination lock. He undid the latches one at a time.

It was impossible ever to take too many precautions against betrayal and theft. Enemies were everywhere. Never could he be complacent, never could he let down his guard. Even his detestable oatmeal could be prepared by nobody but himself.

"You are wise," he told Kyle Ridley as he snapped open the valise, "to trust no one. Even as a child I knew this." He unzipped the lining to expose bricks of hundred-dollar bills wrapped in rubber bands. "I grew up under

Hoxha, the dictator, a monster. Spies and informers in every village. They would tell on you to the secret police for anything you said or did, or for no reason at all. Then you were never seen again."

The girl did not appear to be listening. She stared at the bricks of cash as he stacked them neatly on a counter. Five bricks, ten thousand dollars apiece, to be added to the $50,000 he had already paid.

"Persons of your age," he went on, indulging in his reminiscences though he knew she cared nothing for them, "have no memory of communism. To you it is ancient history, eh? But I lived it." He spoke with a survivor's pride. "I escaped when I was seventeen, on a fishing boat that carried me to Corfu, across twenty miles of open water. I paid the smugglers all the money I had, money I had earned in many dangerous ways. Even so, it was understood that if a patrol boat gave chase, I would be thrown overboard. This was a risk I accepted." He added with a shrug, "I cannot swim."

He picked up the first of the five bricks but deliberately delayed handing it over. He enjoyed the feel of the thick slab of bills in his grasp.

"From Kassiopi in Corfu I went west across the island, then over to Italy. In Genoa I booked passage on a cargo ship—a humble vessel, not so grand as the *Mazeppa*. To pay my way, I swabbed decks, scrubbed toilets. On my eighteenth birthday I arrived in New York. I knew no English, had no money, no family in America, no future. Yet here I stand."

She held out her hand. Grudgingly he surrendered the first wad of cash. She stuffed it too eagerly into her purse.

"You did not carry a handbag before," he said, noticing it for the first time.

"It's hers. Parker's."

"Oh." He chuckled. "Looting her body before she is even dead."

"I need to pass for her, don't I? The hat is hers, too. Stylish, huh? You know, if it was 1932."

He handed over a second brick of cash. "You got to know her, I think?"

"Only a little."

"Why did she not kill Shaban?"

"She's trying to reform." The girl said it with contempt.

Arian thought he understood Kyle Ridley very well. His grandson, on the other hand, would understand Bonnie Parker much better.

"Is not easy," he said, giving her the third brick, "to reform. Those in our business—we must kill and keep on killing, until we die. Is no other way."

Kyle pushed the money deeper into the purse. "I suppose she's finding that out."

"It does not trouble you to betray her to me?"

"Why should it? You do what you have to do. It's all about looking out for number one."

"Ah. Yes. I know this expression. A very American attitude."

As for himself, he cared not at all about Parker's fate, or what agonies she would suffer in the hold. There was an unlimited quantity of pain in the world. Any pain he contributed was no more than a raindrop in the sea.

He surrendered the last two bricks. "There it is," he said. "The balance of your payment. The deposit, you have obtained already. Perhaps you have it with you."

She smiled. "No such luck. It's someplace secure."

Arian nodded. "Most prudent," he said mildly.

He did not need to trick her into revealing the money's whereabouts. He knew very well where it was. On the day of their last meeting, his man Raco had been tasked with following her. Raco had seen Kyle Ridley go into a bank and rent a safe deposit box.

Naturally the girl had suspected nothing. Such was the

way of youth. So cynical, and yet so trusting.

He closed the briefcase and replaced it in the locker. "You will get all this contraband onto the airplane without trouble, I am sure."

"I've smuggled kilos of heroin. I can handle wads of cash."

He had no doubt of it. "You will use Newark Airport?"

"I'd rather not say."

"But wherever you depart from, you will drive her Jeep there, and leave it in long-term parking."

"Of course. As we discussed. Don't worry about it."

Arian nodded. He was not worried.

He accompanied her out of the side room, onto the bridge. It was a long narrow space like a railroad car—but this railroad car was on the seventh story of a tower, its wide windows offering panoramic views of the freighter's bow and stern. So different from the freighter that had brought him to America, so modern and computerized, and yet, standing here, he might have been on that other ship, a boy of almost eighteen, breathing the briny wind.

He passed the conning station, the ship's wheel nestled amid rows of mysterious consoles, a bewildering technological array. In a far corner, a man with a white streak in his beard stood studying a chart. Otherwise the bridge was empty.

Arian moved carefully, with the slow shuffle of age. The girl took quicker steps, eager to be going now that she had her windfall.

At the door to the bridge wing on the port side, he stopped. "You do not need an old man to slow you down," he said graciously. "I will linger here and watch as the last containers are loaded. You take your money and enjoy your new life."

Kyle pulled the purse closer to her body, an unconscious protective gesture, like a mother cradling her child. "Say hello to Shaban for me. And say good-bye."

He did not find this amusing. It was not a fit subject for humor. Still, he said nothing, merely bade her a wordless farewell with a courtly half-bow.

She left the bridge, heading for the central stairway that would take her down to the deck six floors below. He stepped out onto the wing, an unroofed deck high above the water, and through narrowed eyes he watched her go.

Her plan to impersonate Parker was a good one. But she had failed to take into consideration two things. First, Arian Dragusha was not concerned with the police. He owned too many of them. Anyway, without Parker's body they could prove nothing—and her body would vanish into the ocean four thousand miles from here, with all identifying features removed.

And second, Kyle Ridley had betrayed Parker to save herself. Surely she could betray Arian Dragusha no less easily. She believed, after all, only in looking out for number one.

Glancing back into the bridge, Arian curled a finger in a silent summons to the bearded man.

"*Xhaxhi?*" Raco Prifti approached with a quick step.

"You recognized the girl who just left?"

"*Po, Xhaxhi.* Do I follow her again?"

"Is not necessary. I know where she will go. To the same bank she visited last time. It will open at eight thirty on a Saturday. You will be there."

"*Unë kuptoj.*" I understand.

"She will retrieve the contents of her safe deposit box. She will drive off in Parker's Jeep. Probably she will go directly to an airport."

"Yes?"

"At your first opportunity, kill her." Arian shut his eyes as his long-fingered hands curled slowly into claws. "And bring me back my money."

33

FOR BONNIE, IT was a long descent through the dark. The smells of mildew and machine oil closed over her. In the claustrophobic space she found it hard to breathe.

With her hands chained together, she could hold on to only one of the two side rails. She made slow progress. Elvis and Ringo, descending after her, yelled incomprehensible things at her, obviously demanding more speed.

Her sneakers slipped on a rung. She clutched the railing tighter to keep from falling. Above her, the driver let loose a new stream of Albanian curses to encourage her in her efforts.

"Eat shit, Elvis," she muttered.

She had wondered why they'd made her go first. Now she realized that if one of them had preceded her, she could have dropped down on top of him, dislodging him from the ladder and maybe breaking his legs. Apparently they weren't complete morons.

And they'd done this before. Like Ed and Edna Goodman, they were experienced at this sort of thing. But the Goodmans, at least, had killed their victims without pain. A little laughing gas, and it was lights out.

No laughing gas this time.

The shaft ended at a metal landing lit by a fluorescent bulb in a wall sconce. A metal stairway like a fire escape dropped from the landing to a lower story, which in turn would lead to a still lower floor. The landing itself extended to matching doors on both sides, affording access to a walkway that ran the length of the bulkhead. There must be a whole series of those walkways, one for each level in the descent.

The landing looked out at the interior of the cargo hold, fully loaded, a subterranean city crowded with eight-story skyscrapers of corrugated steel, the rectangular boxes lashed together at the corners by orange webbing, nested inside crosshatched metal frames welded to the hull. A lightless city, or nearly so, illuminated only by the scattered auras of fluorescent tubing.

From above came creaks and groans and the clank of chains, as still more containers were piled atop the closed lid of the hold. Down below, there was no sound and no movement, only a vast haunted stillness.

She must have stood gazing at the scene for a long moment. Ringo, impatient, planted his hand between her shoulder blades and gave a hard shove, directing her to the stairway. "*Kreni!*"

She went deeper into the belly of the ship. Staircase after staircase, a succession of landings that all looked the same, until finally she was at the bottom, standing on the floor of the hold with columns of crates towering over her.

Between the bulkhead and the first row of crates lay a narrow stretch of open floor. The doors of all the crates were secured with locking bars—except for one, which was unlocked. The men led her toward it, Elvis threw open the double doors, and light spilled out. Her accommodations for the voyage.

Her heart sped up. Her mouth was dry.

The container was a utilitarian steel box, maybe eight feet wide and twenty feet long, painted a dull green. The walls and roof were corrugated sheet-metal. The floor was plywood.

216

Its interior was raised off the floor by six or eight inches. She had to step up, lifted by the two men.

No cargo inside. Instead they'd turned the shipping container into a kind of man-cave. Folding chair, card table, scatter of dirty magazines. Boombox on a mini-fridge. Long fluorescent tube affixed vertically to a wall near the doors, an electrical cord snaking through a drilled hole to an outlet outside.

And against the back wall, a tool chest on rubber wheels. Many drawers of different sizes. She didn't want to know what was in those drawers.

Elvis gave her a vicious shove that knocked her to the floor. She landed heavily, skinning her palms.

The floor was dotted with rust-colored stains. They predominated near the center of the room. She looked up and saw a large eyehook embedded in the ceiling, directly over that spot. A long beltlike strip—one of the orange packing straps—ran from the hook to an identical hook on the wall.

She didn't need them to draw her a diagram to see where this was going.

The boombox came on, brought to life by Elvis, and some awful Eastern European hip-hop spilled out. Jiving to the music, Ringo pantomimed a drumbeat against the scuffed metal wall. Elvis playfully punched his arm. Kids joking around.

There was something unreal about it all. The container with its blood-flecked floor, the disco beat and stupid laughter, Elvis with his monster BO and Ringo with his noxious cigarette and swamp-gas farts. Being killed was one thing, but to go this way, a prisoner in a fucking tin can, worked over by brain-dead mopes until her heart gave out—

It wasn't right. It was fucking unacceptable.

She thought about that, and she felt something stir

inside her, something roused from long sleep.

Something familiar.

Elvis quit messing around and yanked her to her knees. Ringo grabbed the strap that dangled from the ceiling and passed it under the handcuff chain, then tied it into a loop in a series of complicated knots. She stayed very still, putting up no resistance. There was nothing she could do.

The webbing must be the same stuff that was used to lash down the containers. Some kind of woven polyester, flexible as rope and tough as steel. She could never cut through it, even if she had something to cut it with, and she was sure she couldn't undo Ringo's knots. The guy must've earned some serious merit badges.

When he was done, he said something to Elvis, who'd positioned himself by the hook in the wall. Elvis took hold of his end of the strap and drew it in, hand over hand, winding it around the hook. Bonnie had known what was coming, but somehow it still took her by surprise as the strap tautened, pulling her arms up over her head, then lifting her off her knees in a series of stops and starts.

The steel cuffs bit into the sides of her hands. She arched her back against a pulse of pain. Her legs straightened. The floor dropped away. Bright lines of burning heat shot through her shoulders.

Now her feet were barely touching the plywood. She could just balance herself on the toes of her sneakers. It was the only way to get any relief from the stretched agony in her arms.

This kind of thing had looked like a lot more fun in *Fifty Shades*.

Now she was really starting to wish Elvis had double-locked the cuffs. As it was, downward pressure would move the ratchets, drawing the cuffs progressively tighter until her wrists were painfully squeezed, the blood circulation to her hands cut off. The only way to relieve that pressure was to keep herself precariously balanced. Even then, the edges of the cuffs sawed into her wrists, chafing and biting, drawing blood.

Elvis tied the strap in position. She was left dangling from the ceiling with her feet just barely in contact with the floor.

Ringo gave her a little push. She began to revolve, the room wheeling around her. He blew a gust of noxious cigarette smoke in her face.

She hung there, slowly spinning. Her feet sought purchase on the plywood but kept missing it. She was forced to grab hold of the strap to prevent the cuffs from notching tighter on her wrists. But her hands were sweaty and their purchase on the strap was tenuous at best. She felt one of the cuffs click down another notch.

Probably they wanted her to scream or cry. She wouldn't. Fuck them.

Finally she steadied herself. She touched the floor and made the slow revolutions stop. Head lowered, she struggled to breathe.

She'd been suspended like this for only a minute or so. Arian had said she might last ten days. Ten days before it was over, before her body went into the ocean.

Elvis stepped away from the wall. He and Ringo studied her, grinning like jackals.

Then Ringo raised her shirt—the short-sleeve tee emblazoned *You Can't Handle This*—and removed the cigarette from his mouth. He pressed the burning end against her bare abdomen, twisting the cigarette, stubbing it out on her flesh.

Still she didn't scream. Teeth gritted, she bit back any protest. But her eyes watered, and she knew her face was streaked with tears.

The cigarette came away, leaving the ragged blister of a burn mark.

Elvis leaned up against her and pantomimed humping her with loud grunts and big thrusts of his pelvis. Ringo laughed, and Elvis laughed, and Ringo farted, and they both laughed louder, and the music throbbed and blared.

And all the while the thing inside her grew, taking shape, as it had in a mobile home in the desert.

Ringo slapped her ass. His buddy gave one of her tits a hard squeeze. Big fun. Wild hilarity.

"Laugh now, assholes," she muttered.

She would be the one laughing later. How she would manage it, she had no idea. But she wasn't going to die in a damn shipping crate, dangling like a side of beef.

Elvis unsheathed the knife on his arm. He turned it in his grip, letting the blade flash in the fluorescent light. Letting her see it, admire its sharpness.

She watched almost without interest, feeling no fear, only the strange calm of pure and perfect rage, the unblinking eye of a storm.

The knife traveled to her side, then descended, slitting her pants leg, not yet cutting flesh.

The flaps of fabric parted, exposing her bare leg from her hip to her ankle. Ringo whistled. Elvis leered, breathing his bad breath into her face. She stared back.

"Bring it," she said slowly. "Bring everything you got."

He might not understand English, but he knew she was issuing a challenge. Daring the two of them to hurt her. To do their worst.

Elvis raised the knife again. He licked his lips. He had ideas now. He wanted to get busy.

"*Ti ndal*," Ringo said. Anxiously he pulled his partner aside to confer with him. Bonnie could guess the gist of the conversation. These two were expected on deck. Kyle had said Arian wanted all his men to take part in the ambush he'd planned for Shaban.

Ringo's argument carried the day. Grudgingly, Elvis sheathed his knife. Ringo silenced the boombox.

In the doorway Elvis paused to blow her a wet kiss before flipping down the light switch. Ringo followed him outside, releasing a final burst of intestinal gases as he went.

The double doors clanged shut, sealing her in darkness. She heard the slide of the lock bars, the clicks of padlocks. After that, fast footsteps retreating across the floor, and the distant clang of footfalls on the metal stairs.

She was alone. Locked in. Chained like a prisoner in a dungeon.

She knew how it would be when her new friends returned. They would strip her naked and then use the knife and cigarettes and whatever they had stowed in that tool chest. And there would be more rust-colored stains on the floor.

She could take it. Whatever they did to her, she wouldn't die. She would find a way to work herself free. She'd done it before.

She would get loose and she would arm herself and she would hunt them down and kill them—all of them—Elvis and Ringo and the crew from Brighton Cove and old Arian Dragusha himself.

And Kyle Ridley. Oh, yes.

Definitely Kyle.

34

SHABAN ARRIVED AT the docks at three o'clock. Lou and Joey rode in the Porsche with him. He'd tracked them to a nightclub in Manhattan and spent time pouring coffee down their throats to sober them up. They hadn't been happy about leaving the club, where they were both convinced they were going to score with a couple of cheap-looking pickups. But they'd gone with him, because they were loyal. He could trust them, even if he could trust no one else.

The guard at the terminal gate knew him by sight and let them in without asking questions. He drove directly onto the pier. He was parking a few yards from the freighter when he spotted a woman striding down the gangway.

At first he thought it was Parker he saw. The hat on her head and the purse over her shoulder confused him. But as she came closer, he made out dark hair and big eyeglasses and Kyle Ridley's face.

If Kyle was leaving the ship of her own volition, without Parker as an escort, then she had not been a prisoner. Something else was going on.

She had never seen his car, and she didn't realize he was there until he threw open the door and sprang out, grabbing her by the arm. To her credit, she barely flinched.

"Where is she?" he asked.

"Who?"

He slapped her face. "Where is she?" he asked again, without raising his voice.

"I don't know what you're talking about."

"Why are you here?"

"Let go of me."

She had come here to meet Arian, her employer. This much he knew. But he saw no reason for it. She had failed in her assignment. She should not have been willing to risk seeing him again.

His gaze strayed past her face to the looming bulk of the *Mazeppa,* immense against a moving wall of fog. A dark figure stood on the bridge wing, looking down.

His grandfather. Watching them.

Shaban studied the distant silhouette. He could not see the old man's eyes, but he could feel their angry, hateful intensity, powerful as an electric current.

And he understood. It had been a trap. A trap for Parker—and for himself, too, maybe.

He wasn't worried about himself. And he had no personal feelings for Bonnie Parker. She meant nothing to him. But he had given his *besa* to her. He had sworn there would be no retribution on account of her involvement with Kyle Ridley. If she was in trouble now, the fault was not his directly, but his family had done it, his *fil.* And that made it his responsibility.

Joey and Lou were beside him now, silent and bewildered. He returned his attention to the girl.

"Give me the purse."

Her mouth twisted in a scornful smile. "You robbing me?"

"Give it."

She unslung the purse from her shoulder and handed it over. He looked inside. He saw bricks of cash, many of them, and he knew why the girl had come.

Exploring further, he found a hidden compartment, and in it, a Walther .22 and a silencer. Parker's gear. He recognized the gun from the motel room.

"Is she alive?" he asked Kyle.

She gave up on her pretense of ignorance. "Yes."

"In the hold?"

"I don't know where they put her."

This was probably a lie. But it didn't matter. The question had been unnecessary. Shaban knew where prisoners of the *Mazeppa* were kept.

He took the gun from the purse, leaving the silencer and the cash inside. The gun went into the side pocket of his jacket. He gave the purse back to the girl. He cared nothing about the money. Let her have it—if she survived.

"I'm leaving now," Kyle said firmly.

"Not yet. I talk to Parker, find out what's going on. Anything we still don't know, you will fill in for us."

"Why would I?"

"To save yourself pain."

"I thought you gave your word you wouldn't hurt me."

"Sure, yes. So I did." He smiled. "But Parker did not."

She took that in. He saw a slight tremor in her throat, her first sign of fear.

"Come on," he said, pulling her toward the gangway, with Joey and Lou trailing behind. "We go to her."

"Your grandfather won't like it."

Shaban tossed another glance at the silent, immobile figure on the bridge.

"This I know," he said grimly.

35

THERE WAS PAIN in her wrists and pain in her shoulders and a hot brand of pain at the nape of her neck, but none of it mattered. All that mattered was survival, and Bonnie was savagely sure she would survive.

She only needed to get out of the handcuffs. Free her hands, and she could slip out of the noose Ringo had tied around the chain.

She knew all about picking locks, and a handcuff lock was especially easy. You could defeat it with nearly anything narrow and bendy. A paperclip or a bobby pin. She had neither.

If she'd worn a watch, she might have been able to use the metal tongue on the watchband's clasp to poke around in one of the handcuffs' keyholes. She wasn't sure the method was practical, but since she didn't wear a watch, the point was moot.

Moot? She was starting to sound like Kyle, with her gang aft higgily-piggily bullshit.

There was the underwire of her bra. Nice thought, but she'd need an extra pair of hands to reach it. Other than that, she had on nothing but sneakers, jeans, and a short-sleeve shirt.

Hold it. There was one more item. The plastic bangle on her right wrist, her shooting gallery prize.

No, it wouldn't serve as a picklock.

But as a shim ...

225

ON THE BRIDGE wing, Arian stared after Shaban and the others as they made their way forward on the main deck.

To Raco he said, "Give me your radio."

The man handed over a walkie-talkie. Arian hit the transmit key and raised Zamir.

"Did you take care of the prisoner?" he asked in Albanian.

"Stowed and secured." The man's voice echoed. He and Timir must still be on one of the ladderways in the scuttle leading up from the hold. "She is a tigress. Will be fun to break her."

Arian cared nothing about that. Parker was unimportant, a mere detail.

"Where are you now?"

"Climbing up on the starboard side."

"Go back down."

"Sir?"

"Shaban is here," Arian said briskly. "He is headed for bay number three with some friends. He intends to free the prisoner. You must stop him."

"Free her? I don't understand."

Arian very nearly told him he did not need to understand, only to obey. With effort he mastered himself. "Parker and Shaban are working together. Shaban sent her to kill me. Now he has come aboard the *Mazeppa* with his accomplices to free Parker and finish the job. Do you see what you must do?"

A long pause followed. Arian knew Zamir was consulting with his partner. He could only wait. Probably the two would accept his story. They'd had little contact with Shaban, and Arian thought he might be able to trust their loyalty. But he could not be certain. Not about them. Not about anyone.

◉

SHIMMING A HANDCUFF was simple in principle. You slid a narrow strip into the ratchet mechanism, then clicked the ratchet over a notch or two. While the teeth lifted off the pawl, you forced the shim in deeper, preventing the ratchet from engaging again. After that, the cuff's swing arm would just drop open.

Bonnie had been unhappy with Elvis for not double-locking the handcuffs. But maybe he'd done her a favor. A double-locked cuff couldn't be shimmed. A single-locked cuff could.

And the bracelet on her wrist just might get the job done.

FINALLY ZAMIR'S VOICE crackled over the walkie-talkie. "Who is with Shaban?"

"Luan and Jozef," Arian said. "And also the American girl, Kyle Ridley."

"That one? She gave us Parker."

"Only to save herself. She has been playing a double game." Arian was losing patience. "You have your orders. Can I count on you?"

"Yes, sir."

The words were all right, but Arian detected a troubling note of doubt. "For this service," he said, "you will receive a bonus. Fifty thousand dollars American—apiece."

That would be more money than the men had seen in their lives.

"Thank you, sir." This time there was no doubt whatsoever.

Arian gazed across the tops of the stacked containers. On the main deck, Shaban and the others were approaching one of the two hatchways to the hold.

"They will start down in a minute or two, using the

227

port hatchway. Set up your position below and take them by surprise." Arian tightened his clutch on the handset. "And kill them all."

◉

To use the bracelet as a shim, she first had to break it so there would be a leading edge to push into the slot. She rotated her wrists until the fingers of her left hand came into contact with the bangle on her opposite wrist. She began to bend the plastic, weakening it.

Six times ... seven ... ten ... fifteen ...

Snap.

◉

Zamir climbed swiftly down the ladder, Timir just below him. The two of them had nearly reached the open hatchway when the old man had raised them on the radio. Now they had to retrace their steps, and do it fast.

This new development was unexpected and a little troubling. Ordinarily, Zamir had no qualms about killing. He had grown up slaughtering chickens and goats. The chickens had bored him, but the goats had given him much laughter. They were so frolicsome and childlike, nearly human. He had enjoyed cutting their throats.

Later he had found more joy in cutting other throats.

No, killing in general was all right, but taking out Arian Dragusha's grandson was serious business.

Zamir understood very little of the ways of great ones, and the Wolf was the greatest man he knew. Always he operated on the premise that the rich and mighty had good reasons for their actions, however baffling those actions might be.

The old women of his village had called him *budalla*, slow. But he knew how to use what brains he had. With dogged devotion he had ingratiated himself with Arian Dragusha. He who leans on a big tree will never lack shade, so the proverb went.

Timir was younger, less far-seeing. He liked his work. He liked everything. Zamir had seldom seen him frown. People said he was a fool, a *tarallak*, with his noisy farts and his idiot grin. But he, too, had proven his loyalty to the Wolf, and like Zamir, he would not lack for shade.

So all was well. He and Timir had found their place in the world, and they were satisfied. And now, out of nowhere, had come the order to kill Shaban Dragusha. It worried him. Because here was the thing.

There were big killings and little killings. Most of the victims who had gone into the container had been little killings. The girl, Parker, for instance. An individual of no account.

Shaban Dragusha, though—he was a big killing. And for a big killing, there were always repercussions.

Zamir arrived at the highest landing and followed Timir down the first of the many staircases called ladderways by the crew.

"His own grandson." He spoke the thought aloud.

Timir glanced back at him. His round, stupid face was untroubled. He looked eager and cheerful. He might have been on a picnic. He had considered no consequences beyond the promised $50,000 in American money. Doubtless he was already making plans to spend it on women and drink and a shiny new car. Maybe that attitude was best.

There was another proverb from the old country: He who hesitates, regrets.

Zamir nodded, having persuaded himself. He would trust in the wisdom of the Wolf.

And if this youngest cub of the litter, Shaban Dragusha, must die—so be it.

NOW TO GET the bracelet off her wrist.

She tweezed the plastic strip between two fingers and pulled it free, then tugged at it, deforming the material and flattening it out.

It was in her left hand, but she would have better control if she could transfer the bracelet to her right. Tricky business, though. Her fingers were damp with sweat, the bracelet was slippery, and if she dropped it—game over.

Slowly she passed the broken ring of plastic from one hand to the other. For a bad moment it almost squirted out of her grasp, but she held on.

ARIAN SET DOWN the radio and stared down at the deck. His mind, like a chess master's, was tracing all possible consequences of the move he had just made.

Zamir and Timir were simple men. Less intelligent than his grandson. Their ambush could fail.

Even if it succeeded, there were other risks. They would surely talk. What they said might raise questions in the minds of men more inquisitive and insightful than themselves.

His decision reached, he turned to Raco.

"Muster yours squad and wait by the portside hatch to bay three. If Zamir and Timir should fail, you will get it done, right?"

Raco had seen Shaban come aboard, had seen the cold look he gave his grandfather, had heard the radio conversation. Unlike Zamir, he did not hesitate. "If they fail, *Xhaxhi*, I will not."

"And if they do not fail ..." Arian let the thought trail away like smoke.

Raco raised an eyebrow. "Maybe me and my guys, we give them their reward?"

"Will you do this?"

"They are stupid peasants. For killing the grandson of Arian Dragusha, they deserve to die."

Arian bared his teeth in a smile.

"Good boy," he said, patting the young man's shoulder. "Good, good boy."

NEXT SHE NEEDED to feed the strip into the ratchet mechanism. It would have been easier if she could see. As it was, trapped in darkness, she had to work by feel.

After several tries, she eased the shim into the slot, where it butted up immediately against the locked ratchet. To slide it farther, she would have to click the cuff a notch or two tighter. She'd practiced the technique at home many times.

But everything was easy when it was only practice. This was the real deal, life and death, and she hadn't forgotten the evil promise in Elvis's eyes when he'd blown her a kiss from the doorway.

ARIAN PACED THE bridge, leaning on his cane. He believed he had the crisis well in hand. Zamir and Timir would eliminate Shaban and his friends. Raco and his crew would eliminate Zamir and Timir.

And Parker? He had forgotten about her. Well, she would be left unattended throughout the voyage, to perish alone in the container. Her body could be disposed of in Durrës.

A good plan, but it had a weakness. Raco was intelligent. He had agreed to go along, for now. He would do the job. But later, when he had time to think …

That was the problem. People were always thinking. Arian did not trust thinkers. They were prone to misgivings and regrets, and they asked questions.

The difficulty, however, could be managed. All that was necessary was to take care of Raco and his men at the appropriate time. He could arrange it. Perhaps something like what he had arranged for Sokol, all those years ago.

As always, the thought of Sokol pained him. How he had hated to issue the fatal order. And there had been no positive proof that Sokol was conspiring against him. Still, in the end he had chosen the prudent course. His most trusted lieutenants had carried out the deed, far from the city, where there would be no witnesses.

These days he trusted no lieutenants. He trusted no one at all. Even so, he could find a way to have Raco and his crew eliminated, perhaps by newcomers from the old country or even by a rival syndicate.

By the time it was all over, his personnel would have been thinned considerably. An unfortunate outcome, one he had hoped to avoid by having Kyle Ridley deal with Shaban. Now it could not be helped. He had to kill them all—Shaban, Luan and Josef, Zamir and Timir, Raco and his crew. Others, maybe, before he was done.

It was the only way he could fully protect himself. The only way to be sure.

36

BONNIE EXERTED STEADY pressure on the shim while tugging against the handcuff chain. The ratchet clicked. But the shim hadn't broken contact between the ratchet and pawl. It was still obstructed by the metal teeth.

Another try.

Click.

Still nothing.

The cuff on her left wrist was noticeably tighter.

Maybe this wasn't going to work. But it had to. There was no fallback position, no Plan B.

She was tensing for another try when she heard a clang of shoes on metal treads and an echo of distant voices. Elvis and Ringo, climbing down the stairway. Coming back—too soon.

She'd thought she would have more time. That was the thing. You always thought you had more time.

ZAMIR HAD WORKED it all out during the long climb down. As he and his partner took the last ladderway, he explained his plan.

"We hide in the container, the lights off, the doors open only an inch. When Shaban and the other three come down into the hold from the other stairway, we open up on them from inside."

The steel doors would provide good cover if the targets had time to shoot back. And since Shaban was headed straight for the container—to free the prisoner, the Wolf had said—he would walk directly into the line of fire.

A good plan. Zamir was uncommonly pleased with it. He had not realized he was such a fine tactician.

"What about the whore?" Timir asked.

"Who cares about her?"

"She may try to warn them off. She is working with them, the old man said."

"Do not call him the old man," Zamir chided. "It is not respectful." Actually he was merely annoyed that Timir had thought of a problem he himself had overlooked. "I will knock her out. One punch to the back of her skull."

"But not kill her?"

"Of course not kill her. She is for the voyage."

"We will fuck her, yes?"

Zamir shrugged. "Yes, we will fuck her."

Fucking was just part of the job when the captive was a woman. And a man, too, sometimes. Zamir was not particular.

"I mean," Timir persisted, "do we fuck her right now?"

"Sure, we fuck her. We fuck her as soon as Shaban and the others are dead."

What the hell, it would not take long, and the kid would have earned it.

Timir hopped off the last step, and Zamir followed. Quickly they crossed the open floor.

High above, a booming clang of metal announced that the portside hatch lid had been thrown open.

Shaban and his people were coming. Time was short.

THE FOOTSTEPS HAD reached floor level. They were approaching the container. Moving fast.

Okay, no more dicking around. She had to make this work, and she had to do it *now*.

Still balanced on tiptoe, she tugged against the chain, heard the click of the ratchet—

Nothing.

The shim still hadn't fed any more deeply into the slot. It might be just a millimeter too thick to negotiate the narrow clearance.

The cuff was really tight now. Her wrist was on fire, her fingers going numb.

Still, she thought she could advance the ratchet one more notch.

So this was it. Her last shot.

She clicked the ratchet and felt the shim engage.

In the moment when the teeth had lifted, the stubborn slip of plastic had finally nosed its way deeper into the mechanism, separating the ratchet from the pawl.

Bonnie drew back the swing arm, and the cuff opened.

She dropped down, nearly collapsing as her knees threatened to buckle under her.

Screw that. She didn't have time for weakness.

The footsteps had stopped just outside the container doors.

In darkness she groped her way to the tool chest. She threw open the drawers, rummaging blindly, seeking a weapon. Found knives, grabbed one. Anything else? A small metal cylinder with a trigger. Fire extinguisher? No, acetylene torch. She didn't want to know what the bastards used it for.

The padlocks rattled. The lock bars slid back. She reached the front of the container and pressed herself against the side wall just inside the doorway. The doors opened, Ringo entering first, his hand flipping the wall switch. The fluorescent light came on, throwing its white glow on his face and on Elvis, immediately behind him.

She saw the slight widening of Ringo's eyes as he registered the empty strap hanging down from the ceiling hook. As he turned in her direction, she drove the knife blade into his neck, directly under the chin, forcing it deep.

His beard changed color with a surge of red. Blood sprayed the walls, her clothes, her face. She left the knife embedded to the hilt and hugged the body as it jerked and quivered, using it as a shield.

Elvis was fast. He'd already drawn his Glock. His arm came up, the gun leading, and Bonnie fired the blowtorch at his face.

The shriek he let loose was a wounded animal's cry. His gun fired three times, the shots going wild, rounds ricocheting off the steel walls. She thrust Ringo at him, encumbering him with the corpse, and grabbed his gun hand.

Part of his face—his chin, his lower lip, the edge of his cheek—was a red blister of puckered flesh, his beard scorched off with an acrid smell of burning hair. He held on to the gun. It went off again, the bullet lodging in the plywood floor.

SHABAN HAD BEEN the first one to enter the shaft, and he was first down every staircase. He was nearing the next landing in his descent when he heard a crackle of gunfire.

Frozen, he and the others listened. The shots were coming from the bottom of the hold.

"Is a trap." Shaban pointed upward. "Back. We go back."

They started climbing, with Kyle positioned behind Lou and ahead of Joey.

There was no point in trying to rescue Parker now. Most likely she was dead already. If so, only Kyle knew the details of the plot against him.

"Why did he do it?" he yelled up the stairway at the girl. "Why would he make me his target?"

Kyle glanced down. "He doesn't trust you."

"I have given him no reason for mistrust."

"He doesn't trust anybody. He's just a crazy old man."

At any other time Shaban would not have tolerated this insult to his *krye*. Now he could only nod. The girl spoke truth.

To do what he had done, the Wolf must truly be out of his mind.

◉

IN THE CONTAINER, Bonnie and Elvis were doing a dance.

At least, it might have been a dance, the way they swayed together, hand in hand. She held the wrist of his gun hand, while he had a firm grip on the hand holding the acetylene torch. Both weapons were temporarily rendered useless. But Elvis was stronger than she was, and with slow determination he was lifting the gun, struggling to get it into position to fire into her body.

"*Kurvë*," he muttered through his blistered lips. "*Lavire*."

Ringo's corpse was sandwiched between them, a bloody ménage à trois. Bonnie had never been in a three-way and she wasn't happy about being in this one. But with the gun climbing higher, it didn't look like she would be in it for long.

Elvis knew it, too. The part of his mouth that hadn't been seared like flank steak curved into a smile.

In another few seconds the gun would be pointed in her direction, and he would squeeze off a shot.

All right, improvise.

She released his gun hand. Before he could react, she plucked the knife out of Ringo's neck and thrust it forward.

The gun fired again, the shot just missing her, as the knifepoint plunged through Elvis's right eye and punched into his brain.

He fell against the open door and collapsed, half inside the container and half out.

Bonnie staggered back, letting Ringo drop heavily on the plywood floor. Two corpses. And they wouldn't be the last.

She hadn't been kidding around when she'd sworn to take out all the bad guys. They'd messed with her, and now she was going to mess with them, and they were not going to like it.

You could ask Anton Streinikov about that, or Frank Lazzaro, or the Long Fong Boyz.

It occurred to her that she taken a pledge to reform. To play by the rules, color within the lines. To call the police if she was ever in a situation like this—not take the law into her own hands like a goddamn vigilante.

Yeah, that was what she'd promised. But who was she fooling?

She was a loner and a killer, and the only rules she played by were the ones she made up as she went along. She would fight her own battle, and she would spill blood and make corpses, as she had been born to do.

She knew the thing inside her, that bright, compacted diamond of crystalline rage, would settle for nothing less.

SHABAN AND HIS party reached the next landing and started up. The only option now was to go to the bridge and confront his grandfather. The two of them must speak face to face. No more of this sneaking around, this secret suspicion. Let the chips fall on the table—he believed this was the American expression. Or was it dice?

New gunfire tore into his thoughts. Not from below. Above.

At the top of the staircase Lou screamed and toppled backward, dislodging Kyle and Joey behind him.

More shots pinged off the walls. A shooting party was on the landing above, firing down.

Shaban jumped onto the lower landing and kicked open the door to the walkway. He crouched in the doorway, taking cover there. Kyle and Joey scrambled to join him. Joey was bleeding, his tan shirt rapidly turning red. Lou lay sprawled on the stairs, unmoving.

"Ambush," Joey said, his teeth chattering in terror or shock.

More shots from above. Shaban pulled Joey deeper into the niche afforded by the open door. When he glanced over his shoulder to check on Kyle, he saw that she was gone.

She must have run off while he was distracted. The door at the far end of the walkway was slowly swinging shut on pneumatic hinges.

"Can you walk?" he asked Joey.

"No."

Shaban could not leave a man behind. To do so would be cowardly, dishonorable.

"Can you shoot?" he asked.

Joey nodded, lifting his Smith 9.

"Okay. Cover me." With retreat impossible, the only choice was to advance. Launch himself up the stairs and trust to Joey and St. Bessus to protect him.

And to his *American Gangster* gun, of course. The FEG 9mm, loaded with fifteen rounds.

Gripping the pistol tightly, he threw himself to his feet and took the staircase at a run.

KNEELING, BONNIE RETRIEVED Ringo's gun. It was a Sig Sauer .380 with a full magazine, six rounds. She rifled his pockets and found one spare magazine, which she slipped into the side pocket of her jeans. On Elvis's body she discovered a handcuff key. With it, she removed the cuff from her left wrist. Both wrists were sore, chafed, bleeding a little. Didn't matter. She would live.

She took Elvis's walkie-talkie from his back pocket, but his hand stubbornly refused to give up the Glock. His fingers had tightened around it in a death grip. The guy was a pain in the ass right to the end.

She returned to the toolbox and wiped the blood off her face with a rag. In an odds-and-ends drawer she found a spool of duct tape, which she used to repair the long slit in the leg of her jeans. She didn't need it flapping around and tripping her up when she was on the move.

Elvis's radio started to sputter. "Zamir? Zamir?"

Arian's voice. He sounded worried, which he ought to be.

Bonnie thumbed the transmit button as she stepped over the bodies, out of the container.

"Sorry, asshole. Elvis has left the building."

SHABAN CHARGED HARD up the stairway. Below him, Joey fired off a series of shots directed at the higher landing.

He was almost to the top of the stairs when Joey's gun fell silent. Out of ammunition, maybe.

Without covering fire, Shaban was abruptly unprotected. Retreat was impossible. His only option was to keep going, even as gunfire opened up from above.

He was hit once—twice—leg and arm—but the shots were panicky and most were wasted. He saw Raco, the one with the white stripe in his beard like a badger's marker, and the three men in Raco's crew, and he picked them off, Raco first, then the others, pop-pop-pop, and then he was on the landing and men were scattered around him, groaning and bleeding, stunned by pain.

He had to fight the impulse to deliver the coup de grace. It would not be the Christian thing to do.

Returning to the lower landing, he checked on Joey.

His friend was slumped sideways, the Smith dangling from his slack fingers. His shirt was all red now. In the middle of the gunfight he had bled out, dying as easily as falling asleep.

"Bless you, my friend," Shaban said, gently closing Joey's eyes.

His FEG 9mm was empty now. He pocketed it and took out Parker's .22. He ascended the stairs again, ignoring the men who writhed on the upper landing. Perhaps they would live. Perhaps not. He did not care.

The Wolf was the only man who mattered now.

37

ELVIS HAS LEFT the building ... Elvis has left the building ...

Arian Dragusha had no idea what this meant. The words were impenetrably cryptic. But he had recognized the voice that spoke those words, and that was enough.

Parker had outmaneuvered Zamir and Timir. Killed them, undoubtedly. She could not have commandeered the radio otherwise.

How could she have gotten loose? Evidently they had not secured her properly. *Gomarë.* Donkeys. They deserved to die.

With them out of the way, the burden was entirely on Raco and his men.

They, at least, would not fail.

THE SLOW DRIP of blood from an upper landing on the port stairwell caught Bonnie's attention as she headed up. She slowed her pace, but only a little. She was past fear, past caution, in a strangely calm zone of pure, driving rage.

On the landing she found two young men, both dead. One had tumbled down the stairs, his chest pockmarked with bullet holes. The other was slumped in a doorway.

She took the next set of stairs. As she neared the top, she heard low groans and a rustle of clothing. Someone was alive up there. Several someones, it sounded like.

Emerging onto the landing, she surveyed the area, counting four men on the floor. One guy had to be dead; he lay facedown in a maroon puddle. The other three were breathing, but all shot up. It appeared the odds against her had just improved considerably.

She took a closer look at the victims. One of them was the hitter with the striped beard Brad had described to her. The other three must be his posse.

Their leader, half-waking as he became aware of her, groped feebly for a gun that lay just beyond his reach.

"Pretty sure you guys were looking for me a little earlier," Bonnie said standing over him. "Congratulations. You just found me."

She shot him in the face. A red puff of brains decorated the floor.

With quick precision she dispatched the other two who'd shown signs of life. She did it without vindictiveness, just two trigger pulls at close range.

Spots of blood led up the next staircase. Shaban's blood, she was guessing. He hadn't been among the casualties.

She climbed higher, following the blood trail.

SHABAN WAS BREATHING hard by the time he emerged from the shaft. His wounds weren't bleeding too badly, and no bones were broken, but the pain was beginning to wear him down.

Strangely, there had been no pain at first, only a peculiar numbness. The first intimations of pain had reached him on the last of the staircases he'd climbed, and by the time he'd scaled the ladder, both his right leg and his left arm had been pulsing in hot agony. It hadn't stopped him, though. Prayer had given him strength. Prayer—and the teeth-clenched determination to face his grandfather.

As he climbed out, he heard gunshots from below. Three shots, evenly spaced, as precise as the ticks of a metronome. He didn't understand it. But it didn't matter now.

He approached the deckhouse, struggling to keep his balance as his right leg trembled under him. An exterior door whose sign warned *Restricted Area* led him into a narrow hall on the main floor, where the galley and lounge were located. Not far away there was, thank God, an elevator. He did not think he could have climbed the six flights of stairs to the bridge.

It was possible that his grandfather was no longer on the bridge, even that he was no longer aboard the *Mazeppa* at all. But the bridge was where Shaban had last seen him, and he did not think Arian Dragusha would run from a fight.

The elevator doors opened. Shaban lurched inside and slumped against the wall. With effort he pressed the button for the highest floor.

As the car ascended, he steadied himself. He wished he had some water. Possibly he should have detoured into the galley to get some. He was terribly thirsty. Thirsty and hot. His face felt flushed. His vision was not as sharp as it should have been.

When he looked down, he saw blood pooling around his right shoe. The wound in his leg was bleeding worse than before. The exercise of climbing must have opened it wider. He thought of how Joey had bled out on the landing. What he needed was a tourniquet. The bullet had sliced through the meaty part of his calf; if he could tie off the leg just below the knee, he could stanch the flow. Even the sleeve of his shirt would do the job. He pawed at the sleeve but gave up. He lacked the strength to tear it off, much less to secure it to his leg.

The doors slid open. He tensed, half expecting another volley of gunfire. If his grandfather had bodyguards with him, they would surely kill him on sight.

There was no gunfire. The corridor that faced him was empty.

He staggered out of the elevator and down the short

hallway. The floor was illuminated with red LEDs, like the exit lights in the aisle of an airplane. A dim red tunnel, like a passage into hell. He went past the chart room, onto the bridge. Just inside the doorway, he stopped.

The Wolf was there, standing alone in the middle of the long room, waiting.

"You have killed them," his grandfather said, not asking a question.

"I got past them. Some may live."

"Luan, Jozef?"

"Dead."

"Kyle Ridley?"

"Missing."

"Parker?"

"I do not know. I never got that far."

The Wolf nodded. He leaned more heavily on his cane, both hands clasped tightly on the polished knob. "She may have lived. She killed two of my people."

Shaban remembered those last few shots. "Yes," he said slowly. "It is possible."

"I underestimated her."

"You underestimated me, *gjysh*." Shaban took an unsteady step forward. Parker's gun was in his hand, pointed vaguely in Arian Dragusha's direction, but he had no intention of firing. Not yet. "You make such big plans, but now all your plans are fallen apart."

"Was bad luck, that is all."

Or God's grace, Shaban thought. "Kyle Ridley says you distrust me. Is this so?"

"It is so."

"I have given you no cause to question my loyalty."

"Your very existence is a cause. You are a dangerous man, Shaban. Perhaps you do not even know it yourself. But there is much of your father in you."

It was the second time tonight that Arian had made this point. "What about my father?"

The old man shrugged. "Sokol was like you. Young, ambitious. Popular with the others. I began to notice how they looked to him for leadership. The same way men like Jozef and Luan had begun to look to you."

"I never tried to gain their loyalty."

"It was not necessary for you to try. You could accomplish it without trying. Just as he did."

Shaban focused his eyes on the frail figure who stood watching him from yards away. "What happened to my father?"

"He was a threat to me. I had him killed."

"You ...?" He could not complete the question. Could not think.

"I sent Sokol to Rome, in upstate New York, on a pretext. Men I trusted took care of him there. It was blamed on a rival clan. Only the men who'd done the job, my most trusted lieutenants, knew the truth. No one else. Except Saranda."

"My mother?"

"She guessed my secret. She said nothing, but I saw it in her face. But she was wise. She left this country and returned home. She did her best to keep you there. She knew that if you were to come to America and learn the truth, you would feel bound by duty to avenge your father."

"And now—now I do know."

"Indeed." His grandfather lifted his head. There was something gallant in the way he stood, unprotected, unafraid. "You have a weapon. Use it."

Shaban had nearly forgotten the gun in his hand. He took a long look at it. Slowly he advanced a few steps farther into the room.

"Did you distrust me," he asked "because you feared I would learn about my father, or because you thought I was ambitious like him?"

"I distrust everybody," Arian Dragusha said evenly, "for

all reasons." He added in a lower voice, "I have lived a long time."

The words were not a boast. They were perhaps a kind of apology. To have lived so long in the world he inhabited, a man must learn to trust no one.

Shaban stopped six feet from his grandfather. He raised the gun. It was a small weapon, yet heavy in his hand. The pain in his leg, he noticed distantly, had receded again. He was numb down there. Numb below the knee. His left arm, too, hanging useless—it was empty of sensation. He wondered if he would ever feel anything in those limbs again. Ever feel anything anywhere.

"Honor," he whispered.

The old man cocked his head. "Eh?"

"Honor demands the satisfaction of blood."

"This I know."

Shaban's mind worked slowly. It was true that his father's blood pleaded for vengeance. But it was also true that he had sworn undying loyalty to the man before him. To kill him now would be to confirm his grandfather's suspicions.

And yet to cancel the debt—to leave his father una-venged—and Joey and Lou—to set aside all that, and the insults to himself ...

It was much to ask. The harder path, by far.

His hand opened. The gun clattered on the floor.

"Here is how I prove my loyalty, *baba*. I take no re-venge. I seek no power. I honor my word to you."

His grandfather stared at him. "I have misjudged you," he said softly.

"Sure, yes. So you have. But I forgive."

"Come to me, *dashur*."

The word meant *dearest*. A word Shaban had never before heard from Arian Dragusha.

In three long shuffling steps he closed the distance between them. He embraced his grandfather.

"You never had anything to fear," Shaban whispered. "Always I take the course of honor."

Shaban heard a soft click. He had time to think that the cane had shifted in his grandfather's grip, and then a sudden paralyzing pain tore through his rib cage.

"Stupid boy," Arian Dragusha said. "In this country there is no honor."

The old man stepped back, and something long and sharp slid out of Shaban's chest like an infinitely painful needle.

A stiletto. Polished steel. Secreted in the handle of the walking stick until, with a click of the knob, it had sprung to hand.

His grandfather smiled. "The Wolf is old, but he still has claws."

Shaban fell on his side. His mouth was open. He tasted copper. He thought of his mother in Elbasan. Of a puppet show they had seen together when he was five years old. He had laughed and laughed. Silly puppets, battling over nothing, dancing on their strings. A good show. How he had laughed ...

His body shivered all over, and then it did not move again.

ARIAN DRAGUSHA WIPED the blade of the stiletto on a handkerchief, then carefully replaced the dagger in the cane. It was a true antique, dating to the 1820s, owned originally by a French aristocrat. The hidden knife had saved his life more than once, and he did not doubt that it had done so again.

His grandson's magnanimity was noble, yes, but Arian did not trust noble gestures. He knew how readily second thoughts could creep in, making such gestures look hollow and foolish. Shaban had been injured, weak, confused. Were he to recover, who could say what his frame of mind might be in a day, a month, a year?

Better to dispatch him now, while he was helpless and trusting. Saranda, naturally, would be distraught—and yet not surprised. She must have foreseen this outcome all along.

All was over, then. Zamir and Timir, Raco and his men, and Shaban—all dead or incapacitated. The two females might live, but they were of no great moment, and each could be hunted down in time.

He had won. Oddly, he felt no exhilaration at his triumph, nor even the milder pleasure of relief. He felt nothing. Well, he was not young. Age had blunted his emotions. But it had not dulled his cunning.

He smiled at that thought, his lips stretching to bare his teeth under his beard, and then in the doorway of the bridge he saw Bonnie Parker.

She was not smiling.

BONNIE HAD CLIMBED to the main deck and followed the blood trail to the elevator, but she'd chosen to take the stairs. She didn't trust elevators in a situation like this. There were too many surprises possible when the doors opened.

The deckhouse's central stairway took her to the top floor. She heard voices from the bridge. Shaban and his grandfather. Then a soft thud, like a body falling. By the time she approached the doorway, the old man was tamping a knife into the top of his cane, and Shaban was dead.

Now she regretted not taking the elevator. She might have arrived a few seconds sooner. It could have made a difference. She would never know.

Arian Dragusha caught her gaze. He showed no fear.

His smile did not fade.

"You killed my men," he said, sounding more curious than concerned.

"Elvis and Ringo? Yeah. The others Shaban got, I think. I just finished 'em off."

"And now you will do the same to me."

"That's the plan."

He pointed to a safe in the corner. "There is money inside. Cash money, a lot. I will pay you—"

"Save it. How many people have you put aboard this boat anyway? In that container?"

"I cannot give a number. Many. No one important."

"I guess I wasn't important, either."

Arian thought it over. Then, surprisingly, he laughed. Not one of his hoarse death-rattle chuckles, but a rich laugh of genuine merriment. "This is true. Your life meant nothing to me."

"No one's life means anything to you. Not even his."

She let her gaze flick to the body on the floor.

"You cared about him, yes?" Arian asked.

Had she? Not really. Shaban Dragusha had been a drug importer, a mobster, and he would have killed her if he'd had the chance. But ...

"He was a better man than you," she said quietly.

Arian nodded. "He was the better man. That is why he had to die."

Bonnie squeezed the trigger twice—a double tap, one in the forehead, one in the heart—and the Wolf crumbled, his frail body simply folding up, all but disappearing under a wrinkled heap of clothes.

38

SHE STILL DIDN'T trust the elevator. Making her way down the central stairway, she fumbled in her pants pocket for the .380's spare magazine.

What she found was a hole. Elvis's knife had done more than just slit her pants leg. It had torn open the pocket, allowing the magazine to drop out at some point while she was on the run.

Shit. How light on ammo was she? She did the math. Six rounds to start with. Three shots on the landing to dispatch the wounded gangbangers. Two shots to kill Arian Dragusha.

One round left. She hoped she wouldn't need it.

As she neared the main level, she heard footsteps in the corridor below.

She paused, peering over the railing. A slim female figure breezed into view. Her face was invisible, but Bonnie recognized the hat.

Kyle, Kyle, Crocodile ...

She'd assumed the girl was already off the ship. She'd expected to have to chase her in the outside world—maybe all the way to Honolulu. But Kyle had just made it real easy.

The girl's head tilted as she threw a nervous glance up the stairwell. She saw Bonnie, froze, then broke into a run.

Bonnie plunged down the last flight of stairs and went after her. Only one bullet left. But that was okay.

One was all she would need.

From a doorway down the hall came a clang of metal. She looked in. The galley.

The overhead lights were off, the room dark. There was no sign of Kyle, but above a long stainless steel island, a row of hanging pots and pans swung as if jostled.

The girl had taken cover behind the island. Bonnie had glimpsed the purse strapped to her shoulder. The Walther still ought to be inside, and by now Kyle must be thinking about using it. She was waiting in the dark like a shooter in a blind.

There might be a way to pinpoint her location, if Bonnie could get her to talk.

"Yo, Croc," she called from the doorway.

"Fuck …" The answer came from someplace in the shadows.

"You don't sound too happy to see me."

"I was hoping you were dead."

"Not me. It's everyone else who's dead."

"Everyone?"

"Afraid so. I've been doing some killing."

"I thought you'd reformed."

"Yeah, well, best laid plans … You know how it goes."

She eased through the doorway, along a wall, staying low. She didn't anticipate an immediate attack. She was pretty sure the girl wouldn't be eager to trade shots with a professional killer.

"I expected you to be halfway to the airport by now," Bonnie said, still trying to zero in on Kyle's voice.

"Shaban caught up with me. I got away and hid until the gunfire was over. Then I came up the other stairway, the one on the starboard side."

She'd missed the dead bodies on the landing, then. "Why'd you duck inside this building?"

"I was afraid Arian would see me from the bridge. He sent killers after us. After *me*." She sounded baffled and outraged. "I—I can't trust him now."

"You never could. But Arian's not a problem any-more."

Still in a half crouch, Bonnie made her way to one end of the island. Kyle was somewhere on the other side. Probably with the Walther in her hands, ready to fire off a volley of shots as soon as she had a target.

"You could just walk away," Kyle said. "It's your most intelligent option."

"I'm not very intelligent, remember?"

"I never said that. There's a difference between education and—"

"Save it."

"I only did what was necessary to survive. There's no reason to, you know, take it personally."

Bonnie thought of the hook in the ceiling of the cargo container, Elvis and Ringo capering around her, the cigarette burn on her belly, the spatter pattern of dried blood on the floor. Her mouth tightened in a smile.

"I don't like you, Crocodile," she said softly. "And I'm not planning to forgive and forget."

Kyle didn't answer. Her last words seemed to have come from about halfway down the island. Maybe six feet away.

Bonnie figured her best move was to pivot into the long alley between the island and the counter, then trust that she could pick off Kyle before the girl nailed her. It was chancy, but if she stayed low and kept her cool, she ought to be able to make it work.

Anyway, she was bored with this conversation. And she really wanted Kyle Ridley dead.

She spun around the island, the gun out in front, and squinted into the dark. Directly alongside her, there was movement. She had time to think Kyle had fooled her, had doubled back to this end, and then the heel of Kyle's foot struck her right forearm just below the wrist.

Oh, yeah. Kickboxing. Right.

The hard shock of pain hit her a split second later, in time with the realization that she'd lost the gun. It had flown free, spinning into the dark.

Bonnie stepped back and straightened up. Kyle stood, facing her. No hat on her head. No purse in her hands. No gun.

Shaban must have taken it, or she'd lost it some other way.

So it was mano a mano. Bonnie was okay with that. The girl had some moves, yeah. But this was no strip-mall dojo. And Bonnie had learned her skills on the street.

"You wanna go, Crocodile?" she whispered.

Kyle's answer was to shift into a kickboxer's stance—feet set wide apart, knees bent, elbows drawn close over her neck with her fists raised high.

She looked almost confident. Well, she always did overestimate herself.

The girl snapped a kick at Bonnie's abdomen, but the blow was weak, delivered off-balance. Bonnie side-stepped a second kick and grabbed the first item within reach, a carving board. She feinted low, making Kyle drop her hands, then swept the board upward and caught her on the jaw.

Kyle staggered, her chin bloody. She looked momentarily confused, like an actress who'd forgotten her lines. Recovering, she threw a jab at Bonnie's midsection with her left hand, followed by a right cross to the face. Bonnie blocked both moves with the board. Kyle launched a high kick at her chest. She was impatient, easily frustrated, going for a knockout strike instead of inflicting damage by degrees.

Bonnie spun away from the kick and closed with the girl, delivering another hit with the board that tore open her cheek, then retreated, avoiding a clinch.

Kyle stumbled backward, tripped herself up, and landed helpless on her butt.

She stared up at Bonnie. Her glasses lay crooked on her face. Her mouth was lathered in red froth. A long gash ran down her cheek.

"Looks like you got some skin in the game now," Bonnie said.

"Fuck you," Kyle mumbled through bloody lips.

It would be easy enough to finish her off. Instead Bonnie tossed the carving board aside and stood catching her breath. The girl scrambled away, clawed at the counter, pulled herself to her feet. Her eyes were big and wild and just beginning to look scared.

On the counter was a knife rack. She dumped its contents and snatched up the biggest knife, one with a wide serrated blade. She held it in front of her in both hands, daring Bonnie to approach.

Bonnie took the dare. The blade came at her belly. She dodged it and kneed Kyle in the crotch. It wasn't just guys who didn't like taking hits down there. Kyle doubled over. Bonnie seized her by the hair and slammed her face into the counter. Again. Again. On the third try, there was a wet snapping sound, like the crunch of a snail. The girl's nose, breaking.

The impact shook the knife out of her grip. Bonnie chucked it aside and hopped back. Kyle spun, lashing out with an elbow strike at her head, just missing.

Close one. The kid could have done some damage if she'd connected.

Bonnie stomped on her left foot, breaking some toes, and drilled three snap punches into her gut. Kyle fell against the counter, leaning drunkenly, spilling a ribbon of vomit down her blouse. Her nose was almost comically askew, her face masked in blood and snot. Her glasses were gone, lying in pieces on the counter. Her eyes darted, seeking escape.

Not far away was the doorway to the hall. She lunged for it, nearly falling, her shoes slippery with her own puke. Bonnie took a moment to slow her breathing, then followed, not running. She knew the girl wouldn't get far.

In the hallway Kyle nearly fell against the wall, blinded by blood and pain. She swerved into the nearest room, a lounge where the crew could relax and watch videos on a flatscreen TV, or maybe play a little pool. A safe, inviting place.

Bonnie came down the hall after her. On the threshold, instinct jerked her backward just as an empty coffee carafe exploded against the doorframe. The girl, hiding beside the door, had launched it at her face.

"Missed me," Bonnie said indifferently, though in fact a few slivers of glass had embedded themselves in her cheek. She entered as Kyle retreated.

The door to the hall was the only exit. The girl was trapped in the room, and she knew it.

Kyle snatched up a pool cue from the green baize table, wielding it like a spear. Her hair was all over her face, and her shirt collar was stiff with blood. She wasn't giving up, though. Cornered, she would fight.

But it wouldn't do her any good.

Bonnie rounded the pool table. The cue stabbed at her, never connecting. Kyle backed into the narrow space between a futon and a beanbag chair. The cue was her only weapon. She clutched it in two white-knuckled fists.

Bonnie waited for the next wild jab, then grabbed the stick and wrenched it toward her, pulling the girl with it. Kyle fell against the pool table, losing the cue. Bonnie laced her fingers through one of the girl's belt loops and heaved her onto the table, flipped her on her back, then jumped up and straddled her. Kyle's fists flew up, hammering at Bonnie's face. Bonnie caught her by the thumb of her right hand and wrenched it out of its socket. Kyle shrieked. Her arm fell away, and Bonnie directed quick punches to her belly, cracking ribs. The girl's one good hand came at her, digging into her neck with her nails, scratching, gouging. Bonnie slugged her in the mouth, rocking her sideways, and punched again and again, widening the gash in the girl's cheek, almost stripping the skin from her skull. Kyle was screaming, crying. She might have been saying, "Stop." It was hard to be sure over the steady smack of fists on meat and bone.

Arms flailing, the girl writhed under her. Her head whipsawed. Blood flecked Bonnie's face. She blinked it out of her eyes. She punched again, tearing Kyle's lip like paper, then grabbed a second pool cue off the table, raising it high.

Kyle saw the weapon poised to strike. There was only fear in her eyes now. Bonnie brought it down, but in a last act of self-preservation the girl squirmed sideways, and the strike missed, the green baize ripping as the shaft cracked. Bonnie gave the cue a hard shake to throw off the broken end. She lifted the remaining portion of the cue, the jagged point bristling with splinters.

Kyle stared up at her out of a tangled mass of black hair dripping with blood.

"Please," she whispered.

Bonnie slammed down the cue with her full strength, driving the splintered tip through Kyle's neck. The girl thrashed, gargling blood, until with a twist of her wrists Bonnie ripped out her throat.

She gave a final spasm and lay still.

Then it was finished, and Kyle Ridley was only a dead thing on the table.

"Aloha, bitch," Bonnie said, climbing off.

39

BY THE TIME Bonnie got home, Mrs. Biggs was already up and about, banging around in her half of the duplex. It was what she did. She rose at dawn and banged. Bang bang bang. Around 8 PM, exhausted from a hard day's banging, she went to bed.

The banging didn't bother Bonnie. Nothing bothered her right now, not even the various pains that had been announcing themselves throughout the morning as she left the freighter, wrapped in a sailor's oilskin coat, then drove her Jeep out of the terminal and headed south, stopping to dispose of Kyle's money in a river.

In her bathroom, she washed her face. The water that spiraled down the drain was pink with blood.

She reviewed the contents of her purse. Though the Walther was gone, the silencer was still there. That was good. She was pretty sure she could get it to fit her other .22. If so, she would have a use for it tonight.

You know, it was true, what they said. A woman's work was never done.

She thought about breakfast. Normally, after seeing action, she was famished. Today she had no appetite. She decided to tend her wounds.

Rolling up her right sleeve, she saw a badly swollen purple bruise below her wrist, a reminder of Kyle's surprise attack. With a little more force, the kick might have broken her wrist, and things could have turned out very differently.

She popped some painkillers, then bandaged her cuts and the cigarette burn, smoking a cig of her own while

258

she did so. She was tweezing out the last of the glass slivers in her cheek when Sammy, still in her purse, started singing "I Will Survive."

"You and me both, pal," Bonnie said agreeably.

The caller was Mrs. Mitter, who wouldn't be requiring Bonnie's services any longer. "Bill and I—we had a talk. And ... well, everything is out in the open."

Bonnie played dumb. "He come clean about the other woman?"

"It's, um, something like that."

"Well, that's good, Gloria. Not that he's cheating, I mean. But at least he's being honest. No more lies."

She knew it was hypocritical as hell for her to say this. Her whole friggin' life was a lie.

AROUND FIVE O'CLOCK she woke up on the living-room sofa and realized she'd been down for six hours. Well, she wasn't as young as she used to be. Couldn't pull these all-nighters anymore.

She nuked something unhealthy and ate standing at the sink. A couple of cups of coffee washed it down. She'd already taken a shower, but she took another one. Somehow it was just hard to feel clean.

She changed her bandages, took more pills, and put on a shirt bearing the message *Club Sandwiches Not Seals*, a nonviolent sentiment disarmingly at odds with her purpose for the evening. By seven she was on her way out the door, with the suppressor and a Beretta .22 in her purse. It was the 1952 pistol, the one she hadn't taken last time because it was old. She figured it was okay for tonight. Edna Goodman was old, too.

Leaves were falling around her as she backed out of the garage. Halloween was coming up. She intended to give it a pass this year. She'd already been through her own personal horror show. Dracula and Frankenstein had nothing on Elvis and Ringo, and the Wolfman was no match for the Wolf.

As she was pulling away, her phone pinged with a text. The caller wasn't identified. The message was one word: *Office*.

With a secret smile, she detoured to Main Street, parking in the empty lot outside her building. She entered through the front door and climbed the staircase to the second floor.

He was waiting in the hall. He'd parked his personal car on the street—no one would find it suspicious for him to park downtown—and had entered the building through a back door, unseen. He was a cop; he had a key.

"Hey," Brad said. His face changed as she came nearer. "Whoa. What happened to you?"

"Tripped and fell."

"Must've been a heck of a stumble."

Naturally he said *heck*, not *hell*. She kinda loved that about him.

"I don't suppose," he added, "it has anything to do with what went down at Port Newark."

She hadn't turned on the news all day, but it was no surprise that the shootout had gone public. "What about Newark?" she asked innocently.

"A bunch of Albanian gangsters got shot up. Strangely enough, four of them were the same crew that came to town last night."

"Sounds like those guys really got around."

He leaned against the frame of her office door. "They might not be the only ones. Dan thinks you were involved."

"Does he? He hasn't come calling."

"He has no evidence. Just a feeling in his gut."

"Yeah, well, he should lay off the burritos. We just gonna stand out here and talk?"

"You know we're not."

She unlocked her office. They went in together, as they'd done so many times since May, when after two months of separation they'd reconnected. It had been his idea, not that she'd had anything against it. He'd simply pulled her over one day, and instead of writing up a ticket, he'd said, "I miss you."

She knew what it cost him to say that. It was more than a matter of pride. He liked to see himself a certain way, as a straight arrow, one of the good guys, someone who followed the rules. Given what he knew, he shouldn't allow himself to have anything to do with her.

But what was the old saying? The heart wants what it wants.

This time they'd been more careful. They never met at his apartment anymore, and he never went anywhere near her home. Her office was their little love nest. Only after hours, when the rest of the tenants were gone for the day. He always made a purchase at one of the stores nearby, just to cover himself in case anyone questioned why he'd parked on Main.

It was all about sex. No dinners out, no trips to the movies, no romantic getaways. Just the two of them together on the new sofa she'd bought to replace the ruined one. Sometimes they shared a drink; she kept liquor in a drawer of her desk. The booze was always warm, but that was okay.

The oddest thing about it was that it was probably the most normal relationship she'd ever had.

She was shutting the blinds when he said, "Dan knows about us."

Startled, she turned. "You're shitting me." She'd been sure they'd both done a good enough job of playacting last night to fool the chief, who normally wasn't all that hard to fool anyway.

Brad hung back, just inside the doorway, reluctant to

proceed until all the blinds were closed. "I shouldn't have put it like that. What I mean is, he knows we were seeing each other up till around February. One of my neighbors blabbed. But he doesn't know ... about this."

"He thinks it's over?"

Brad nodded. "That's why he's willing to cut me a break. Of course, if he ever finds out different ..."

"If the situation's getting too hairy for you, Walsh, you can always walk away. I won't hold it against you."

"I'm not walking away. I tried that once."

"Yeah, I'm a hard habit to break." She shut the last of the blinds, and he came all the way into the room, closing the door to the hall.

"You were on that freighter, weren't you?" he said quietly.

"Really want me to answer that?"

His eyes half-closed in resignation. "You just did."

"They were bad people." She approached him, slipped her arms around his waist. "You have no idea how bad. And a lot of it was self-defense."

"A lot. But not all?"

"Not all. But nobody died who shouldn't have. At least"—she thought of Shaban—"nobody I was responsible for."

His hands came up. Slowly, almost against his will, he took hold of her hips. "You're never going to quit, are you?" he breathed into her ear.

"I tried. You don't know how hard I tried."

"For all I know"—his voice was low and bitter—"you're planning to kill somebody tonight."

"For all you know, I am."

"I think I still hate you sometimes."

"Do you?"

"Yeah." His lips found hers. "But not enough for it to matter."

40

At 8:30 Bonnie drove into the Locust Hill RV Park on Devil's Hook Island. No guards patrolled the property, so she was able to tool around the compound unobserved. In most places, her vandalized vomit-green rust bucket would have drawn attention to itself. Among the aging campers parked on patches of dead crabgrass, it fit right in.

It occurred to her that Walt Churchland, a.k.a. Sparky, was probably getting it on with Charlotte Webb right about now. Her good deed for the year, she'd called it. But that wasn't quite right, was it? Getting rid of Ed Goodman had to qualify as a good deed in somebody's book.

And now it was Edna's turn.

According to the address on Ed's license, the mobile home was parked at 63 Screech Owl Lane. Bonnie tracked it down, memorized its appearance and location, then left the RV park and ditched the Jeep in the pine woods that bordered it to the west. She returned on foot, hiking through the tall stands of trees in the moonless dark.

As she approached the edge of the woods, she pulled on cotton gloves, then screwed the suppressor into the Beretta. She held the gun down at her side, the long tube brushing her thigh.

Silently she crept along the perimeter, past the rear ends of various RVs, using the trees to shield herself from sight. A small cluster of folks sat under an awning. They were grilling hot dogs and chatting. One guy strummed a guitar, singing a John Denver tune. Or was it Bob Denver?

One of them was a folk singer, and one of them was Gilligan. She could never remember which was which.

She was glad she'd brought the suppressor. These RVs were packed close together, and it was a safe bet the walls weren't soundproofed.

The camper in 61 Screech Owl Lane, next door to the Goodmans, was occupied; Bonnie saw the flicker of a TV in the window. Just past it lay a battered wreck of a camper sprawling on soft tires in a spread of weeds. Dim light glowed in one window, but there was no sign of activity. If Edna Goodman was home, she wasn't making it obvious.

Bonnie took a step toward the motorhome, then paused, half expecting another flashback. The situation was the same, after all—the stealthy approach to a camper at night. She might have been back in Purgatory Canyon. But she felt nothing. Evidently, getting rid of old Ed had been just the therapy she needed.

She reached the back of the vehicle and ran her hands along the grimy aluminum siding, trying to feel the vibrations of footsteps inside. Nothing. Was the woman in there or not?

Then she heard it. A soft current of music wafting through the closed windows. Some classical shit, like the stuff they'd played on that other night. The volume was low, barely audible from outside, but it was all she needed to hear.

Edna was in the camper, listening to one of her records on the phonograph. And waiting.

Waiting for her.

Boldly she circled around to the side door. The knob turned in her hand. Unlocked, as it had to be.

She opened the door and went in, not hurrying, nothing dramatic, just a neighbor dropping by for a chat.

In an armchair, haloed in the glow of a table lamp, sat Edna Goodman. She was knitting, of course. She glanced up from her needlework with a twitch of recognition that was almost a smile.

"So it was you," Edna said. "I thought it must be."

Bonnie looked her over. In eleven years she'd turned gray and gained weight. Gone were the cowgirl clothes she'd sported in Arizona, replaced by a colorless smock. Gone, too, was the deep sunburn that had reddened her face and made her look almost healthy. Now she was as pale as a slug, with a thick neck and a fat face and flat, empty eyes.

"You knew it wasn't a botched robbery," Bonnie said evenly.

"Sure I knew. Ed would never have checked out that way. It was an avenging angel who come for him. And for me, now."

"I'm no angel."

"I suppose not. I really don't know who you are. We never did learn your name."

"You never will."

"Back then you were scarcely more than a child. All grown up now, aren't you? Filled out real nice. You look good."

"Do I? You look like forty miles of bad road. The newspapers said you killed fourteen in all."

"Fourteen in the canyon. There was more in other places, ones the police never found."

"How many more?"

"I've lost count, child. Too many."

"You did a good job getting away."

"Ed had it all planned out. He was always thinking ahead. We had new identities already made, and a little money, and a car. Even so, we made it just by the skin of our teeth, you could say."

"Ed told me you kept doing it."

"It was him who kept doing it. Couldn't stop. Just stayed at it, year after year."

"Purifying the world."

She waved a fleshy, languid hand. "Oh, that was mostly talk. He needed to justify himself at first, so he came up with all that fire 'n' brimstone stuff. Losing Lily, our little girl—it made him crazy, I think. Or maybe he was crazy all along, and Lily just brought it out. In later years, he didn't go on so much about sin and the Bible. Towards the end, he got it done with hardly no talk at all."

"Who was the last one?"

"Hitchhiker in Ohio. Nice young fellow. Shame."

"That why you came to Jersey?"

"Not exactly. We moved a lot after Palm Garden. Ed was always looking over his shoulder, jumping at shadows. Coming home in a fright, saying someone might've recognized him and we had to go. For a time we was up in Canada, in the north woods, where nobody would know us. You have any notion how cold it is in those parts? How lonely?"

"Ed blamed me for all that, I guess," Bonnie said.

"Sure he did. That phone call to the police—it's what got the bodies found and brought the real heat down on us."

"Yeah, but here's the thing. I didn't make any phone call."

"Didn't you?" Edna said in her dull, curiously affectless voice.

"I should have, but I must've been shock or something. I intended to call when I got to El Paso, except I read in the paper that someone else already had. They'd called it in that same night. The police said it was a woman who spoke in a whisper. I'm thinking it was you, Edna. You, with your throat damaged from the needle I stuck there. I can still see the scar."

"You're a smart one, aren't you?"

"I've been around."

Edna put down her knitting and folded her hands in

her lap. "I wasn't sure I could count on you to do it. Your kind don't always talk to the police."

"Okay."

"So I patched myself up as best I could while Ed was still out cold, and then I used my cell. In those days, the police couldn't trace a cell-phone call. At least the police in Palm Garden couldn't. I made out like I was the victim. Like I was *you*. I told 'em all about the crazy people in the camper in Purgatory Canyon. I told 'em to come quick before those awful Goodmans got away."

Edna sighed, remembering.

"It would've worked, only Ed came to, and he was frantic to run. He was sure the biker girl—that's what he always called you—the biker girl would go straight to the cops. Naturally I couldn't say I'd phoned 'em myself. We flew out of the canyon like a bat out of hell. Switched the camper for the car Ed had hidden—we knew everyone would be looking for an RV—and headed out of state, running north, then west. By sunrise we was on the outskirts of Bakersfield." She glanced at the record spinning lazily on the turntable as the music swelled. "I always liked this part. Mozart, you know."

Bonnie didn't give a damn about Mozart. "What I want to know is why you called. Why'd you want to get caught?"

"Because I was tired, and scared, and tired of being scared. I used to do my needlework during the executions so I wouldn't betray my nerves. Even then sometimes my hands got so shaky, I'd drop a stitch. I knew if Ed ever suspected I was getting cold feet, I would go into the ground with the rest of them. I was scared of him, you see. And I was his prisoner, as much as you ever were. I tried to tell you so, that night, when you came at me, but you wouldn't listen. And I knew if I ever left him, he would hunt me down. My only hope was prison for us both."

"You could have called the police at any time."

"Not without Ed knowing it was me. You were the only one who got away. If the call came on any other day, he would know I'd made it."

"So what?"

"That's a real good question. Maybe I always thought he'd find a way to get to me, even if we were in separate cells in separate jails. Or maybe I just couldn't bear to have him know I betrayed him. I still loved him, see. Loved—and hated and feared. The human heart is a funny thing, isn't it?"

"Yeah," Bonnie said quietly, "funny."

"Whatever way it was, my courage always failed me. I was brave only that one time. And last night, when they came and told me Ed was gone, finally gone, I felt only blessed relief. Even though I knew I'd be next." She gave Bonnie a shrewd, knowing look. "None of this surprises you, really."

"I was sure you wouldn't run. You wanted to be caught then, and you'd want to be caught now."

Edna nodded placidly. "I've been sitting here waiting. Would have been disappointed if you hadn't come. There's a weariness that settles over you, and a helpless, trapped feeling. It's your life, you know? And there's no way out. Except the one way."

"Nothing you've told me is any excuse."

"Don't you think I know that? Go on, do what you have to do. While the music's playing. I like to hear it."

She reclined in the chair and shut her eyes as if settling down to sleep.

"Tell me just one thing," she added, her eyes still closed. "Did we make you what you are? What we did that night—did it, you know, *turn* you?"

"I was turned already."

"That's good to know. I thought as much. There was a hardness about you, and a wildness. There still is."

"Yeah, I was never any good at coloring inside the lines. That's just not how I play the game."

"Is that what this is? A game?"

"Point-and-shoot. Like Ed's booth on the midway."

Edna showed a slow, sleepy smile. "That game's rigged, child. You can't win anything that matters."

"I know," Bonnie said, raising the gun. "But I keep playing anyway."

AUTHOR'S NOTE

READERS ARE INVITED to visit me at www.michael prescott.net, where you can find links to all my books, news about upcoming projects, contact info, and other stuff.

Skin in the Game is the fourth book in a series that began with *Cold Around the Heart* and continued with *Blood in the Water* and *Bad to the Bone*. A fifth book featuring Bonnie Parker is in the works. The next one probably won't have any body parts in the title, though. After heart, blood, bone, and skin, I've run out of ideas.

As always, thanks to Diana Cox of www.novel proofreading.com for another meticulous proofreading job. And thanks to all you good folks who keep buying—and reading—my books, even in this highly competitive ebook environment.

—MP

ABOUT THE AUTHOR

AFTER TWENTY YEARS in traditional publishing, Michael Prescott found himself unable to sell another book. On a whim, he began releasing his novels in digital form. Sales took off, and by 2011 he was one of the world's best-selling e-book writers. *Skin in the Game* is his most recent thriller.

Made in the USA
San Bernardino, CA
03 March 2019